Wild Ones

LEIGH GOODISON

SHEFFIELD PUBLICATIONS

The text for this book was set in Garamond.

Printed and bound in the United States of America.

10 9 8 7 6 5 4 3

Leigh Goodison

Wild Ones / Leigh Goodison / 2nd edition

Summary: After a series of disastrous foster homes, Breeze Jordan finally finds happiness at a state school for troubled teens, but when circumstances change she is forced to make choices that will change her life forever.

[1. Teen problems-Fiction 2. Foster care-Fiction 3. Horses-Fiction] I. Title

[Fic]

ISBN-13: 978-1-945136-00-9 (Sheffield Publications)

DEDICATION

For my mother,
Mary Goodison,
who loved to read.

Wild Ones

LEIGH GOODISON

ONE

The summer before my mother died and I became a Ward of the State, she took me to the Steens Mountains in southeastern Oregon to see the annual wild horse round-up. Back then anyone with a few dollars in their pocket for the adoption fee and a trailer to haul away a horse could take home one of the mustangs, feral creatures that rarely encountered humans.

We'd driven nearly two hundred hot, dusty miles from our home in central Oregon, the road spanning precipitous cliffs, crossing dry reservation land, and finally bisecting lush dairy farms. Soon we could see the county fairgrounds that sprawled across the crisp brown August grass and gravel parking lot like scattered pieces of dirty red Lego. After parking the Jeep we wove our way between the parked cars to the enormous covered arena where the auction would take place.

While I pressed close to my mother so we wouldn't get separated, eager kids pushed forward through the crowd, straining to be free from their parents' hands so they could get a closer look. A few dads hoisted their kids up to sit on their shoulders, as only a tenuous line existed between excitement and danger. But my mother and I were mesmerized, oblivious to the flying hooves and rolling puffs of dust as hundreds of wild horses fought for freedom. A boiling sea of terrified horseflesh whirling around the steel-pole holding corrals in the huge fairgrounds arena.

"I didn't think there were any mustangs left in the wild,"

I said, wiping my stinging eyes free of the hoof-blown grit. When my mother didn't answer, I turned. Tears coursed down her cheeks, carving snake-belly trails through the dust.

A little embarrassed, I glanced away from her, hoping no one else had noticed. A sliver of sunbeam had squeezed through a hole in the tin roof of the arena and shone down on her head, igniting highlights that looked like copper wire in her dark brown hair. At that moment, she didn't seem much older than me. Her sad expression made me realize it wasn't the dirt making her eyes water. I'd seen her look like that before when she talked about my father.

She flashed a smile that disappeared as quickly as it arrived. Then, as if ashamed by her show of emotion, her eyes couldn't meet mine for a few minutes. Instead, she fumbled in her pocket for a tissue and not finding one, wiped her eyes on her sleeve. As a kid, she'd bought a pony with babysitting money, spending every spare minute grooming, riding, or just sharing secrets with him. It wasn't the first time that I wondered if the plan to adopt a horse was more for her benefit than mine.

"Wild horses *will* become extinct if these guys have anything to do with it," Mom sniffled.

Not bothering to disguise her anger, she gestured toward a group of khaki-uniformed, Bureau of Land Management agents. The men, each armed with a clipboard and stack of papers, appeared to be making a deal with a group of potbellied cowboys in dirty jeans and western hats, looking like extras on the set of a John Wayne movie.

I found a crumpled tissue in my pocket and handed it to her. She blew her nose in a soft, ladylike way, and tossed the tissue in a garbage can. Then she turned and hurried away in the direction of our old green Jeep, squeezing between the grandstands of the arena. Left standing there, I had no choice but to break into a trot to catch up to her.

"What do you mean? Didn't you say that these horses were up for adoption? That they'd go to a good home where kids like me could train them to ride?"

My mother unlocked the doors to the Jeep and flung them open one at a time to let out the heat. She shook her head in disgust.

"I overheard a conversation between a few of the men who won the right to *adopt* them. Before the BLM guys got here, they were talking about the price of horse meat in Canada."

The corn dog I'd eaten for lunch began to roil in my stomach. For a moment I didn't believe her. She'd taken me to the roundup to try and adopt a horse of our own. We'd made arrangements to keep it at a neighbor's farm in return for cleaning extra stalls, because apart from the price of hay and board, we only had enough money for the adoption fee and the use of his trailer. But our name hadn't been drawn and so we would have to try again next year. I didn't know then that there wouldn't be a next year. Five months later my mother was dead, killed by a drunk driver on her way home from work.

TWO

The first day at a new school has to be the most traumatic, nauseating event in a teenager's life. At least it's always been that way for me. You'd think that after four years of foster care and dozens of new schools it would have gotten easier, but it never did. Because we'd moved around a lot, my mother had mostly home-schooled me and we used to joke that she had more library cards than credit cards.

Now between foster homes, I would be temporarily housed at a State-run school until another home could be found. One part of me dreaded the process: getting used to the quirks of unfamiliar teachers, and fitting into the inevitable cliques. But the part of me that loved an adventure looked forward to it. A new school meant new friends. Right?

Yeah, right.

Stark School, and from my initial impression appropriately named, consisted of two environmentally friendly, snot-green, wood-frame buildings, one for the boys and one for girls. It was discretely separated by a 12-foot wire fence so thickly covered with English ivy it looked like it was upholstered in leaves. A caseworker with the Children's Services Department told me that the school had been founded by a man named Joseph Stark who grew up on the streets and went on to make a fortune. A place for troubled or homeless kids. From what I'd seen so far in the outside world, there were plenty to fill it.

My caseworker had left me standing outside the

Principal's Office, a Mrs. Watkins according to the brass plate screwed onto the door. Then the caseworker hightailed it back to her dented government-issued vehicle as if she were afraid she'd catch a case of empathy. Though my stomach flip-flopped a bit as it always does in new situations, I knocked, then waited until I heard a voice telling me to enter.

Mrs. Watkins sat behind her desk smiling at me like an enormous pink frog in a flowing algae-colored dress. Her throat had about three folds of skin where a normal neck should be. But her smile was sweet and genuine, so I didn't laugh when she started to speak and her voice sounded like a croak.

"Breeze," she began, clearing her throat. *Got a frog in your throat, Mrs. W?* I sucked my bottom lip in between my teeth and bit down on it until I felt I was safe from giggling. Especially important because I tend to snort when I laugh.

"Breeze," she repeated, "welcome to Stark School." She rose to her feet and once standing I realized she was hardly taller than when she'd been in her chair. I probably looked like a moose next to her.

"Let me show you around the school and get you settled into classes," she said, grabbing an obese folder from her desk that I figured must hold my entire life history.

She opened the file, removed a sheet of paper and handed it to me. "This is your class schedule. We'll go to your dorm so you can put your things away, then I'll take you to first period."

She waddled out the door, waiting for me to move out so she could lock it. Then she headed down the hallway. I was left with no choice but to follow her, my normal long-legged stride curtailed to keep pace with her shorter steps.

Stark's classrooms turned out to be on the bottom floor of the building. I could hear teachers' voices intoning their particular subject material as we passed, but otherwise it was rather quiet. I glanced down at my schedule and tried to note where my classes were located so I wouldn't get lost trying to find them later on. With long wide hallways, accented by students' artwork, posters announcing upcoming events, and a glassed-in case containing school trophies, it was pretty standard as far as schools went. Only one thing set it apart from other schools I'd attended: I'd be here 24/7. Unless I was sent to a foster home, there was no hope of escape until I was eighteen. And if that wasn't the definition of a prison, I didn't know what was.

We hiked up the first flight of stairs and while I waited for Mrs. Watkins at the top of the landing, she puffed, "The top two floors are subdivided into dorms; the second floor is where they've assigned your room." I could tell from the disappointment in her voice she wasn't thrilled about another climb. I don't know what she would have done if there'd been a third level.

We finally stopped at one dorm at the far end of the second floor corridor. Mrs. Watkins opened the file and looked inside, then at the number on the door and beamed up at me.

"You'll be sharing this room with three other girls," she said, throwing the door open.

The room appeared painfully cramped to house four girls, I noted with dismay after seeing the two steel bunk beds. It looked more like a barracks than a dorm, furthering the prison effect. There was a small wooden table with four mismatched vinyl chairs stuck in the corner. Posters of Justin Bieber, Taylor Lautner, and One Direction were taped to one wall. The bunk nearest the door had a stuffed pink giraffe on the top bed. The bottom bunk beside the window had an oversized pillow with the name "Tyesha" embroidered along the edge. As long as I had a choice I might as well have a room with a view, I thought, and slung my jacket over the dull blue comforter.

Although it seemed odd that the room held no closets, one entire wall had been dedicated to a series of waist-high gray metal, file-like drawers. Four small mirrors had been mounted on the wall just above the surface top. A couple of the mirrors had brushes, lotions, hair clips, nail polish and other girlie stuff in front of them, leading me to understand the surfaces substituted for dressing tables.

Mrs. Watkins ambled over to the cabinets and opened a top drawer. "You can put your things in here."

I frowned. I didn't have much, other than some mementos and photos of my mother I carried in my book bag, but I didn't want to lose them. I glanced questioningly at Mrs. Watkins.

She read my mind and shook her head. "Sorry. School regulations don't allow locks."

I shoved my belongings and what clothes I had as far to the back of the drawer as I could. Then I grabbed my school supplies and followed her out the door. After taking several breaks for Mrs. Watkins to catch her breath, we ventured down the stairs to the classrooms.

She came to a stop outside a room with a door that had been propped open by a large clay bust. It looked like someone had attempted to immortalize Elvis. And not in a flattering way. From inside the room came the murmuring of students working together, punctuated by occasional laughter. Mrs. Watkins rapped twice on the door and all talking ceased as we entered. It was an art class. There were four or five girls to each long table, some working on sculptures, a few sketching, and several were painting the portrait of a more-nude-than-draped, live female model perched on a stool in the middle of the room.

Mrs. Watkins' face seemed to catch fire right down to the neckline of her dress. Then she cleared her throat as if getting ready to speak. A ripple of nervous nausea coursed through my stomach. This was the hardest part for me, the introduction. For with it came the inevitable, excruciating questions and misuse of my name. *"Breeze?* What kind of a name is *that?"* "How about we call you Sleaze?" Of the seemingly limitless variations, I'd pretty much heard them all at one time or another.

Mrs. Watkins handed my file to the willowy, black-haired teacher who glided up to us. Mrs. Watkins turned and smiled at the class then said, "Good morning, everyone. I'd like you to welcome Miss Jordan to Stark School." With that she squeezed my shoulder and moved out the door, presumably back to her office.

"I'm Eve Huntington," the teacher said, taking my arm. "You can call me Eve." She led me to a table and pulled out a chair beside a pretty blonde girl who looked about ten and had stopped sketching to watch. "Carla, please share your supplies with Breeze until we get her some of her own."

Carla rolled her eyes in an exaggerated way then made a sour sort of face that Eve couldn't see. She ripped off a sheet of her sketch pad, placed a couple of pencils on it, and slid them toward me. I heard a couple of kids behind me snickering and tried to tell myself it wasn't about me, or my name. They were probably just sharing an inside joke. It made me uncomfortable to have my back to anyone. The same feeling I got once when faced with a pack of vicious dogs: show no fear, don't turn your back, and don't make confrontational eye contact until you have sized up the enemy.

Though I was hardly able to look at the model long enough to try and sketch her, I forced back the embarrassment of seeing someone half naked and began to draw. Several minutes later Eve peered over my shoulder at my paper. Self-consciously, my hand crept over the drawing to cover it and I glanced up. Eve gently moved my hand away and smiled.

"You're quite a talented artist, Breeze," she commented. "I'm glad we have you in our group." I heard one of the girls mumble something and I swiveled my eyes to meet her gaze. But the looks returned weren't resentful of my praise, just inquisitive. I felt my self esteem ratchet up a notch.

The remainder of my classes passed by in the kind of blur that comes from too many things happening at once. Though I received stares from the other girls, no one talked to me or attempted to make friends and I didn't make the effort either. It gave me time to assess my surroundings and watch the cliques. Which ones I'd fit into or even want to be involved with. And which to avoid. It felt unnatural attending a school with only females, except for the occasional male teacher. Would there be conflict without boys? I wondered. Then I rationalized that if you put any two girls in a room there'd eventually be conflict.

Finally, after dinner we were allowed to return to the Common Room to watch TV or go to our rooms to read until lights out. I opted to return to the dorm and get settled in. I discovered the occupant of the bunk below me had arrived. Tyesha, if the name on the pillow was correct, a slender African-American girl with skin like creamy coffee was stretched out on her bed, her toes almost reaching the end.

"Hi," I said, giving her a tentative smile. She inclined her chin in acknowledgement but didn't say anything. Great, I thought, a silent one. Those were the hardest to get to know. But her olive-colored eyes hadn't shown animosity.

I went to the cabinet and removed a book from my drawer. Then I climbed up the ladder to my bunk, trying not to make the ladder creak as I got into bed.

"I hope you're not one of those people who rock and roll in bed all night," came the voice from under my bunk. I grinned.

"I hope you're not one of those people who kick the bottom of the mattress to get them to stop," I replied. From the long silence that followed it appeared we'd essentially marked our territory.

"I hope you're not one of those people who fart in their sleep, gassing out the person below them," she shot back, apparently not satisfied with me having the last word. I heard her muffled giggling as if she had her face in a pillow. I let her have that one and picked up my book.

Soon I could hear gentle snuffling snoring from below, which told me that Tyesha was asleep. I was just about to jump down and turn out the lights when the door opened. The blonde girl named Carla who had shared her art supplies with me walked in and stopped dead, surprised to see me.

"Oh, so you're our new roommate." She glanced toward Tyesha's bed and seeing no movement said, "Did they give you your assigned list of chores?"

I shook my head. She frowned.

"Well, don't assume we have servants and staff here, because that's not the case. If they haven't given you a list then you can have some of mine if Tyesha hasn't burdened you yet."

It occurred to me that when I got my list then I'd have double the work but I didn't say anything. Just go with the flow for now, I thought. The playing field will even out later.

At that moment, Tyesha turned over and muttered, "Will you tell Talking Barbie to put a sock in it? I'm trying to sleep."

Carla rolled her eyes the way she'd done in art class and walked over to the cabinets. She pulled out a pair of flannel pajamas, turned and headed to the door.

"I'm going to the showers," she announced loudly, "if anyone wants to know where I am." Tyesha's pillow hit the door just as it closed behind her.

As I lay there trying to accustom myself to my new surroundings enough to be able to fall asleep, I thought, today wasn't so bad. No one was particularly friendly, but they weren't mean either. There was still one unoccupied bunk in the room. I couldn't help but wonder what that girl would be like.

THREE

That night I dreamed about my mom. I was starting school in a new town, but she was still alive. Sometimes I missed her so much it hurt. Other times I could hardly remember her. In the crazy, terrifying days after her death, I'd tried to stay optimistic about what would happen to me, but she was the only family I had. If there were grandparents, aunts or uncles, I'd never met them. And she'd never mentioned anyone other than my dad, but he was dead, too.

The day she died, the principal had come to my classroom and taken me to his office. Waiting there was a social worker and a policewoman who broke the news to me about the accident. It didn't sink in that mom wouldn't be coming back until I was taken to a temporary shelter. Though I was still numb, I could hear strangers huddled in groups talking about me and about my future as if I wasn't there, and nothing I wanted or cared about mattered. All our possessions were taken and given to Goodwill, leaving me with only my clothes and a few personal items. And fading memories of my mom.

I awoke to the sound of girls talking and decided to pretend I was still sleeping while I eavesdropped. That might sound sneaky but it wasn't as if they didn't know I was there.

"If you used a little mascara and blush you'd be gorgeous," I heard Tyesha say.

"To hell with that," Carla replied, "Why would I want to look like one of my stepmothers?"

Tyesha made a grunting noise and I figured that now was

as good a time as any to let them know I was awake. I swung my legs over the side of the bed and dropped to the floor without benefit of the ladder, making a loud thump. Startled, they both spun around.

"There are dorms below us. If anyone squeals to Mr. Simonson about the noise he'll have you writing enough lines to fill a novel," Carla cautioned.

Despite looking so young, Carla had a figure like that of a twenty-year-old. She reached into one of the drawers and pulled out a pair of oversized jeans that looked like the ones boys wear halfway down their butts then slipped a T-shirt and a heavy grey hoodie over top. I couldn't figure out why someone so pretty would cover up like that. With straight brown hair, unremarkable brown eyes and a nose with a weird turned-up tip, I considered myself pretty homely. I'd have killed to look like her.

She twisted her long blonde hair into two shiny braids as if she were in kindergarten. Then she noticed me watching her.

"Why don't you take a picture, it lasts longer," she said, and headed down to the cafeteria for breakfast. Tyesha raised her eyebrows and proceeded to get dressed.

"Never mind Carla. She's a little rough around the edges until you get to know her."

"Nothing I can't handle. She's awfully tough for someone who looks like that."

Tyesha laughed. "Don't let appearances fool you here. Carla's dad is a serial womanizer. She dresses like that to piss him off. While he was on his third honeymoon, Carla hitchhiked to her mother's place in Florida, then went out and shoplifted at some store and got caught. She's been at more fancy boarding schools than Paris Hilton, yet she always runs away. Though her dad has custody her latest step mom talked him into having her classified as a habitual runaway. So she got sent here."

She shrugged and stopped at the door for a moment, giving me a shrewd once-over. "We've all got baggage," she said, "some more than others." Then she headed out the door after Carla, leaving me alone. Realizing that if I didn't get moving I'd be late for breakfast and classes on my second day, I hurriedly threw on my clothes and followed them.

At lunch I saw Carla seated alone at a table in the far end of the cafeteria. I loaded my tray and made my way over to her. As I squeezed between tables and chairs, out of my peripheral vision I saw a foot snake out from underneath a table, a deliberate attempt to trip me and send my tray flying. Without breaking stride or acknowledging its owner, I lifted my sneakered foot and planted it down hard on theirs. I heard a sharp intake of breath and a muffled snarl of pain. Someone spat, "Bitch!" as I passed. But I just ignored them and when I reached Carla, I sat down, uninvited.

Carla didn't appear to mind. She'd arrived at Stark only two weeks before me and hadn't formed many friendships yet. Also, unless something changed, I had the feeling that it wouldn't be too long before she'd be making a break for it and running away again. I couldn't imagine running away from someplace unless I had someplace to run to.

"How long has Tyesha been at Stark?" I asked through a mouthful of instant mashed potatoes that contained hard lumps, which in my opinion isn't what mashed potatoes are supposed to be like.

"She told me she's been here a year, off and on. Her mother dumped her on her grandmother when she was a baby and took off, but now her grandmother is going into a nursing home and can't take care of her."

I frowned. "Doesn't she have any other family? A dad or something?"

Carla shook her head. "Her dad disappeared before her mom did. She has an aunt, but the aunt has kids of her own and is unemployed. Besides, she's seventeen, so she's almost out of here." She shrugged. "Why so nosy? It's none of your business."

"I just like to know things about people, that's all."

She pushed her fork into a pile of chicken stew. "Well,

being too inquisitive can get you into trouble. MYOB is my advice."

I went back to eating my lunch and we finished in silence.

Carla was right, of course. Being shuffled around from foster home to foster home didn't give you a lot of time to form long-lasting friendships. A part of me wanted to get to know these girls. We might have stuff in common or maybe not. But another part of me cautioned that Stark was probably temporary, if not for me, for some of them. Still, it would feel great to be able to talk about my mom with friends. I just needed to make some.

That afternoon a new girl was brought around to the classrooms the way I had been the day before. Remembering how I'd felt when I arrived, I tried not to stare at her the way the others did. But it was hard not to. She was the unhappiest looking girl I'd ever seen. Her bright, carrot-orange, fuzzy curls were cropped as short as a boy's and she depended on thick, black-rimmed glasses to see.

A roll of white skin that looked like something popped from a Pillsbury can, had escaped from under the edges of a dirty Hello Kitty! T-shirt and sagged over top of her baggy jeans. From her face to her exposed belly, her skin was freckled all over. I looked away and got back to my math lesson. Suddenly I felt eyes on me. I glanced up.

"Breeze?" Someone snickered and I suddenly realized Mrs. Watkins had been addressing me. "Deanne is going to share a dorm with you, Tyesha and Carla." I tried to make my expression welcoming but this girl had absolutely no personality. None. I wondered how she'd fit in with sarcastic Carla and the serene Tyesha. And me, of course.

I smiled at her but it kind of froze on my face because her eyes didn't even focus on me, almost as if she were looking at something in the distance. She settled into a chair to my left, and plopped her text and notebook on the desk. I suppressed a sigh and went back to my work.

That night the three of us had already bunked down but Deanne hadn't yet arrived. Probably in the shower, I figured, because she'd laid out pajamas and a tattered crocheted throw blanket on the bunk above Carla's. Carla was tossing around in her bed, restless and bored. Finally she sprung up and threw her legs over the edge of the mattress.

"Anyone want to look in her stuff before she gets back?" she said.

I rolled over to look at her. "I thought you told me we should MYOB."

She shrugged. "Sure, but we have a right to know who's moving in with us. She might be a serial killer."

"Don't you think if she was a serial killer she'd be in maximum security, not minimum security?" came Tyesha's voice. "Now shut up and leave her alone."

"We're not in jail," I protested.

"Really?" Carla challenged. "Okay then, try and leave and see what happens. If you can't leave, then we must be in prison, right?" I hadn't thought about it that way.

"Anyhow, you gutless wonders, I'm going to have a look." With one glance at the door she climbed out of bed and headed for the file drawers. "Cover me," she said, and though we disagreed with what she was doing, I knew one of us would warn her if Deanne showed up. I turned back to my book.

"Whoohoo!" Carla hooted. "Look what we have here! A diary!"

"Put it back," Tyesha hissed.

But Carla was already turning the pages of a small coil notebook. At that moment the door opened and I turned to see Deanne standing in the doorway. She didn't move or say a word, her face remaining that blank freckly slate I'd seen when she was introduced. Carla quickly thrust the diary back in the drawer and feigned sorting out her own cabinet. But we all knew Deanne had seen it in Carla's hands and I wondered why she didn't say anything. In spite of that, the four of us settled into a respectful, though without much camaraderie, nights sleep.

Although sharing a dorm forced us to be semi-friendly, the turning point in our relationship came a few days later. We'd had a particularly hideous version of corned beef hash for dinner that most of us couldn't eat. I was virtually starving when I went to bed, and my stomach started to growl. Unfortunately, it was already past 'lights out' and there was nothing I could do to stave off my hunger.

"What the *hell* was that?" Tyesha's whisper was loud enough to wake the other two girls. She kicked the underside of my bunk.

"Ouch! Knock it off! It's my stomach, you idiot. I'm dying of hunger." I rolled over to see Carla shoving a blanket into her mouth to smother her laughter and keep the hall monitor from hearing.

Tyesha swung herself up until her head appeared at the level of my mattress. "Then we need to feed you or I'll never get to sleep."

I shook my head, but she was determined. She dropped back down, then crouched to floor level and crawled over to Carla's bunk.

"Carla!" she hissed. "Breeze is hungry and so am I. We're going to the kitchen."

"It's not worth it," I heard Carla growl back. "You'll get caught and we'll all get detention."

"I don't care. We need to eat and you're coming with." I heard a squeaky protesting noise from Carla as Tyesha yanked her blankets to the floor. Then she whispered to me to get my ass out of bed. No one bothered Deanne, who had her back to us and appeared to be sound asleep.

My stomach aching too much to care about the consequences any more, I followed Tyesha. The three of us sneaked down to the kitchen, taking turns keeping lookout. There we discovered a pan of cinnamon coffee cake and a jug of orange juice the cook had prepared for breakfast the next morning. We managed to spirit it back to the dorm without anyone seeing.

Deanne woke up just as we closed the door, staring expressionlessly at us. Using a nail file, Tyesha cut a piece of cake, placed it on a Kleenex and handed it to Deanne. That was the first time I saw Deanne smile. Then Tyesha passed around the jug of orange juice and we drank commune-style right from the bottle. It took us only a few minutes to polish off the entire cake.

After stashing the empty pan and jug under Tyesha's bunk we crawled into bed, our stomachs finally full. I felt nauseated from all the sugar.

"Wonder what's for breakfast now?" Deanne muttered from her bed near the door. Then I fell asleep to the sound of Carla snickering.

The next morning all hell broke loose when the cook discovered her scheduled breakfast was missing. We ended up with Pop Tarts and Kool-Aid instead of what she had planned. Every teacher we passed raked us with interrogative glares, making my nervous stomach quiver worse than it had from the hunger pangs I'd had the night before.

When I was in Chemistry class an announcement came over the PA system that I was to go to Mrs. Watkins' office. I arrived to find Tyesha and Carla already there. A downcast Deanne followed soon after. Apparently the janitor had discovered the empty pan in our dorm before we were able to return it.

"I'm disappointed in you ladies," Mrs. Watkins said, trying to look stern while tactfully suppressing a smile. "Stealing is a serious offense at Stark. I have no choice but to give all of you detention."

"Deanne wasn't part of it," I said. "I did it."

Mrs. Watkins shook her head. "Since every one of you has absolved the other of blame, you'll all receive the same punishment: one-hour of detention after classes for a week, with no T.V. or internet. Now go to your classes."

As we walked out the door I heard Deanne mutter behind me, "We should have told her giving us poison and starving us are serious offenses, too."

We all had to stuff our fists in our mouth to prevent Mrs. Watkins from hearing us giggle. Deanne had nothing to gain from keeping quiet about our part in the theft, but she'd definitely earned our respect.

After that we got bolder. Though no one actually said the words 'I dare you,' dreaming up new adventures to alleviate the boredom flooded our conversations. Carla took a bottle of White-Out from a teacher's desk and used it to give us all French mani-pedi's. Deanne stole two bottles of vanilla and a quart of cream from the kitchen and made us Brown Cows. After puking our guts out we swore off alcohol. Fortunately neither of them got caught and we blamed our sickness on food poisoning. The bonus was that we got to stay in bed all that day instead of going to class.

One day on my way to the girls' locker room I glanced down at an open gym bag that I knew belonged to Mr. Pulaski, the PE teacher. A pack of cigarettes lay alongside a book of matches. Smoking on school grounds was forbidden for both teachers and students. Some devil must have been sitting on my shoulder because it was just too tempting. When he was busy setting up the gymnastic equipment, I stole a few of the cigarettes and the matches. Because even having cigarettes or matches was against school rules, I knew he wouldn't report it. He could only wonder what had happened to them. As if he wouldn't figure out that a student took them.

A couple of hours before 'lights out' I brought out my contraband and showed them to Carla.

"Jesus, Breeze! You're going to get us expelled," she said. Then a smile crossed her face and I could see a plan hatching.

At that moment I realized what I'd done was pretty stupid, though I could see the admiration in Deanne's eyes.

"You're right," I said, "I'll just toss them in the garbage before we get caught with them."

"No," said Tyesha, "I think we should go outside to smoke them. My cousins and I snagged my aunt's all last summer without her knowing. Come on, we don't have much time."

We filed out the door and headed behind the school where we wouldn't be easily seen. Tyesha pulled a cigarette from the pack, lit it and took a long drag. She blew a couple of smoke rings into the air then passed it to me. I sucked in like an old pro and started to cough so hard I almost threw up. I handed it to Carla, who inhaled, made an involuntary gagging noise and spat on the ground.

"God! Does anyone have some gum?" she choked. She offered the cigarette to Deanne who waved it on. Tyesha snatched it from Carla and took another puff. At that moment we heard the caretaker heading out the door in our direction, dragging his rattletrap cart that contained mops, brooms, cleaning and gardening supplies, down the steps. Tyesha dropped the cigarette and we bolted back to the dorm.

The fire alarm went off an hour later, jangling us out of our sleep. My stomach flip-flopped when I heard it because I realized in our haste Tyesha had forgotten to stamp out the burning butt. The still-lit cigarette must have started to smolder in the bark dust around the flowerbeds that lay beside the school wall. Having practiced our fire drills, we all filed dutifully out of the school in our pajamas, shivering as we watched the old wood siding catch fire like kindling.

Within minutes it had turned into a three-alarm fire. Fire trucks, men and hoses were everywhere. It was exciting for a while as everyone scurried out of the school like ants exiting a stirred-up anthill. We entertained ourselves by making jokes about how 'hot' the firemen were. But it wasn't so funny later when we were finally allowed back into the school and Mrs. Watkins called me into her office.

I don't know how she knew it was me who stole the cigarettes. Either one of the younger kids had seen me and ratted, or Mr. Pulaski had more guts than I'd given him credit for and had noticed me passing through. I figured I'd get shipped out of Stark faster than you could yell "FIRE!" But after denying that any of the other girls were involved and it was all my doing, Mrs. Watkins just gave me a stern warning and another week of detention. Then she told me to set a better example for the younger kids and sent me back to my smoky dorm.

Three nervous, expectant faces greeted me when I entered the room. It smelled terrible, the residual smoke making me sneeze.

"Well?" said Tyesha.

"Doesn't she want to see us, too?" Deanne ventured.

I shook my head. "I confessed and told her it was all my doing." I hopped up on my bunk and swung my legs. "You know what's weird? She didn't even suspend me."

"Not so weird," said Carla. "Mr. Pulaski is Mrs. Watkins' brother-in-law. She knows he smokes at school sometimes. All the teachers here are in collusion." She hugged her knees to her chest. "It sucks."

Tyesha rolled her eyes. "Figures."

"That was a crazy thing to do," I said. "I'm sorry I almost got you guys into trouble. Again." I tried to keep a straight face, but couldn't help but burst out laughing when I thought of how green Carla had turned when she'd inhaled the cigarette smoke. Even Deanne's face cracked into a wry smile.

"You're a lunatic, you know that, Breeze?" said Carla. She thought about that for a few minutes. "Actually, we're all lunatics, or why would we be here?"

"We're Stark raving lunatics," murmured Deanne, and we all stared at her.

"Oh my god," said Carla. "We should form a club or something and call ourselves the Stark Raving Lunatics."

"That's really juvenile," said the sophisticated Tyesha, but even she looked intrigued. So we did just that. We became the Stark Raving Lunatics, and everyone in the school knew who we were. And although I'd led the last few escapades, we did not officially have a leader. It seemed that without even trying, each of us raised havoc and chaos on an equal level.

After we'd formed our club, we created a pact and wrote Commandments as part of our rules. A Credo for us to live by.

Tyesha knew her Bible pretty well as her grandmother had taken her to church every Sunday and sometimes on other days just to cement the lessons. She came up with The First Commandment, which was: "Thou shalt not cry." Then we borrowed directly from the Bible for the second: "Thou shalt not steal." And so on with the third: "Thou shalt not tell lies."

But Tyesha thought we needed more latitude than restrictive blanket rules that applied to everything. So we amended the Commandments to read, "Thou shalt not cry, *in front of anyone other than each other*" and "Thou shalt not steal, *from each other*," and "Thou shalt not tell lies, *to, or to hurt, each other.*" And so it went with the other rules. We were banned from committing offences, *but only against each other.*

One night at dinner I sat picking at my Shepherd's Pie and steamed peas. I'd been in a crappy mood since English class where Mr. Simonson, the English teacher, had berated me over a late assignment. He was always on my case about a paper I'd done wrong or some reading I'd forgotten to do and made it his personal mission to embarrass me in front of everyone else in the class. He hadn't liked me from day one, or maybe that was week two; he had probably heard about my involvement with the fire.

"What crawled up your butt and died?" Tyesha asked as she slid her tray next to mine and pulled out a chair.

"Mr. Simonson," I growled. "Only he didn't die. Unfortunately."

She took a mouthful of her food and made a face, then chewed and swallowed with a gulp.

"He does single you out over everyone else."

"You *think?*"

Carla had joined us. "Yeah, I don't get it. It's not like you're not good at making up stories and shit."

I kicked her under the table.

"Hey!" she said, glaring at me. "There must be something we can do about him. It's not just you. He picks on Deanne, too."

Sharing the misery didn't help. It upset me even more when someone took their problems out on Deanne, who did nothing to stir the pot. She never missed handing in homework assignments and was always on time getting to class, which was more than I could say about the rest of us. It was clear to me that Mr. Simonson would have to go.

I lay awake half the night hatching a plan. After recalling the behavior of a former foster father, the next day I went to our counselor and told her that I'd seen Mr. Simonson peeking in the girls' locker room through a crack in the wall. Tyesha and I had created the crack earlier by prying away at the wood with a stolen dinner knife. Although Mr. Simonson hotly denied it, Carla backed me up and actually added some lies of her own. Of course, neither Carla nor Mr. Simonson, nor even I, could indisputably prove our case. But because Mr. Simonson wasn't related to Mrs. Watkins in any way, shortly after that he was transferred to another school.

FOUR

At Thanksgiving, Carla went home to her family, and Deanne headed out to stay with her father. Tyesha and I were left feeling lonely and bored. Carla was the chatty one and although Deanne hardly talked, having four girls in the room instead of only two made it a lot livelier. One night I'd just gotten to sleep when Tyesha kicked the bottom of my bunk.

"Hey!" I yelled, startled awake. "Knock it off."

Tyesha's head popped up beside me. "Shut up," she whispered loudly. "I can't get to sleep. Let's sneak out of here."

"And go where?" I muttered, rubbing my eyes.

"Yesterday I talked to a boy on the other side of the fence. He's going to meet me tonight. I need a lookout to make sure we're not seen."

"Well, it's not me," I said. "I can do without detention this week." But I was intrigued. My limited experience with boys consisted of either babysitting the younger ones or being ignored or teased by the older ones. And then there was the obligatory suspicious foster mom who was convinced you were after her husband. I'd had a few crushes and a little flirting at some of the schools I'd gone to, and at one foster home the son had tried to feel me up before I clobbered him, but that had been the extent of it.

"Grow up," Tyesha said. "What else have we got to do?"

I sighed and crawled out of my bunk. Tyesha was already dressed and waiting impatiently.

"Wear black," she hissed. "And layer up because it's starting to rain."

I dragged the darkest jeans and sweatshirt out of my drawer and pulled them on. "I got a bad feeling about this," I said. She just shrugged and opened the door carefully, peering up and down the halls.

"Safe," she whispered.

"How are we going to get out?" I asked. "They lock the doors at night."

"They lock them from the inside, so we can unlock them no problem. We just need to jam something in the door so we can get back in."

At the rear exit I searched around for a rock while Tyesha held the door open, then we stuck it in the doorway so it wouldn't latch on us. I followed her silently through the shadows until we reached the wire fence. She made her way along nearly its entire length and then stopped and knelt. In the light from the street lamp I saw that someone had snipped the ivy and the chain links, allowing her to raise the fence to make an opening and slip through.

"What am I supposed to do?" I whispered.

"Stay there and play guard, or come through, too," she said. "I don't give a shit."

Figuring I'd be less likely to be seen on the other side, I crawled through after her. I scrambled to my feet, then rubbed my hands on my jeans to clear away the mud and pebbles embedded in my palms. I glanced around to see two boys standing awkwardly with their hands in their pockets, staring at me. Tyesha was already talking to a boy near the bushes. I could barely make them out in the shadows. The shorter of the two boys walked over to me.

"Hey," he said. He wore a dark hoodie that he flipped back to reveal brown hair with spiked blond tips.

"Hey," I replied. He chewed his lip nervously but didn't make a move. In my peripheral vision I could see Tyesha and the boy with their heads together, either kissing or lost in private conversation.

"Do you want to smoke a joint?" Alarmed, I shook my head. "Aw, c'mon," he teased, "you'll like it." He lit what looked like a cigarette, though it smelled like burning socks, took a drag and passed it to his friend. His friend inhaled and held his breath, then offered the joint to me.

"No thanks," I said, remembering how much I'd enjoyed smoking before. I scanned the darkness for Tyesha and her friend, wondering if she was ready to leave. I was a nervous wreck by now and wished I'd stayed on our side of the fence.

Then, almost like bugs flitting toward a street light, both Tyesha and her friend appeared at our sides. Tyesha's guy grabbed the joint from the boy and took a drag. He held it out for Tyesha, who sucked on it hard. When he offered it to me I shook my head, glaring at Tyesha. She ignored me.

At that moment I heard the other boy hiss, "Someone's coming." He whirled and raced back in the direction of his school. The blond-spiked boy glanced at me, winked and bolted after him. Tyesha's friend tossed the joint into the bushes, gave her a quick kiss and suddenly he too was gone. She was left standing rubbery-legged beside me.

"Let's get out of here before we get caught." Like Alice's rabbit she disappeared through the hole in the fence and I scrambled after her. I felt my sweatshirt snag on the wire and I gave a hard jerk, tearing a small piece out of the back. I half-fell through the fence and stood to see her grinning at me from the damp ground.

"Wasn't that *fun*?" she said. She started to giggle.

"Not really," I muttered. I grabbed her hand and dragged her up from the dirt. We sneaked back to the school, Tyesha stumbling ahead of me toward the propped door.

"Shit!" she hissed.

"What's the matter?"

"The rock fell out or someone found it. We're locked out."

The bottom of my stomach twisted into knots. It had started to drizzle and November in Portland could be miserable. We might die of hypothermia out here. I was pissed at Tyesha but even angrier with myself for going along with her plan. Which hadn't been fun at all for me. Especially now.

"We'll just have to break back in through a window," I said.

I made my way to the north side of the school where it was least likely to have teachers or caretakers around. I knew a place where the windows were routinely left open for ventilation. The art room. I tried three windows before the fourth moved. Sliding it back I hoisted myself up then crawled in through the opening. I leaned back out and held out my hands to Tyesha. She was heavier than she looked, but eventually dragged herself through and fell to the classroom floor. From there we were able to creep back to our dorms without being seen.

"Wasn't that fun?" she enthused again, once we were back in our bunks. "Kudos to you for remembering the art room window!" I heard her sigh. "God, I'm hungry."

"Shut up!" I muttered. But at the back of my mind I felt a small thrill. Even though I wouldn't admit it to Tyesha, the night hadn't been so bad after all. I fell asleep with a smile on my face, thinking about the spikey-haired boy who hadn't even had a chance to tell me his name.

Just before Christmas the buzz of excitement around Stark quivered through the school like an electric current. Not only would some of the girls be able to go home for two weeks to their families, if they had them, the co-ed dance would be held just before break. The other Lunatics and I were nothing short of a nervous-sick for days, planning what we'd wear for meeting up with the male half of the school. I wondered if the spike-haired boy I'd met was still at Stark, or if he'd been sent to a foster home.

Tyesha had some knowledge about protocol as this would be her second Christmas dance. The boy she'd sneaked out to meet at Thanksgiving was named Zach, and he was all she could talk about. That she hadn't seen or communicated with him in a month didn't seem to matter. Suddenly he had become the Zac Efron of Stark. It annoyed the hell out of the rest of us.

"Did you kiss him?" curious Deanne wanted to know.

"Yes," Tyesha breathed, closing her eyes. "We made out for hours when we met at Thanksgiving." She lolled back on her bunk, hugging herself as if in ecstasy.

"Liar!" said Carla, laughing. "You wouldn't know how to French-kiss if a Frenchman kissed you."

"Screw you," Tyesha retorted. "God, Carla, at least I've been with a guy."

"French kissing could end up getting you pregnant," Carla warned. "You'd better be careful or there'll be a little Zac-ette running around. And I don't think Stark is going to create a nursery just for you."

"You know an awful lot for someone who looks like they should be in kindergarten," Tyesha shot back.

"I do know a lot," Carla said. She gave a shrug. "It's like the Playboy channel every night at my house."

We were all quiet for a few minutes, trying to erase the picture of Carla's dad and her step mom that had been involuntarily burned into our retinas.

"I had a boyfriend last summer. My dad was too preoccupied to even notice until he caught us together in my bedroom."

I glanced at Carla, shocked. "*Dude!* Seriously?"

She nodded, chewing her lip for a few minutes. "He called the boy's dad and threatened to have him charged with statutory rape." She gave a humorless laugh and glanced around at our dismayed faces. "Hey, it's okay. We didn't go all the way." She turned to Tyesha. "I'm just sayin', be careful." But Tyesha threw Carla a poisonous look and wouldn't talk to her for the rest of the night.

In spite of their squabble, we practiced for days putting makeup on each other, sitting around in our room like caged chimpanzees grooming and primping. The night of the dance even Deanne joined in by letting Tyesha erase her freckles with a nearly white foundation she'd pilfered from someone. With makeup and her luxurious blonde hair swinging loosely down her back, Carla looked like a Barbie doll, as Tyesha referred to her when she was being annoying.

Tyesha, though she'd spent the day bitching about a zit that only she could see, was elegant and poised as usual, with glistening lips and eyes that shone as green as a cat's underneath a dusting of mascara. I put my long dark hair into a ponytail and chose to go lightly with mauve eye shadow and eyeliner, adding just a bit of colored lip gloss as a final touch. Wearing the nicest clothes we had, we followed our chaperone out the front gates of our school, and through the otherwise forbidden gates to the boys.

When you build up something as much as we did that dance, it's bound to fall short of expectations. I guess we all thought we looked so gorgeous that boys would immediately come up and ask us to dance. Of course, that didn't happen. We all stood around on one side of the gym, looking like unwanted stepchildren beneath the red and green streamers and helium-filled Christmas-themed balloons, staring at the boys clumped across the room who were probably feeling the same way. No one had the nerve to ask the other to dance. My spike-haired boy was nowhere to be seen and apparently Tyesha's Zach wasn't either.

Finally, bored out of our skulls but stuck there until the chaperone was ready to take us back, Tyesha and I ventured out onto the dance floor and danced together. Before too long, several of the other girls were dancing with each other as well. Might as well make the best out of a bad situation. I had lost track of Deanne and hadn't seen Carla for over an hour. It never occurred to me that they weren't doing the same thing as the rest of us.

Then out of the corner of my eye I saw a couple huddled together near the bleachers, locked together as if there were plungers stuck to their faces. With a jolt I recognized that bright golden hair. Tyesha noticed me staring and turned to look. She froze and I saw her fists clench involuntarily.

Carla was in the arms of a tall boy with olive skin and wavy, coal black hair. She pulled back, her arms still around his neck then led him out to the dance floor. I could feel the simmering resentment bubbling up inside Tyesha, who still stood beside me, her breathing getting faster and faster. And suddenly I realized that the boy with Carla was Zach. An icy shiver passed through me as if someone had opened the gym doors. But it was just the shock of knowing that here was something that could sever our friendship as nothing else could.

Although Carla hadn't realized that the boy she had kissed and the Zach of Tyesha's dreams were the same person, that night in the dorm she got the cold-shoulder treatment from Tyesha. Carla apologized and promised never to let it happen again. But for a couple of days Tyesha avoided Carla, and if Carla was with Deanne or me, gave all of us the evil eye. Not that any of it had been our fault.

Nearly a week passed and still the coldness in the room was so tangible I couldn't stand it anymore. Finally when we were all together just before lights out I said, "Look, you guys. Our friendship is too important to let a stupid boy ruin it." I took in Tyesha's sullen expression and Carla's unhappy, downcast face. Then I caught Deanne's reassuring smile. They were stubborn, but I was determined. "Right?"

Tyesha shrugged and though she remained stiff while Carla gave her a hug, eventually she relented and gave her a hug back.

"Group hug!" yelled Deanne, and we folded together like the Lunatics we were, falling to the floor giggling.

As we extricated ourselves from the pile, Tyesha said, "I've just thought of another Commandment: 'Thou shalt not covet *another Lunatic's boyfriend.*' Carla laughed nervously, but Tyesha threw her arms around her and all was forgiven.

With Tyesha going to her aunt's for Christmas and Carla heading to Hawaii with her dad and latest step mom, I was making plans for how Deanne and I would celebrate

Christmas on our own at Stark. All four of us had squirreled ourselves away for long periods after class, coming up with the best things we could think of as gifts for the others.

Not having spending money of my own, I couldn't buy anything, but I had been drawing caricatures of the teachers since I'd arrived at Stark. When I was photocopying assignments for one of the teachers I made copies of my drawings, stapling them into a book that included sketches I'd made of each of the Lunatics. They were amazed at my work and it embarrassed me a bit to see how much they loved my gift.

Tyesha gave us each a bracelet she'd twisted into glowing coils from copper wire taken from the art room. We slipped them on, vowing never to remove them. Carla, whose lawyer father gave her gobs of cash as if it were a replacement for parenting, had purchased prepaid cell phones with additional minutes so we could keep in touch. We were ecstatic. At first we thought Deanne hadn't come up with anything, not that it mattered, then she pointed to our book bags. She'd embroidered our initials, followed by the letters "SRL", on the front of every bag.

Before they left, Tyesha and Carla took me aside.

"There's something not right with that girl," Tyesha said, glancing at Carla.

Carla chewed on her bottom lip, a frown creasing her forehead. "She's right, Breeze. We've been worried about her. Watch out for her, will you? I know she doesn't open up much, but at least she won't be alone with you staying here. She talks to you more than us."

So it wasn't just me, even Carla and Tyesha had noticed the change in Deanne since Thanksgiving. I reassured them that I would look after her, though I wasn't sure how I'd go about it. That night after the case worker had delivered Tyesha to her family and Carla was picked up by her father, Deanne and I were left alone in the dorm.

"Why aren't you going to your dad's over Christmas?" I asked Deanne when we were alone. She gave me a dark look and didn't answer at first.

Finally she said, "Can't. He got his ass arrested."

I was so taken aback that for a few minutes I couldn't think of anything to say. Since Thanksgiving break, Deanne had retreated into herself again and was almost as reticent and distant as when we'd first met her. Even though the weather was warm when she'd returned, she wore long sleeves to hide the bruises I caught sight of once when she was undressing. She'd chewed her nails so short the tips of her fingers looked like speed bumps. Most of the time she appeared so depressed she hardly spoke to anyone. It was none of my business, but she was my friend and we had gotten her to open up a lot over the past three months. It gnawed at me to lose the closeness we'd shared.

"What for?"

She turned away so I couldn't see her face. "I don't want to talk about it. I'm just glad I have an excuse not to go back." I saw her shoulders begin to shake and though I held back for a few minutes because I felt awkward about it, I moved toward her and gave her a hug. She began to sob uncontrollably against my shoulder, leaving me feeling helpless at how to console her.

"Did he hurt you?" I asked.

She stumbled to her cabinet counter and got a tissue to blow her nose, all the while keeping her back to me. "How do you define hurt? I wouldn't even know where to begin."

She turned to face me and leaned back against the counter, her pale freckled face splotched and reddened from crying. She studied me for a long time as if weighing my level of trust. Finally she said, "You have to promise you won't tell *anyone*. Not even Carla and Tyesha." And though I gave her my word, what she confided to me was too dangerous to keep secret.

The next morning I stopped by the school counselor's office and asked if I could talk to her for a minute. The counselor was a tiny, elderly woman named Mrs. Smart (which I thought was an enormous misnomer) with thin grey hair pulled into a bun. I'd been sent to her office a couple of times after my escapades to discuss why I was 'acting out,' to quote her. Maybe it was because she had been born six generations back, but she was not the easiest person to confide in. Still, I needed to share my concerns about Deanne, whose mood became more melancholy every day.

When I explained why I was there to see her, though, she as much as waved me away, saying, "Breeze, I can't discuss another student with you. I'm sure Deanne is just going through that awkward teenaged girl time that you'll all experience sooner or later. It's called growing pains. Her moodiness is most likely due to hormones. She'll grow out of it just like all girls do."

With those antiquated pearls of wisdom Mrs. Smart ushered me out the door. "Have Deanne come to see me and I'll give her something for cramps."

I just stared at her for a few minutes realizing that she was so close to retirement, or death, that she had no comprehension about what today's teenaged girls might be experiencing. Especially the girls at Stark who came with so much baggage, as Tyesha had once remarked, that they could have packed for a month long cruise vacation. I left her office feeling worse than when I'd arrived. No way was Deanne going to talk to a counselor, of that I was quite certain. It was up to me.

"It feels strange not to have a foot hit my kidneys every time I turn over," I said that night as I lay on my bunk.

From the other bed I heard Deanne laugh. I smiled to myself. She didn't laugh often. But her silence was never an uncomfortable one. We'd all gotten used to it over time.

"Do you want to tell me about your dad?" I ventured.

Deanne didn't respond for a long time, so long that I thought she'd fallen asleep. I heard her long intake of breath as if she had been working up to a reply.

"My father isn't what you'd call a good guy. My mom left because of him and basically just disappeared from our lives so he could never find her. If I ever see him again it'll be too soon."

I could hear the pain in her voice. A parent would have to be freaking awful for a kid to never want to see them again. I was too young to remember my dad because he had joined the National Guard and had disappeared somewhere in Afghanistan when I was just a baby. MIA, which meant Missing in Action, my mother told me. She never talked about him much and when I asked questions, that look would come and she would get so sad, I began to realize it was best to avoid the topic completely. But I knew for certain that if he'd been cruel, my mom wouldn't have deserted me the way Deanne's had. I didn't know what to say to make her feel better so I didn't say anything at all. Maybe being her friend was enough.

In the spring, Stark presented us with an amazing opportunity. Twice a week, those who wanted to participate, were bused to a local equestrian center where we could learn to ride, groom and clean up after horses. Deanne and I loved it; Tyesha and Carla wrinkled their noses the first day and decided that volunteering at a seniors' center was less obnoxious to their senses.

Sometimes grooming our horses seemed to loosen Deanne's reserve. Once after I'd made a comment that my mom had a pony when she was a kid, and that we'd once tried to adopt a horse for me, she said, "Do you think your dad would have let you buy a horse?"

I shrugged. "Maybe. I never knew him, but I think so. Even though my mother didn't share much, I know she loved him."

Deanne was silent for a while and only the sounds of soft brushing came from the other side of her horse. Finally she said, "But your dad was a hero, right? Mine's anything but. He would never even let me have a kitten."

She didn't elaborate any further and I didn't pry, even though I wanted to. Sometimes keeping your opinions to yourself is the best policy. As Carla said, MYOB.

I had spent eight months at Stark when one day I got called into Mrs. Watkins's office. This concerned me a bit because I hadn't done anything punishable, at least in my opinion, for a while. Still, there were kids who resented the popularity of us Lunatics and often tried to frame us for their indiscretions. But when I entered the principal's office, she gave me a welcoming smile and didn't appear upset at all.

"Sit down, Breeze," she said. "I've got wonderful news for you."

My heart started beating irrationally. Though I had no idea of what was to come, I was filled with dread. Why do people say they have good news when it almost always turns out to be the opposite?

"We've got a new foster family who wants to take you in."

A wave of panic welled up in my stomach. I liked being at this school. Actually I loved it. With rare exceptions, the food didn't make me sick. In fact it tasted better than most of my foster moms' cooking. I got a healthy respect from the other kids. And I lived for our trips to the equestrian center, a half-hour bus ride away. Deanne and I doted on the horses which, like us cast-off kids, had been donated.

"Oh," I said, trying to sound more interested and excited than I felt. "Who wants a sixteen-year-old girl?" Other than someone who needs a babysitter, I thought bitterly.

She thumbed through my bulging, paper-fat file as if she were looking for an important document, though I knew she'd rehearsed her sales speech already. No matter how much a kid protested or came up with rational excuses for not going to a new foster home, Children's Services always had a convincing argument that would eventually break them down.

"Their name is Thompson, Emily and Frank Thompson."

"Do they have any other kids?" *One can always hope not.* I mentally crossed my fingers.

"Another foster child they've had with them for nearly a

year," she said. "A special needs child. None of their own, though."

Yup, another unpaid, live-in babysitting job. I sighed, knowing special needs meant special duties, but it might be more pleasant and challenging than changing diapers.

"Did you tell them anything about me?" That would cinch it if she had. Once they heard my adventures at Stark they wouldn't want me anymore.

Mrs. Watkins hesitated and her face kind of puckered up. Without looking directly at me, her voice as mechanical as a telephone recording, she said, "I gave them your family history."

I frowned. "Did you tell them about the fire?"

She stared out the window at something I couldn't see. Or more likely she wasn't looking at anything, just recalling one of my finer moments. The fire had been a pivotal point for me. Without even trying I'd had the opportunity of a lifetime drop in front of me; too good to pass up, as they say. And once everything settled down, I began to receive respect and admiration from my peers, becoming 'King of the Castle,' as my mom used to call me when I acted superior.

I could see Mrs. Watkins becoming exasperated at my baiting. She finally met my round-eyed, innocent stare and said, "No, Breeze. I didn't mention the fire. And we didn't put it in your permanent record, either."

I shrugged and cocked my head to one side. "How about the thing with Mr. Simonson? Did you tell them about him?"

Mrs. Watkins sighed and seemed to grow older and smaller right before my eyes. She shook her head, looking very tired. Standing, she closed my file, placing it on the corner of her desk on top of a large stack of what were probably the files of other soon-to-be-released inmates. She gave the stack a couple of gentle pats, as if they were seeds she'd just planted in a garden.

"Breeze," she gave me a cold, narrow-eyed look that matched her voice, "I know what you're trying to do but it's not going to work. The Thompsons are aware that you've had a rough life these last few years and that's all they need to know." She took a deep breath and inflated, reverting back to her original size, and looking like a frog getting ready to say 'ribbit'. "If you give it a chance, you might actually learn to like living with them."

I kept my mouth shut then. There was no point in arguing the case now. If I wanted out, which I knew I would, there were plenty of ways to get sent back.

FIVE

As the days neared for me to meet my new foster family, I decided I would behave myself and give living with the Thompsons a try. At least for a while. I more or less had to because being underage, the choice was not mine. The Lunatics gave me a make-over as a send-off. Deanne, who fanatically trimmed her own curls nearly every day, cut my long wavy, brown hair that I kept in a ponytail to a more manageable shoulder-length. Carla showed me how to put on makeup, but it made me feel like someone else so when she wasn't looking I washed most of it off.

"I'll bet you twenty bucks you'll be back in a week," Tyesha said.

I chewed on my lip at that because I didn't have twenty dollars to spare, especially on a bet that would probably work out in her favor.

"Just because the longest I stayed in foster care before coming here was a few months, doesn't make me a candidate for automatic rejection," I protested.

"Make it forty," Carla followed, adding, "and if they kick you out before the end of the month you have to do our bathroom duty for the rest of your life. Or at least, till you leave Stark permanently."

I pulled a nasty face and stuck my tongue out at her, but she only flipped me off and laughed. We'd gotten to know each other pretty well. Deanne didn't say a word, she just shot me a tight-lipped smile as if she were going to miss us all being together.

Of course, they weren't the boss of me, but between the three of them they outnumbered me. So since we were going into summer break I agreed to their bet and decided to give it three months. Less than half the amount of time I'd spent at Stark.

"How many foster homes have you guys been in?" I asked the others one night after lights out.

"They never send me to foster care, just boarding schools," said Carla. "When those didn't work my dad figured I might do better in a residential treatment center, so I ended up here."

"I've had only one," Tyesha chimed in. "It was okay but some of the other kids they had didn't like me. They were there first so I got sent back. How about you, Breeze?"

"I've gone through four, no five before Stark," I corrected, "I almost forgot the Dahl family because I only lasted two weeks."

"Wow!" Carla let out a whistle, "what makes you so special?"

I shrugged and tried to appear nonchalant, but the fact that none of my foster homes wanted to keep me on longer, or even adopt me, still hurt at times.

"You'd have to ask the foster families. I think maybe I wasn't a good mix with other personalities." I left it at that. The truth was that I had never really been given a good reason for them not wanting me to stay.

Carla scrutinized my face for a moment then turned to Deanne. "How about you, Deanne?"

"I've never been in foster care," came Deanne's quiet voice. "I think there's a stigma against ginger kids."

The three of us burst out laughing. I'm not sure that Deanne meant it as a joke as she didn't chime in. Then we heard a sharp rap on the door, which was a 'be quiet' warning from the hall monitor. At that we quieted down and finally fell asleep.

Because I would be leaving soon, I began hanging out with the Lunatics as often as I could. They were the first real friends I'd had since my mother died. It was difficult to admit to them, much less myself, how much I was going to miss our time spent together. Without becoming mushy, I wanted to share my feelings, I just didn't know how. But with only ourselves to count on, we had sworn loyalty to the death. So maybe they knew, after all.

The night before the Thompsons were to meet me I hardly slept at all. I was so jumpy I was almost sick to my stomach a couple of times, not helped any by Tyesha kicking the underside of my mattress because I kept her awake with my restless tossing. By morning I was a wreck. My brown eyes had matching brown circles underneath, like reverse eye shadow, from lack of sleep. And I had a headache, which put me in a bad mood. Still, I showered, put my newly shortened hair into a ponytail, and got dressed in the best clothes I had: a pair of khaki cargo pants and a pale yellow sweatshirt with the 'SRL' logo Deanne embroidered, and a white collared shirt underneath.

Most of us, except for Carla, relied on donations and school hand-me-downs for clothes, so there was no opportunity for us to get uppity about fashion. Chances were I'd inherited my clothes from a girl who had 'graduated' from Stark, just as the clothes I outgrew were passed down to the younger ones.

As I nervously waited in Mrs. Watkins' office for the Thompsons to arrive, I chewed on my cuticles, a habit that had driven my mother crazy. Reminded of this I shoved my hands in my lap and tried to sit patiently. Then there was a knock on the door and Mrs. Watkins stood up. I turned in my seat to see my new family.

Mr. Thompson reminded me of a giraffe, tall and thin, with wrinkled skin like saddle leather, tanned dark brown from the sun. I could see white skin peeping out from the neck of his yellow and brown plaid shirt, which compounded the giraffe resemblance, and realized that probably the tan ended where the shirt started. He smiled at me, looking a little shy. When he took off his cowboy hat and revealed a nearly bald head it made him appear much older.

Mrs. Thompson, on the other hand, looked too young to be married to him. She had lots of curly hair the color of wheat that bounced around her shoulders, and her eyes were such a pale blue they could have been water. The scent of her perfume wafted over to me, which I recognized as lilacs. She said, "Hello, Breeze," with a strange accent I didn't recognize. In spite of my natural reserve with strangers, they both seemed nice enough. Mrs. Thompson reminded me of my mother a bit, although she looked nothing like her. Then I saw their other foster child.

I tried not to stare, I really did, but I couldn't help it. The kid was about five or six and missing half of his left arm that just tapered off, and on the right a sort of flipper appendage with a couple of stubby, incomplete fingers. He wore ridiculously thick-lensed glasses held tight to his head by a band that went clear around the back. He grinned at me with what was left of his front teeth. I remembered going through that gap-toothed stage during first grade. I tried to smile back at him but I was in such shock that I felt if I did it would just look more like a grimace. I gave a kind of stiff nod and glanced away.

Mrs. Watkins took control of the awkward moment and invited us all to sit. Jonathan, that was the kid's name, just stared at me, grinning the whole time, making me even more edgy. I was dead scared, certain I was going to laugh or cry and get into deep trouble, so I forced myself to stare at Mrs. Watkins and kept a tight smile on my face.

"Mrs. Watkins tells us you like working with horses," said Mrs. Thompson with that odd accent. I didn't answer because I was struck mute with nervousness.

"That's wonderful," she continued, "because we live on a ranch in southeastern Oregon and have several Quarter Horses. We also have a few hundred head of cattle and could sure use another rider to help move them onto range land."

I got so excited when she said that I almost lost my practiced reserve. But I couldn't let on that I knew there was no way this would work out. The foster families usually got tired of me, or their expectations of what I could do for them was too high, and I would always get sent back. There was no doubt in my mind that this would be the case with the Thompsons, too. And what if I started to like it there? No, I resolved, I would not let myself get attached. It had happened to me once or twice before and it had taken me months to get over it. I'd bluff it and get them to let me stay just long enough to win my bet with the girls and then they could send me back.

"I guess I'm pretty good with horses," I said keeping my voice cool and level. Then I told one of the biggest lies ever. "But I don't really like them. I don't really like much except television."

"Oh dear, that's too bad." Mr. Thompson had finally found his voice. "We don't own a TV." He smiled, kind of bashful and apologetic, his brown face crinkling at the corners of his eyes. "And though we've got a computer, we're not hooked up to the internet."

From the glare Mrs. Watkins shot me I realized my mouth must have been hanging open in shock. As I couldn't think of one thing to say I just stayed silent because everyone else had excited grins on their faces. Miserable, I stared across the room and caught Jonathan's eye, squinting behind his lenses like a carp trying to see through a fish bowl.

The next three months were going to be torture.

SIX

By comparison to the interview, the trip to the ranch had all the suspense of sitting in a dentist's chair, knowing that you were about to undergo a root canal. The Thompsons came to get me in an enormous blood-red pick-up truck, so high off the ground Mr. Thompson had to reach down and give me his hand to pull me into the cab. I wondered what on earth anyone needed a vehicle the size of a train for, but then realized that on a ranch there were probably plenty of uses. For some reason they hadn't brought Jonathan along, for which I was grateful. A three hour drive with him staring at me the whole time and me trying to avoid looking at his flipper would have been excruciating.

"Do you want to listen to the radio?" Mr. Thompson asked and without waiting for an answer turned it on. I am no fan of country music and of course, that's what he liked. Even more annoying, he sang along with it, and oh joy, Mrs. Thompson sang along with him, just like they were Tim McGraw and Faith Hill doing a duet. I thought I was going to be sick.

It hurt to say goodbye to the Lunatics, even if I was only going to be gone for three months. Uncharacteristic for her, Tyesha was a little wary as she approached me, her hands behind her back. Forced to bring them forward for a hug goodbye, she relinquished a coral sleeveless tank top I'd always admired.

"Thought you'd like to borrow it this summer," she

mumbled, trying not to let me see tears in her eyes, "just don't get any horse poop on it." The tank had once been a sweatshirt she'd reworked after coercing it from another student, and I knew how much she liked it.

"I'll take good care of it until I can get it back to you," I promised. "I'll even wash it by hand."

Carla walked up to me, stood on tiptoes and pinned my bangs back with a couple of her favorite butterfly clips. Then she whirled and bolted away without so much as a hug.

Deanne scowled at Carla's back then turned to me with a shrug.

"I'm lending you my book of Emily Dickinson poems. You can keep it unless you don't last three months. In which case, I get it back."

I clasped it in my hands, hugging it to my chest until I recalled that it was the only thing she had left from her mother. I pressed it back into hers and said, "You keep it for me to read when I get back. It will give me something to look forward to."

She nodded, her eyes and mouth downcast. Then I felt a hand on my arm and heard Mrs. Watkins clear her throat. I turned to see the Thompsons waiting patiently beside their truck. I blew a kiss to Tyesha and Deanne, for Carla was nowhere to be seen, and mentally said goodbye to Mrs. Watkins and Stark. But only until the end of summer.

As I stared miserably out the window, missing the Stark Raving Lunatics already, I watched miles and miles of pretty much nothing pass by. It occurred to me that this probably wasn't much different from the Thompson's ranch: acres of scrub and fields and cows as far as the eye could see. My lip quivered so I bit down on it to keep from getting weepy. Just then I caught Emily smiling at me in the rear view mirror. It was time for 'the talk.' The one I knew to be inevitable.

"So," I said as casually as I could, "what are your rules?" Mrs. Thompson turned to me and smiled again, a puzzled expression crossing her face. Obviously she couldn't hear me above the radio. I repeated the question. She reached over and turned the radio down to just a hum, narrowing her eyes quizzically.

"We don't have any rules, Breeze. You'll find that life at the Double-T Ranch is probably nothing like the other places you've lived."

I shook my head, frowning. "No, I mean, like, what's my curfew, stuff like that?" The Thompsons glanced at each other and fell silent for a few minutes.

"Well," Mr. Thompson began, inclining his head to look at me, then back to the road ahead, "there's really no need to have a curfew because there's nowhere to go. The nearest town is an hour away. If you needed something we'd all go together." He gave Mrs. Thompson a quick grin. "Right, hon?" She returned his smile and patted his arm.

Nowhere to go. Wasn't that just the story of my life, I thought. I stared out the truck window, hoping to see something interesting out there. But it was like watching the scenery in cartoons, identical frames passing by over and over again, like the kid watching isn't going to notice the same barn, the same trees, the same horses. It became so boring with the nasal droning twang of the awful country music I fell asleep, only to wake up an hour later to see the same damn thing, all over again.

Suddenly I remembered I had my cell phone. I text-messaged Tyesha, "OMFG GMO!" and saw that the phone had gone into Roam mode and the message couldn't be sent.

Things were getting worse by the minute. Could Mrs. Watkins have known the kind of place she was sending me? Surely this didn't fall into the Stark School rules of finding homes for the kids. I might as well be in prison. Stuck on a huge farm with no T.V., no internet, no email, no friends. Only dogs, horses and cows. And Flipper-boy.

We stopped for dinner at the only restaurant in a tiny town whose name I didn't catch because I must have blinked. The town was too small for any franchise fast food places, and when we walked in the cook and waitress seemed really glad to see us. I couldn't help but wonder how these people made a living. We were the only customers in the place, an old fashioned, renovated barn with a red and white checked tablecloth draped over a table that rocked and creaked whenever one of us leaned on it.

The waitress, who had a couple of teeth missing in front that she kept trying to hide behind her hand while she told us about the day's special, gave us actual sit-down menus. After we'd eaten and Mrs. Thompson paid the bill, I saw Mr. Thompson go back to the table and leave a tip that was more than the price of the whole meal. For some reason that embarrassed me. I couldn't help blushing as we left the restaurant and I heard the waitress give a subdued squeal of joy, but no one else appeared to notice.

Back on the road again for another hour and then suddenly there we were. At the Double-T Ranch. I don't know what I'd been expecting, maybe something like the ranches you might see in the movies? A white, three-story wood frame house with a wraparound porch, a lazy old herd dog sleeping on the front step. A curved driveway lushly framed with trees. Hitching posts. This had none of those. A double wide mobile home with faded blue siding and peeling white shutters squatted between a couple of twisted Ponderosa pine. Half-dead azaleas, with a few desiccated blossoms left hanging, had been planted around the dried-up lawn to complete the landscaping.

We drove through two tall wood gateposts with an enormous curving, hand-carved wooden sign that spanned the space between them. It said "Double-T Ranch," with a logo of two 'T's', one right side up, the other upside down. Off in the distance, an enormous weathered-gray barn cast a giant shadowy square across the yard. That was about it. Pretty much a dry, yellow-brown wasteland with wire fencing around the outside. I tried not to look as disillusioned as I felt.

As we slowed to a stop, I saw the house and barn were now bathed in deep tangerine from the lowering sun. It was nearly dusk. The Thompsons jumped out of the truck, and when I followed I heard what sounded like thousands of cows all bellowing at once. Then the whinnying of the horses started up. The Thompsons slammed the truck doors closed, leaving my backpack that contained my belongings inside. I opened the door and started to reach into the back for it.

"We'll get it later. The livestock need to be taken care of first," Mr. Thompson called out as he headed toward the outlying fields. I couldn't help wondering if Jonathan was in the house, but no one mentioned him.

Finally Mrs. Thompson, remembering she had a new 'child' in the family, turned to me and said, "Do you want to help with the horses?" I didn't have much choice; that was what I was here for, right? Overnight I'd been promoted from babysitter to farmhand. I nodded.

She strode off in the direction Mr. Thompson had gone, toward the field surrounding the barn, pivoting back to me as she walked. "By the way, you can call me Emily. And it's okay to call Frank by his first name, too. We're not so formal here as to require you to call us Mr. and Mrs. Thompson."

I was glad she'd clarified how I was supposed to refer to them because I had been wondering about it. I didn't want to sound rude or too forward. There are a lot of things people can say about me, but being impolite is not one of them. Usually. I bent to tuck my cargo pants into my sock tops so they wouldn't get dirt or horse manure on them, then hurried to catch up to her.

"How many horses do you have?"

She opened the gate to let me through and then latched it carefully behind us.

"We have five. Four are rideable. There is a nice, older mare who is the mother of the filly I ride now that might be suitable for you."

I nodded, a little disappointed again because by giving me an old horse she must think that I was a novice rider, which I wasn't. I tightened my lips. I guess I would have to show them what I could do. As we reached the pasture where four horses were lined up, they began pacing and whinnying expectantly.

Emily introduced me to her horses, all of them stocky, Quarter Horses, bred primarily for working cattle. They were friendly and sweet, two chestnuts and two palominos. Eager faces pushed forward, greedily jostling each other for the expected treat of peppermints that Emily produced from her pocket.

"This is Honey, the mare I mentioned would be the best horse for you." She pointed to one of the golden palominos, the one with the enormously thick, cream-colored mane and tail. I knew I had my work cut out for me grooming that horse.

"What about the fifth horse? Why can't you ride him?" I pointed to a muscular dun horse with brown striped legs and a matching brown stripe down his back. He was penned in a small corral away from the others, racing back and forth, whinnying his lungs out. Each time he reached the end of the enclosure he'd rear up, spin on his haunches and bolt in the opposite direction. He looked like one of those wild horses my mother had taken me to see years ago.

"He's a Kiger mustang and not broken yet," Emily said. "Stay clear of him. He's a stallion, and in addition to being wild is also unpredictable." But I was fascinated by that horse and could hardly tear my eyes away. What a thrill it would be to ride him!

The origin of her accent had been bugging me all day. I had to ask where she was from, even if she thought I was being impolite. But she only laughed when I apologized for asking.

"I'm from Sydney, Australia originally. A few years ago I came here on a temporary work visa to teach school. Then my visa ran out. I was faced with voluntarily returning home or being deported. I had no family left there and I wanted to stay in America." She hesitated and a flush reddened her face right to her ears. "Anyhow, I met Frank and we got married just in time for me to stay in this country."

I was old enough to know what that meant. She and Frank had gotten married so she could get a Green Card from United States Immigration. People had been doing it for years. I'd even met some foster kids who said their parents had only given birth to them so they would be allowed to stay in the U.S. I felt let down, expecting better of her, I guess, though I had no reason for doing so. I didn't know her any better than she knew me. Nor would I probably get the chance.

I helped Emily turn the four horses out into the loafing shed, a three-sided building where they would have shelter in case of an overnight storm, then we tossed them some hay and filled their water troughs. We did the same for the Kiger stallion, whose name was Diablo, but he stayed separate from the others, even though he kept whinnying long after we'd gone.

"Herd dynamics," Emily explained. "Among other things. He'll get over it."

We headed back toward the house and entered through a homemade wood-frame, added-on room, with a wash stand and sink to clean up before going into the house. After we washed up, I followed her silently as we passed through a tiny laundry room into the kitchen. It was bright and cheerful, with lemons and oranges on the lace-fringed curtains, and a matching tablecloth on the chrome and Formica table. Jonathan sat at the table with a pleasant looking older woman. He gave me that toothless grin and I responded with a sickly wave. The woman stood up.

She looked like she baked. Maybe it was because she was dressed like someone you'd see in a photo on the front of a baking powder container: squarish hips and a half-apron over a full, blue-on-white polka-dotted skirt. She wore her curly grey hair poofy at the top but shaved at the neckline. And at the throat of her open-necked mauve blouse was the most beautiful diamond studded crucifix I'd ever seen.

"Breeze," said Emily, "this is Mrs. Shoemaker. She helps take care of Jonathan. She lives on the neighboring property about a half-mile down the road to the east." Mrs. Shoemaker smiled and held out her pudgy, blue-veined hand. I shook it politely. Where the heck was east from here, I wondered, Idaho?

"I've heard a lot about you," she said, which got me wondering *what exactly* she had heard, but then she finished with, "I'm glad Jonathan will have a big sister to talk to."

I just gave what probably looked like an idiotic grin because I didn't know what else to do. I also couldn't think of a single thing to say. I was in shock. A big sister? That was a first for me. Maybe for a few months. Then I'd be back at Stark with the Lunatics, where I belonged. Or die trying.

SEVEN

At first, when we'd driven up to the ranch and I saw the tiny mobile home where the Thompsons lived, I had the uneasy suspicion that I might have to share a room with Jonathan. This happened more often than not with other foster homes where I'd lived. Multiple foster kids packed six deep, beds lining the room like pencils in a box. There had never been an opportunity to have a room of my own, at least not since my mother died. The Double-T Ranch was to be different.

Emily had relinquished her sewing room to create a private bedroom for me. But she hadn't done any decorating at all. The furnishings consisted of an unpainted three-shelf wooden bookcase with coffee ring stains, a dresser with a streak on the mirror that wouldn't come off no matter how many times I rubbed it with my sleeve, and a single bed covered with a frayed homemade patchwork quilt.

A couple of recent issues of teen magazines and crossword puzzle books had been placed on top of the dresser. I picked one up as if to pretend that I was interested in it, but I never read that stuff. That was Carla's forté. Nor did I like doing crosswords, which Tyesha enjoyed. Whatever. I'd stash them away to take back to the Lunatics. Not knowing what was expected of me, I was rescued when Frank knocked at the door, carrying my bookbag. He set it at the foot of the bed. Even with those few items, the tiny bedroom was cramped. Frank cleared his throat and muttered something inaudible, then backed out of the room.

"I thought you might like to add your own touches," Emily said, leaning through the doorway. "When you are ready we can look through some catalogs and order a new bedspread and curtains."

My mouth hung open in surprise. No one had ever done anything like that for me before. I almost said we could go online and order through the internet when I remembered that they weren't connected. I didn't even want to think about the age of their computer, which probably wasn't even capable of internet access. Emily had offered me the occasional use of their phone to call my friends, but the only one they had was in the kitchen, an ancient black, wall-mounted unit with a dial that I wasn't sure I could figure out. And no privacy at all. I felt a moment of panic. It had been a long time since I had not had access to a phone or the internet. Even the most rudimentary foster family owned a computer.

Or television! I suddenly recalled what Frank had said in the truck. What did people who didn't have television do in the evening? Emily still hovered in the doorway, waiting for me to follow her. Or make some kind of response. One thing was for certain, with previous foster families it had been a lot easier figuring out was expected of me. I gave her a smile because expressing my true emotions was not something I did freely.

"That would be great," I said, then after a little hesitation added, "thank you." And although I really meant it, I couldn't help feeling guilty because I wished I were back at Stark instead, watching 'Glee' with the Lunatics.

When she retreated into the next room I remembered my cell phone and flipped it open to see if there was a signal so I could send a message to one of the girls. But it still read 'no signal available.' I sighed, already missing my friends and the crazy stunts we'd pull behind the teachers' backs, reveling in the danger-rush of getting caught. A heavy, aching loneliness settled over me. Though why I would be lonely living like a rabbit in a tiny warren of a house with three other people was incomprehensible.

As far back as I could remember my mother and I had lived in apartments. Most of the time I'd had my own bedroom, but sometimes I'd had to share with Mom. I didn't mind that because often we'd stay up late at night talking, even if she had to go to work the next day, and me to school. It was like having a sleep-over every night.

The places we lived were never fancy. Mom didn't make enough money as a temp secretary to afford much, especially with my father out of the picture. Some of the apartments we rented were scary at night. Mom would carry her keys laced between the fingers of one hand, my hand gripped tightly in the other. In the daylight we'd see the nasty graffiti and tagging sprayed on the outside walls. A couple of times we'd had our Jeep 'keyed', bad words scratched into the paint.

When the noises got too loud in the next apartment or gangs of teenagers would be sitting on her car in the morning and spit or swore at her when she asked them to move, Mom would look around for a new place to live. She'd let me choose, pasting a map of Oregon across the kitchen wall and covering my eyes with a bandana. Then, almost like I was about to hit a piñata or play 'pin the tail on the donkey,' she'd spin me round and I'd point out our next home. And we'd start all over again. The new place never turned out much different than the old one. So when I thought about it, the Thompson's mobile home wasn't that bad at all.

I hoisted my suitcase onto the bed and began hauling out my things. I pulled open the top drawer in the chest and placed my T-shirts, socks and panties inside. Then I opened the second drawer and squished my jeans and shorts flat so they'd fit. As I did so I felt a rough ridge at the bottom and pulled the clothes back out to have a look. There was something carved into the wood.

The name Kevin Palola had been roughly cut into the bottom of the drawer. It looked as if an attempt had been made to sand it down but the cuts were deep and angular, as if the person who had done the original carving was furious. I traced my fingers over them and got a small splinter stuck underneath my nail. I grabbed a pair of tweezers from my things and removed the sliver, wrapping a tissue around my finger to stop it bleeding. That was stupid! I chided myself. I placed one of the magazines over the wood cuts and shoved my clothes back inside, wondering about this Kevin guy. More likely, the chest was second hand and had passed through a lot of people before it arrived at the Thompsons.

Once I'd finished unpacking, I headed to the kitchen. Frank had heated canned spaghetti in the microwave for our dinner. Probably the closest version of fast food that they ate. Mrs. Shoemaker had gone home and Jonathan sat at the table looking at a book. Maybe he was reading, but I didn't know if he could yet. He held down the pages with the stub of his left arm and turned the pages with the little flipper-thing. Watching him gave me a weird feeling in my stomach. I glanced away quickly.

Frank set the table, then placed the spaghetti in a huge bowl that he transferred to the table. Emily brought a salad out from the fridge and poured two glasses of milk, one for Jonathan and one for me. She motioned me to sit beside him. He looked up and gave me a grin. I kept my eyes averted while I ate, trying not to watch as he made rough attempts on his own and was finally aided by Emily.

After dinner I helped clear the dishes from the table and loaded them into the dishwasher, thankful for at least one modern invention. I wondered if I was expected to head to my room or to perform chores. In other foster homes they made it pretty clear what I was supposed to be doing with my time. Feeling unsettled, I finally asked, "Is there anything else I can help with?"

Emily just shook her head and smiled. She moved to sit in one of two matching red velvet recliners that clashed with the gold shag carpet in the living room. She reached down to a wicker basket and pulled out a half-knitted, variegated green and gold sweater, some wool and knitting needles, and began to click away.

"Why don't you have a look around. We've got lots of books you might be interested in. Or the next time we go to town you can get a library card and check out some books or magazines."

Books, books, books! Is that all they had to do? Read? Although my mom and I had gone to the library every weekend, I hardly read at all any more unless a teacher required it for an assignment. Even though I loved working with horses, I didn't want to read about them. Or try to lose myself in a romance about a dorky girl falling in love. Jonathan must have sensed my dismay. When he spoke I realized with a shock that it was the first time I'd heard him say anything.

"Would you like to play a game with me?" he asked shyly. "I know a whole bunch of card games." I swallowed hard. I really *didn't* want to play with him. More to the point, I didn't want to *watch* him play. And how on earth would he be able to hold his cards? But I couldn't hurt a little kid's feelings either.

"Sure," I replied, "but I don't know any card games."

"That's okay, I'll teach you," he stated with the confidence of a first-grader. "We'll play Crazy 8's."

And then I saw how it was he could play. Frank or Emily had rigged up the sort of paper stand people use at the computer for copy typing, to act as a card holder. And he was quite adept with the little fingers on the end of his flipper. It occurred to me that because he'd never known any other way of life, he'd had to adapt the way that other people did not. I felt so ashamed my face turned red and I got a little teary-eyed. Fortunately no one noticed. Crazy 8's, I thought, a perfect game for me to learn and take home to teach the Lunatics.

EIGHT

The next morning was more or less the same routine with the horse chores, only in reverse. We put them out in the pasture, and cleaned out the stalls, but that didn't stop them from groveling over us, trying to coerce us into giving them treats. Emily had brought a healthy snack, sliced carrots this time instead of peppermints. She handed them to me so I could give a couple to each horse before she turned them out, slapping them on the rump as they passed through the gate. The Kiger stallion was throwing a fit as they left, but they all ignored him.

"We'll saddle up after lunch and see how you do with Honey," she said. But I was still thinking about Diablo and wondering when they were going to train him, so I asked her.

"Frank started working with him until he got too busy with the calves this spring. We'll probably hire a trainer until he has more time to put some skills into him."

Diablo seemed tame enough to me, I thought, as I stroked his neck. "I'll bet you'd let me get on your back, wouldn't you?" I said quietly to him so Emily couldn't hear. He gave me a shove with his muzzle as if he understood what I was saying and the idea of me training him was a secret shared between us.

As we walked back to the house to make breakfast, I noticed that we always ate *after* we'd fed the animals. Even going so far as to first feeding the ancient black Labrador and grey-striped barn cat that stayed close to the barn. I commented on this to Emily.

"They depend on us, Breeze. It wouldn't be fair to feed ourselves first." She gave me a hug. I should have felt bad that I involuntarily went all stiff and didn't respond, but it had been years since anyone other than the Lunatics had hugged me. I sure didn't want it to start here. After all, I'd be gone and back at Stark in three months.

"If you wouldn't mind helping me with the dishes after breakfast, then you have some free time to yourself before lunch," she said. For a moment I felt as if I'd been let out of a cage. No one had ever *asked* me to help. It was always an order. An expected service for taking me in.

"I'll do them for you," I offered, "although I can't guarantee you'll be able to find them again." She laughed and gave me another hug, which made me even more uncomfortable. I gritted my teeth, trying to figure out how I could manipulate things so I could stay long enough to win my bet with the Lunatics, yet still get sent back home when I was ready. I'd have to work on that one.

After we'd eaten a hearty farm breakfast of crispy fried sausages, scrambled eggs stuffed with chunks of melting cheddar cheese, and buttered toast, followed by fresh strawberries, I finished loading the dishes into the dishwasher and went outside. I called Dingus, the old black Labrador, to my side and patted him. Maybe I'd take him for a walk. This was a good plan, in theory, as most dogs yearn for walks, but ancient Dingus headed back home when we hadn't even gotten half-way across the pasture. I tried calling and whistling for him a few times, even making a fool out of myself trying to cajole him into getting up and running with me. Finally I gave up as he was either completely deaf or just ignoring me.

I turned my back on the house and surveyed the surrounding landscape of over-grazed fields and listless aspens, sealed in on the far horizon by grey-blue hills. In every direction, brown and white cattle milled around hay bales the size of Volkswagens. In the center of a moving dust cloud I saw Frank bouncing about on the old John Deere tractor, dropping still more bales in the field. Though each time he dispersed the hay the cattle swarmed around him, they'd part like the Red Sea because he kept the tractor moving at all times for his own safety.

The fence enclosing the cattle looked too flimsy to keep them penned in, but I'd been told it was hot-wired, and the cattle respected it. I didn't understand what Emily meant by hot-wire, so I went over to the fence and touched it. A jolt of humming pain shot through my arm all the way to my shoulder. Hot-wire meant the fence was electrified. And so was I, for about two minutes. I learned the hard way about crossing through fences. After that I gave them a huge clearance whenever I ducked underneath.

The goal for my walk was to head toward the hills, find a place that wasn't brown and dirty or smelled like manure, where I could get away from everyone, and think for a while. I set off, glancing at my watch as I left. I needed to be back in time for lunch and it was already 10 o'clock.

I hadn't been to this part of the state since my mother had taken me to see the wild horses. Even at that I wasn't familiar with the desert-like terrain. After hiking for an hour or more I realized it had been stupid of me to leave the house without a bottle of water or letting anyone know where I had gone. With the heat of the June sun burning down on me, my mouth was dusty and dry. I knew my face would already be sunburned because whenever I blinked it felt like my eyelids were about to split.

For the first time since setting out on my walk, I looked back in the direction of the house and realized that I had gone so far I couldn't even see the hundreds of cattle that would be difficult for even the most nearsighted person to miss. I was certain I must be on range land, yet still those misty-blue mountains remained elusively in the distance.

Not sure of my bearings, I kept walking and lost track of the time. With the sun almost directly overhead, that meant it must be close to noon. I would be late for lunch. Although I was pretty sure it wouldn't be the case with the Thompsons, for some foster families that was enough for them to call Children's Services. Not that different from the way people return bad meat to the grocery store. I turned away from the mountains, keeping them behind me as I made my way back toward the direction I imagined the Double-T ranch to be.

But with the heat so overpowering, my head started to pound. I began to feel dizzy and sick to my stomach. With no trees nearby, the next best thing was a dry, prickly bush. Though it cast almost no shade, I sat underneath as far as possible to take a rest and figure out if I was going the right way. Then in the far distance I could just make out what looked like a house. My heart jumped with relief. I'd rest for a few more minutes, then head in that direction.

Just then I heard a whining sound to my right and glanced over my shoulder. A scruffy coyote, its short, golden-brown coat nearly camouflaged by the surrounding terrain, trotted toward me carrying something in its mouth. When it saw me it stopped and stared, just as I stared back. I held my breath, not knowing what I should do or how I should react. Would it run away if I made noise? Or would it attack?

It did neither. It dropped what it had in its mouth, came toward me and licked my face. Around its neck was a brown leather collar with tags. It was only then I saw that this was no coyote, but a large, male domestic dog. I heaved a huge sigh of relief and started to cry. He turned to leave. Suddenly I realized that he was my way out. The dog could lead me to his home and from there I could get directions and find my way back to the Thompson's.

I scrambled to my feet and grabbed the dog's collar. But at the same time he remembered what he had been carrying in his mouth when he saw me. He half-dragged me over to a tiny body lying in the dust. Just before he was about to snatch it up again, I let go of the dog, reached down and picked up the body. It was a newborn baby rabbit, still too young to have its eyes open. I clutched it close to me because it was scarcely breathing. Then to my dismay the dog ran away.

"Wait!" I yelled, but the dog tore off in the direction of the house I had only barely been able to see before. Now the house had completely disappeared over the horizon. Cradling the baby rabbit in my shirt, I started after the dog. Like the coyote I had mistaken it for, he was swift as the wind and his color blended naturally with the landscape. Soon he was out of my sight.

I dropped to my knees and began to cry in huge, gulping sobs. Both this baby rabbit and I were going to die and no one knew where we were or even cared. I glanced down at the tiny creature in my hands. It made blind, soundless sucking motions, needing to quench its thirst even more than I did.

Then just when I had given up I heard a thumping noise and the sound of panting. I looked up and there was the dog again, but it wasn't the dog that was breathing hard. A person on a big black and white paint horse cantered behind him, and he headed toward me as if he already knew I was there. I stood and waved one arm in the air, folding the rabbit carefully into my shirt with my other hand. The dog bounded toward me and bounced up, trying to get the baby rabbit.

"Cache, get down," ordered the dog's owner. He sat high in the saddle of that large horse as naturally as if he were sitting on a chair. The dog obeyed instantly, lying down in a guilty heap at my feet though his eyes never strayed from the rabbit in my shirt.

"Who are you?" The voice sounded angry. It was a young man's voice. Even from where he sat, I could tell he wasn't much older than me because I could see the pink cheeks that showed from under his wide-brimmed cowboy hat had never felt a razor. He wore heavy denim jeans pulled over scuffed cowboy boots, and a thin blue cotton shirt with fake pearl snap buttons. My mouth was too dry to answer.

"Here," he growled. He swung easily off his horse, removed his hat and placed it on my head. I started to pull it off, but he said, "Wear it until we get back. You're close to having sunstroke, if you don't already."

He handed me a water bottle from a saddle bag and I took it with my spare hand. He watched as I gulped greedily, rivulets of water running down my chin. The water dried before I had a chance to wipe it off. He grabbed the bottle from me.

"That's enough. Too much and you'll be sick." His blue eyes raked scornfully over my dusty, sweat-stained clothes. "Can you ride?"

I nodded, rendered mute from shame and weariness.

He stepped to the one side of his horse and cupped his hands to give me a leg-up into the saddle. When I hesitated he realized I held something. He tried to pry my hands apart, but I pulled away, keeping the bunny covered under my shirt.

"What's that?"

"It's a baby rabbit your dog found," I managed to croak. "It needs to be fed."

He shook his head. "It would be better to leave it and let nature take care of things. There are a million rabbits out here that might find it and nurse it, but you can't raise it. It won't live. It's too young."

That made me mad. "I can take care of it."

He just laughed and that made me madder. "Okay, if you're that stubborn I guess you'll have to find out for yourself. Now climb up on that horse and let's get you home."

I held the rabbit in one hand and grabbed the saddle horn with the other. He boosted me into the saddle and I settled comfortably on the horse. *Home*, I thought. It sounded nice, but it wasn't the home where I wanted to be. He turned and started to walk off. The horse automatically followed, and so did I. As if I had a choice in the matter.

We walked in silence for about ten minutes, me on the horse, the boy's long legs striding effortlessly alongside. I looked down at the dark blond hair that curled up around his ears, and grew untrimmed on his tanned neck. I wondered if he missed his hat because even though I still wore it, my head was close to exploding from the heat. I dared not look down at the rabbit because I knew it was at least as hot from being held in my hands. I shifted it down to my shirt tails and cradled it like it was in a sling. The boy saw this and shook his head but didn't comment.

"What's your name?" he asked finally.

"Breeze."

He gave a short laugh. "Was there a weather system going on the day you were born? Or were you just a gassy baby?"

Glaring at him, I retorted, "A lot of people think it's kind of a cool name."

He shrugged. "What were you doing out here without water or anything else?"

I explained that I'd just gone out for a walk. For some reason I didn't mention the Thompsons. I didn't want them to know I'd gotten lost. But he already knew more about me than I knew about him.

"Frank and Emily have been worried sick about you," he said. "They thought you might have run away. They were going to give you another hour and then they were calling the cops."

I almost laughed out loud. Running away was the farthest thing from my mind, and yet, it was something I had tried in the past with one awful foster home. The Thompsons were probably aware of that or they wouldn't have thought of it. I realized he hadn't told me his name.

"So who are *you*?"

"Jared. Jared Shoemaker." That explained it. He must be Mrs. Shoemaker's son.

"So that's how you knew who I was. I met your mom last night."

"Not my mom," he corrected. "My grandmother. I come here to help my grandparents on their ranch each summer. The rest of the year I live in San Diego with my parents."

I'd lived all over Oregon and mostly in cities, but I'd never been to California. I couldn't help wondering how different Jared's life was back at his own home, away from cows, horses and dust. He didn't seem like my idea of a city kid, more like someone from Carla's world, walking alongside the horse looking as relaxed as most kids are parked in front of an Xbox.

"Are there any kids our age around here?" I asked.

Jared didn't reply for a few minutes. "There are some kids who live in town, but a lot of the farms are being bought up by big conglomerates so most of the families have moved away. I haven't really met anyone I'd like to hang out with." He glanced up at me. "I don't know any girls, though."

I was just about to ask him if he had a girlfriend, which would definitely have fallen into Carla's MYOB category of conversation, when he stopped walking and the horse almost ran him over. I realized we had arrived at his house. The Shoemakers' ranch was what I had expected to see when I'd arrived at the Thompsons: a Spanish hacienda-style ranch house of beige stucco made to look like sandstone, with a four-foot high perimeter courtyard surrounding it. The southwestern architectural style fit in perfectly with the dry starkness of the landscape. A couple of spiky cactus-like plants grew within the courtyard, but otherwise there was no pretension or artificiality of greenness here. I handed the bunny to him as I slid from the saddle and turned to see five people staring at me.

NINE

I guess I expected yelling. There wasn't any of that. Worse was the look on Emily's face. I knew that look. It's one I get it often enough myself. Profound disappointment. I recognized Mrs. Shoemaker from last night, and the grey-haired man standing beside her with the pot belly hanging over his belt buckle must be Jared's grandfather. Frank and Jonathan were staring at the ground as if they wanted to disappear into it. Jared spoke first.

"She got lost going for a walk. She met up with Cache and found this bunny." He held the rabbit up for them to see. "I have to get some fluids into him or he'll die." He set off in the direction of that lovely hacienda, not waiting for anyone to respond. I just stood there, absolutely certain they were about to tell me they were going to have to send me back to Stark. Which was okay except I'd be doing Carla's bathroom duty for a month.

But no one said a word about returning me to Stark. Emily finally said in a tight little voice, "We're just glad you're safe, Breeze, we were worried."

She put her arm around me and steered me towards their red truck. Jonathan skipped in front of us and climbed in first. I heard Frank thanking the Shoemakers as Mrs. Shoemaker handed him a basket of home-baked rolls. Then we were heading back to the Double-T. I didn't dare ask about Jared or the baby rabbit.

When we got back to the ranch, I clambered out of the

truck and was about to head into the house but Emily stayed me with a slight tug on my shirt sleeve. "Breeze, can we talk a minute, please?"

My heart sank down to my socks because I knew what she was going to say, and I was ashamed of myself. In spite of wanting to be back with my friends at Stark, my feelings were torn. I'd kind of been looking forward to riding Honey out on the trails instead of just going around in baby, Merry-go-round circles like we did at the riding stables. This was a record for me: I'd been here just one day and already I'd managed to screw things up. I tried to keep my voice from quivering and making a fool out of me.

"You don't have to tell me, I know. You can't handle me so you have to send me back." I lifted my chin, trying not to look defiant or upset, just resolved. "It's okay. It's not the first time. I didn't mean to get lost. I planned on taking Dingus for a walk but he didn't come with me. The next thing I knew the ranch was out of sight." I didn't want to wait for her to tell me the inevitable. I tried to cheer myself up imagining the reception I'd get from the Lunatics, although losing a bet meant I'd be their servant for a while. The thought made me smile. I was about to go home!

But then Emily grabbed my shoulder. "Breeze, it's not that. We're not sending you back. We're not even thinking about it. Things happen. I meant it when I said we were glad you were back safe. I just wanted to ask you to carry a walkie-talkie or a GPS next time you go out. That way we can locate you if something happens. There are cougars out there, and a lot of other dangers I don't even want to talk about. And as you've probably noticed there is no cell phone signal out here."

"So that's why I couldn't call back home, I mean, Stark School," I corrected, seeing her pinched look.

"Yes," she sighed, "we're pretty isolated." And suddenly I got the impression that maybe the Thompsons had taken me in for a different reason. That perhaps Emily wanted another female to talk to. To share things with. But it didn't change anything for me. With luck, by the end of summer I'd be back at Stark. I just had to figure out what I had to do to make it all fall into place.

We didn't speak as we walked to the house. I could see she was as lost in her thoughts as I was in mine. When we reached the kitchen Emily announced, "Lunch is in the fridge."

Then for the first time she noticed my reddened face and arms and visibly winced, making a 'yikes!' sort of face. "I'd better cut off a piece from my aloe plant to put on your burns. If you're not too tired, we could still go riding after we eat."

To be honest, the day already had me exhausted and the last thing I wanted to do was go riding. After all, I'd just gotten off of Jared's horse. My skin felt as if I'd danced through a campfire. But something told me this was important to Emily and so I said, "Sure. It sounds like fun," though the whole while I was trying to figure out just how I could contact the Lunatics and let them know the way things were unfolding here in the wilderness.

Emily had prepared a delicious lunch of a cold chicken Caesar salad, which we accompanied with Mrs. Shoemaker's homemade rolls. Frank and Jonathan had eaten earlier. Emily had been too nervous worrying about my disappearance to have been hungry, which gave me an unbidden pang of guilt. So we sat down together and wordlessly enjoyed the coolness of the salad, washed down with peach iced tea. Though I offered to do the dishes afterward, she told me to clean myself up a bit and deal with my sunburn then we'd go out and get the horses for our ride. It occurred to me that cleaning up before grooming the horses was probably pointless, but it gave me time to slather her mashed aloe preparation on my burned face and arms.

We walked out to the back pasture together side by side until I set off to catch Honey, while Emily brought in Sage, Honey's four-year-old palomino filly. We brushed them and tacked up, then climbed into the saddle and headed out on the range, much in the same direction I'd taken for my stroll. This time, Emily held up a walkie-talkie that she then tucked into her pocket.

"Now Frank can contact me, or we him, if there's a need." We rode along in silence for several minutes, companionably listening to the four-beat clop of the horses' hooves. "How much riding have you done?"

"My mother started me in riding lessons when I was about ten, but after she died I hadn't ridden until I got to Stark. They started a therapeutic riding program to help some of the kids with anger management, or just for extracurricular activities, and I was all over that."

Emily smiled. "Would you like to go a little faster?"

Before I had a chance to reply she was off, cantering across the open field. Not to be left behind, Honey jumped into a gallop and it was all I could do to stay in the saddle. This was faster than I'd ever ridden before. My heart racing as fast as my horse, I grabbed hold of the saddle horn and hung on. While I didn't need two near-death experiences in one day, I realized she was testing me. But for what, I didn't know.

Then her horse turned abruptly and mine followed. Emily never moved in the saddle no matter how many jigs and rollbacks her horse made around the sagebrush that she used for makeshift cows. I gritted my teeth as Honey followed, zigzagging across the plains. Then just as suddenly as she had started, Emily reined her horse around in a complete circle, it pivoted on one foot, and came to a dead stop. So did Honey, with me halfway out of the saddle.

"Whee!" Emily squealed with laughter. I swallowed hard to keep from bringing up my Caesar salad.

"What was all that about?" I asked when I could finally breathe. She looked like a teenager with her hair all tossed around her, cheeks flushed from the exhilarating ride and the heat.

"Just wanted to see if you could stay on when we drive the cattle out tomorrow."

Tomorrow? I thought in alarm, but before I could ask, Emily whooped again and headed off at a gallop toward the ranch. Despite her age, Honey spun around with no cue from me and tore off after them, and so did I. Eventually Emily slowed her horse to a trot and we rode together, side by side at a more leisurely, less death-defying pace.

After we'd cooled, groomed and put away the horses for the evening, we had a light dinner and I headed to bed early. In the morning we'd be driving two hundred head of Hereford cattle onto summer pasture, range land leased from the Bureau of Land Management. I left Emily and Frank bustling around the kitchen, making preparations for the long day tomorrow.

I opened the door to my room and pressed it closed, leaning against it for a few minutes as I surveyed the meager, yet comforting furnishings. Completely unbidden, a warmth washed over me like a beloved old blanket. My room was a sanctuary; a place where I could be sad or happy, a haven to contemplate my problems and entertain whatever thoughts entered my head. No longer was I in a fish bowl, watched by teachers and other kids. Complete and utter privacy.

After climbing into bed, I turned off the lights and lay there luxuriating in the soft, cool sheets and the sounds of crickets chirping in the grass outside. A half-moon peeped through my curtains, casting a glow across my bed. I sighed in contentment, wriggling around in my own bed like a horse rolling in green grass, relishing the novelty of not having someone kick the bottom of my mattress. For a moment I had a pang of guilt, remembering Tyesha and our little tête-à-tête's each night. Then I forced the memories out of my head for another day. I was tired, though not sleepy, and while the thought of perusing Emily's magazine selection wasn't appealing, reading might put me to sleep.

In such a tiny room I could almost reach one where it lay on the top of the dresser. But as I pulled it toward me it slipped from my fingers and fell to the floor. Out of habit I froze, waiting for the footsteps and the reprimand that usually developed from such a caper anywhere else I'd lived. But no one came. In the dark I leaned over the bed and felt for the magazine with my fingertips, but couldn't reach it and nearly fell out of bed trying.

Crawling backwards with my palms on the floor I gave a final push and rolled back against the bed. As I fell back I heard the crinkle of paper. Curious, I leaned back to the edge of the bed and felt between the mattress and bed frame. The crackling came again but I couldn't feel anything. I switched on the bedside lamp, got out of bed and knelt on the floor facing the bed. I lifted the mattress. A couple of stapled sheets of paper lay pinned between the box spring and the frame, which explained why Emily hadn't seen them when she changed the sheets for my arrival.

I grabbed the papers then climbed back into bed to read what was written on them. It appeared to be a homework assignment. Whoever it belonged to was a lousy student because a large red "F" was written across the top, though they hadn't bothered to write their name on it. The subject appeared to be an English Lit class because the assignment read, "Write a short story, it can be fiction or a personal narrative, about an event that changed your life or the way you looked at life." Damn, I thought, someone got more interesting assignments than I ever had. Still, this person had gotten an "F." How bad do you have to write to fail an assignment like that, I wondered, and started to read.

"I am a foster kid," the narrative began, "I live with a foster family because my parents are both drug addicts and can't look after themselves, let alone me. I live on a ranch and the only reason they have me hear is because they need someone strong enough to work with the cows. I friggin' hate cows. They smell and most of the time they want to kill you. That just makes me love hamburger more than ever. In fact,......"

Then suddenly I stopped reading because what he wrote next made me feel as if I were going to throw up. No wonder this kid got an "F". He should have been sent away to a mental hospital. Maybe he had been. Could he be the same person who had scraped his name into bottom of my drawer? Kevin Palola. I wouldn't, or couldn't, forget that name now. I tore the paper into tiny little pieces and dropped them into the wastebasket.

After reading that paper, sleep was out the question. Remembering that I'd wanted to read a magazine, I located the one that had fallen on the floor. I rolled onto my side, leaned closer to the bedside lamp, and flipped the pages. Finally I stopped at an article about depression in teens. A boxed quotation was inset in the middle of the page. It was a line from an Emily Dickinson poem, which brought memories of Deanne flooding back. It read, *'Because I could not stop for Death, He kindly stopped for me.'*

Shocked, I set the book down on top of the quilt, wondering why Deanne would have wanted to give me such a morose book to take with me. Between her and this Kevin guy I was totally freaked out. To the point where I was close to checking under the bed for monsters this time instead of hidden homework.

But eventually the weird creepy feeling vanished and loneliness took its place. In spite of the minor freedoms I now enjoyed with the Thompsons, I actually missed the scrutiny of the staff at Stark School, the company of my friends who understood me. I yearned desperately to be back with them. Show them Kevin Palola's homework. What would they make of that? I needed to talk to Deanne, ask why she would want to read such morbid poetry. The Thompsons were kind, but at this point I owed them nothing. My sense of self-preservation was stronger than the fledgling affection I'd started to feel towards Emily. I refused to let myself get attached.

Despite knowing that I need to be rested, I tossed in the unfamiliar bed, remaining sleepless until well into the night. I could have sworn I'd scarcely put my head on the pillow when I heard Emily calling my name. I switched on my lamp because the room was dead black. Then I glanced at the window and I saw it was still dark outside. Groaning, I rolled over and prayed she'd let me go back to sleep because the LED readout of the bedside clock on my dresser showed that it was 4:30 a.m.

"Get up, sleepyhead," she said. "I've got pancakes, and bacon and eggs started for breakfast. The men are getting the horses saddled up while we get the food ready. I could use your help."

Put that way, I dragged my butt out of bed, took a splash of a shower and tied back my hair. I glanced in the mirror and grimaced at what I saw, but decided that putting on even a little makeup was pointless. We'd be hot, sweaty and dusty most of the day. Besides, there was no one around to care about what I looked like. Jared was the only boy and he acted like he was pissed at me. My Mom used to tell me I was pretty, but I didn't think I was much to look at, especially if there were other girls around. I always figured I must have resembled my dad because mom had green eyes and mine were just a plain brown that matched my hair exactly. And I certainly didn't inherit her nose because my nose was as long as Pinocchio's with that weird upturned tip.

I sighed. Short of plastic surgery, my looks were out of my control. I got dressed in jeans and a long sleeved cotton shirt then headed out to the kitchen. Emily was already dressed for riding; even her jeans had leather chaps over top, and she'd tied a bright pink bandana around her neck. There was a spare lime green bandana lying on the table at the place where I usually sat. She nodded toward it.

"For you," she said. "It can get awfully dusty out there riding behind the cattle and you'll be coughing for weeks if you don't have something to cover your face."

I saw how she'd knotted hers, and did the same with mine, fastening it around my neck. Then I helped her scramble the eggs, fry up the bacon, and pile golden brown pancakes on a plate. We had just set all the food, pancake syrup, dishes and coffee cups on the table when Mrs.

Shoemaker walked in, followed by Frank, Mr. Shoemaker and Jared. My stomach flip-flopped nervously when I saw him. But though he said 'Good morning' to Emily, he deliberately ignored me and didn't make eye contact.

"Nettie's going to look after Jonathan when he wakes up," said Emily. "We'll be gone most of the day." She ordered us to sit then scurried around making sure no one was missing anything. We dug into the food like we weren't going to eat for days, let alone hours.

I was desperate to find out about the bunny and kept trying to catch Jared's eye, but it seemed as though he made a conscious effort to avoid looking at me. Trying to attract his attention, I made a production of offering to pass around the food and then jumped up to refill coffee cups and juice glasses. Still he paid me no mind so I masked my disappointment by giving up and concentrating on eating my own breakfast.

"How's the baby rabbit doing?" I finally dared to ask through a mouthful of pancake. He exchanged glances with his grandparents then lowered his eyes.

"He didn't make it." When I didn't say anything, just sat there with my lip quivering, he continued, his anger just barely under control, "I told you he wouldn't live, he was too young. You should have just left him there in the field."

"Jared!" his grandmother admonished. "She did what she thought was right."

"Yeah, well, doing what she thinks is right is going to get one of us hurt. It's wrong to take the wild ones out of their environment, they can't survive."

"Jared. That's enough," said Mr. Shoemaker. There was dead silence after that. I felt awful. Everyone considered me stupid for taking in that rabbit. I couldn't have just left him out there to die. Why couldn't they see that? But I wasn't going to let Jared have the satisfaction of seeing me break down. No one could make me cry against my will. I thought of that now as I sat there trying not to cry, *in front of anyone other than my fellow Lunatics.*

TEN

The sun had just begun to peep above those misty-blue hills on the eastern horizon when we mounted our horses and rode out through the pasture to drive the cattle toward the BLM range land. For everyone else the silence was comfortable. They were concentrating on keeping the cattle in one cohesive bunch, and probably wondering what I would do if things changed abruptly. For that reason they had me ride alongside Emily, to learn how it was done.

I had hoped that it would be Jared who would teach me how to drive cattle, but he hadn't even looked at me since our altercation at breakfast. I couldn't help being puzzled at his attitude. Although he appeared angry when Cache first found me, yesterday he'd stood up for me in front of everyone. Today he sounded as if he hated me. What had happened to change things? Maybe the baby rabbit dying had upset him as much as it had me. Then I got mad at myself, wondering why I gave a rat's ass about what Jared thought of me. I forced myself to concentrate on the task at hand, which had to do with cattle.

Two hundred cows are a lot of cows. There were more cows than you could ever imagine seeing in one place at one time. And they made more dust and smelled worse than just about anything. I stared at the herd, pressed so tightly together that as they moved they looked like a giant, rippling brown and white rug. I wondered how Emily and Frank knew for sure they had two hundred cattle here. How could they count accurately when these beasts never stopped milling around? What if there were only 199, or maybe even 201? The thought made me giggle. Emily saw me laugh rather than heard me above the racket. She pulled down the bandana that covered the lower part of her face to give me a smile back. Conversation was impossible. We each carried a walkie-talkie radio with us for communicating.

While we all kept a safe distance behind, Frank worked the far left side of the cattle. Jared rode on the right with Emily and me, and with Mr. Shoemaker in the center, hanging back. We really only had to move them about ten miles in total to get to the BLM land, but there was definitely a skill to it. Our goal was to keep them traveling quiet and steadily, in a more or less single file. If they spread out wide, something spooked them and they decided to stampede, well, we'd be doing a lot of backtracking and probably wouldn't end up with an even two hundred number.

Even though we'd started out so early, the horses' flanks were dark with sweat, and every so often a glob of foam would fall into the dust. My clothes stuck to my body as if they'd been painted on. We each had two canteens full of cold water strapped to the pommel of the saddle, which we all knew would be indispensable. And Emily providing me with the bandana was a stroke of genius: I could feel my nose was already full of dirt and grit and tingled something terrible. Though I tried to stifle the inevitable sneeze, it only made it worse. I let out a loud, squeaky "Ahh choo!" But as sneezes always come in two's, the second one was more of a screech. I reached into my jacket pocket, brought out a tissue and blew loudly into it. Not expecting it, Honey almost jumped out from underneath me at the sound.

I heard Frank yell, "What tha?" as the long stream of cattle bunched together like paper clips to a magnet. Then they were off. Jared and Emily scarcely had time to react. Out of the corner of my eye I caught Jared's glare as he spurred his horse and worked with Frank to ride alongside and even with the cattle. Emily's bandana had dropped down and her lips were set in a straight, determined line. I had really done it this time.

Not knowing exactly what to do, I stayed close to Emily as our horses cantered alongside the bolting cattle. For the first time I became aware of how much danger I'd be in if I fell off the horse. Small calves bellowed in fear as they tried desperately to stay close to their mothers in the blinding trail dust. Just then a steer flung his head out toward Sage, Emily's young and inexperienced horse. Sage leapt sideways, flinging Emily down under the trampling hooves.

For a moment I couldn't see her lying there she was so covered in dirt. Then Sage took off at a gallop after the cattle and I saw Emily. I jumped from Honey, and still hanging tightly onto the reins, walked toward Emily, using Honey's bulk and waving my arms to act as a shield to keep the cattle away. It worked. As Jared, Frank and Mr. Shoemaker carefully turned the cattle around with their skillful horses, miraculously, soon all the cattle slowed down to an uneven jog and then came to a stop. I knelt beside Emily and put my ear to her chest. Her eyes were closed and she hadn't moved since she'd fallen. But she was breathing.

Just then Jared came running up. "Don't move her!" he ordered. He took off his bandana and poured some water from his canteen over it, then gently wiped the dirt from around her eyes and nose. We all held our breath as we waited for a response. Jared leaned close and said in a loud voice, "Emily!" Slowly she opened her eyes and stared up at us, unfocused.

"What happened?" I could feel the burning stares on me, or maybe it was a guilty conscience that made me feel that way.

"The cattle got spooked," Frank said, not looking in my direction. "That's all. Can you feel your fingers, your legs?"

"Yes, I can," Emily said, "I think I'm okay." She started to get up but let out a yelp of pain as she tried to pull her leg under her. Mr. Shoemaker, who had just ridden up, said, "Don't try to stand, your leg might be broken."

He got off his horse, brought out a pocket knife and slit her jeans to the thigh. Her skin was scraped and red, but otherwise the leg didn't look too bad. Not that I could tell what a broken leg looked like.

"Dennis, that was a brand new pair of Levis," she hissed. "It's not my leg, it's my ankle." We couldn't help but laugh at that. Mr. Shoemaker cut the rest of the pant leg off and stripped the Levis into wide bands, then wrapped them around her ankle to keep it rigid.

When he'd finished, he said, "Do you think you can stand now?" She nodded, wincing as she got to her feet, supporting herself on Frank's shoulder.

"If someone catches my horse and can lift me onto it," she said, "I can still make the trip."

Frank shook his head. "No, you won't. You and Breeze are heading back to the ranch so you can get to a doctor. Nettie can drive you once you get there. The three of us can take it from here. Just radio in so she'll be prepared."

For a moment Emily looked as if she wanted to argue but then a flash of pain crossed her face and she realized she had no choice. Jared had caught Sage and led her up. Frank and Mr. Shoemaker lifted Emily carefully onto the saddle, and we started slowly back toward the Double-T.

I had to say something to Jared, even if I was rebuffed. "I'm sorry, I didn't mean...." but he cut me off.

"Maybe when you go to town you should buy some antihistamines and a muffler for that long nose of yours," Jared called out as he rode away.

I desperately wanted to shout back about buying an extra one for his loud mouth, but mostly I wished it had been me who'd gotten trampled. I was going to get sent back and this time I hadn't even been trying. Why couldn't I ever do anything right?

Emily hardly said a word as we rode back toward the ranch. From the tightness around her lips I could tell she was hurting, even though every time I asked, she denied it. Finally I felt too guilty to say anything more. It was my fault that she had gotten hurt. I just hoped it wasn't more serious than it looked.

By my estimation we still had a couple of miles to go when I saw a cloud of dust forming in the distance. At first I thought it might be another herd of cattle being driven to range land then I realized it was a vehicle heading toward us. We were on the wide open range with no drivable roads in sight. I glanced questioningly at Emily, but her face was screwed up in a pensive frown. She pulled Sage to a halt and without looking at me said, "Stop." She didn't appear worried that the driver wouldn't see us, or maybe run us over before he even knew we were there. I wished I had her confidence, but trusted her to know what she was doing. At least I hoped she did because the vehicle didn't show any sign of slowing down.

We sat there on our horses, waiting for the people in the vehicle to notice our presence. I could feel my heartbeat pounding all the way up to my head. The horses began to snort and blow, ready to flee at the slightest cue from Emily or me. And then it appeared the driver finally saw us because the dust cloud began to dissipate as they drove more slowly. Sage jigged on the spot a little as they approached, but good old Honey stood her ground. I gave her a light pat on the neck.

The vehicle came to a stop about twenty feet away. It was a huge SUV, a bright yellow Hummer. I was so busy staring at it I hardly noticed when two men got out and started to walk toward us. A big man with an enormous handlebar mustache, wearing a red and blue striped shirt, 10-gallon cowboy hat, and spotless silver and black cowboy boots approached. A slender man in street clothes hung behind him, looking like he was afraid to get his shoes dusty. When 'handlebar' stood a few feet from our horses he touched his hat brim, and smiled at Emily.

"Hello, Mrs. Thompson," he drawled. Emily didn't reply and when I glanced at her, I saw her face under its tan had gone dead white. Whiter than when she'd been thrown underneath the cattle hooves. I looked back at the man, wondering how they knew each other. She didn't say anything to him, just kept Sage at a standstill, staring at him. It made me uncomfortable, and quite a bit nervous. But apart from her cold silence, Emily appeared to be in control.

"How's the cattle industry this year?" He chewed then spit in the dirt, wiping his mouth with the back of his hand.

I grimaced inwardly at his bad manners, noting the loathing and disgust on Emily's face. Finally she spoke, and her voice was filled with such hatred I hardly recognized it.

"The industry is just fine, no thanks to you, Nolan Barker."

"Who's your young friend?" Nolan persisted.

"That doesn't concern you, nor does the state of our business affairs at the Double-T."

"Your business concerns me more than you think." His tone sounded menacing. I didn't like his smile. It had a nasty sneer to it, like he had some kind of secret and was going to use it against us. Emily didn't flinch. She stared back at the cowboy with as insolent a glare as his.

Then, as if she just remembered I was beside her, she turned to me. "Let's get going." She gave Sage a nudge with her heel and trotted off.

As she rode away, I heard him call out, "Your husband will have to talk to me sooner or later."

Afraid of being left behind where 'handlebar' might ask me questions, I gave Honey a kick and we cantered to catch up to Emily.

"Who was that?" I managed to pant out as I drew alongside her.

"Never mind," she muttered and then as if sorry for her abruptness, she apologized, and said, "He owns the neighboring property on the other side of ours. If you see him again, don't talk to him. Even more important, don't answer his questions or give him any information about yourself or the Double-T."

I nodded, wondering what bad blood the Thompsons

could possibly have with 'handlebar' when they were so chummy with the Shoemakers. For a person as sweet-tempered and accepting as Emily to harbor hatred toward him, it must be terrible. It didn't look like she was about to fill me in, but Jared might know. Although the possibility of Jared actually speaking to me now, even with a different topic of conversation, was probably nonexistent.

We rode nearly all the way back to the ranch in silence. Emily was either too preoccupied for small talk or in too much pain. When we got into walkie-talkie range, she called Mrs. Shoemaker to prepare her for our arrival. As we rode up I could see Mrs. Shoemaker's square, aproned form standing beside the pasture gate, with Jonathan at her side.

Jonathan's eyes were reddened and his jam-sticky face had tear streaks. He hung back from us, looking fearful. Tactfully, Mrs. Shoemaker didn't make eye contact with me as I dismounted my horse, which made me wonder if she'd received any calls other than Emily's. I prayed Jared hadn't told her of the part I'd played in the accident. Together we helped Emily get out of the saddle, while Jonathan came forward and did his best to hold Sage under control with his little fingers. I took the reins from him because he wasn't used to handling horses. With Emily leaning against Mrs. Shoemaker for support, and Jonathan attempting to help from the other side, they made their way into the house.

"I'll look after the horses," I called after them, feeling a horrible mixture of guilt and frustration. But they gave no indication they'd heard me and didn't look back. That only made me feel worse.

Once I was in the house, Mrs. Shoemaker got ready to take Emily into the nearest hospital, an hour's drive into town, and I was left to take care of Jonathan. Still not looking at me, Mrs. Shoemaker gave instructions on how to finish fixing the evening meal for the men who would be returning in several hours after moving the cattle. She must have assumed I knew my way around a fridge and stove, but to be honest, Mom and I had lived out of cans and packaged food most of our lives. The sight of a big side of beef roasting in the oven scared the heck out of me. But I vowed I wasn't going to mess this up. There would be enough dirty looks when everyone showed up.

As I sat, miserably pondering over the events of the day and waiting for the two families to return, I remembered what Jared had said about wild ones. How they couldn't survive if they were taken out of their environment. I couldn't help thinking about how that applied to me. And if I would be able to survive for three months, away from Stark, the only environment where I'd been able to adapt.

ELEVEN

As it turned out, Emily's ankle was broken. Her orders from the doctor had been 'absolutely no riding for six weeks,' something I was sure must have rankled her to the core, because she had that 'yeah, right' expression when she told us. She and Mrs. Shoemaker had gotten home just about the same time that Jared, Frank and Mr. Shoemaker arrived, dusty, hungry, and professing a combined, profound hatred of cows.

I'd done my best to get dinner ready. The roast beef had gotten a little overdone and when I attempted to carve it, the slices bore a strong resemblance to beef jerky. The mashed potatoes and gravy I'd made rivaled each other with their lump sizes. But to my advantage, everyone, including Emily, was starving, and I got more praise for the meal than I deserved. For a while it made knowing that I was the cause of the household upheaval a little easier to bear.

After the Shoemakers left for their own home, things returned to near normal at the Thompson's. Emily sat with her foot propped up pillows while she resumed her knitting. Jonathan and Frank played cards until Jonathan's bedtime. Finally, Frank went out to check on the horses and it was just Emily and me alone in the living room, in a somewhat strained silence.

Emily looked me over introspectively. "You probably saved my life today, blocking those cows with your horse."

My lower lip trembled. "Don't forget that I was the one who caused the whole thing."

Emily smiled gently. "Accidents happen. It was my fault for taking you out too soon. I thought that having you join us in one of our biggest jobs on the ranch, especially being with someone your own age, would make you feel like a member of the family."

I didn't know what to say to that so I just stared at my hands, wishing the floor would open and swallow me up.

"With me laid up for a few weeks, we're going to need you to help with the barn chores a little more than I'd planned."

I nodded. It was only to be expected. They couldn't afford to hire additional farm hands and even with the cattle up in the grazing lands there was still more farm work to be done than Frank could handle.

Emily was lost in thought for a few moments. "I guess we could always ask if Jared has some spare time. The Shoemakers employ several ranch hands on their property and it might be nice for Jared to have someone closer to his age to talk to."

I felt mixed emotions well up in me, and I wanted to tell her that I wasn't sure how the idea would appeal to Jared. Just because of a couple of stupid things I'd done, it seemed as if he disliked me more every time I saw him. I wished there was another girl around to talk to; boys were definitely a pain in the butt. Maybe when I wrote to Tyesha I'd ask her for advice.

I looked up to see Emily giving me a quizzical stare. Then she dropped her head and concentrated on her knitting, trying not to let me see her smiling. I blushed, suddenly realizing that she'd become aware that I was confused about Jared. It embarrassed me that I'd been so transparent. It wasn't as if I'd had much experience with boys, what with being segregated from them at Stark.

Again, just for a moment she reminded me of my mother and I had to blink hard to keep from having tears start up. She must have sensed what I was feeling. Without looking at me, she said, "I lost my mum when I was about your age. She died of breast cancer." She stared out the window as if overwhelmed by the pain of remembering. I didn't say anything, just watched her as she tried to concentrate on her knitting.

"At the time I thought it was the worst thing that could ever happen," she went on, "but I was wrong. A month later my dad shot himself. He'd been so depressed he hadn't been able to see that I felt just as lost as he. It was the ultimate rejection that I wasn't worth him staying alive for. Now I'm older I understand how it can be for a person to get so mired in thoughts of hopelessness that they can't even see the positive things around them."

I nodded, not knowing what to say to comfort her. For a moment, Deanne flashed into my thoughts. Only then did I realize how unhappy and depressed she had been until she joined the Lunatics. I shook the memories away. I preferred to remember the times spent with my friends in the privacy of my room. Especially now I knew how easy my feelings were for Emily to read.

"I felt a lot like that when my mom died," I said. "But the state immediately placed me in a foster home, so I never had a chance to talk to anyone about her. Everyone around me was either too absorbed with their own problems or too busy keeping me busy."

"How about your dad?" Emily had composed herself again. "What do you remember about him?"

"Almost nothing," I admitted. "My mom never talked about him to me and if I asked questions, she'd just say that he was a good man who thought he was doing the right thing. He was lost to us and there was no point in regrets."

Emily looked puzzled. "Are any of your grandparents alive?"

I shook my head. "I don't think so, but mom might not have wanted me to know them. The only information she ever gave me was that her parents hadn't approved of her marrying my dad, but she would never say why. I don't know if his parents are still alive. No one came to see me when my mother died."

Emily sighed. "Parents try to do their best with their children and reading all the parenting books in the library can't change the course of fate."

I nodded, only partially understanding.

"Take Jonathan," she went on. "His teenaged mother abandoned him at birth, maybe because he was different, or it could have been because she knew raising him would always be a challenge. Or perhaps she wasn't ready to be a mother at all. Whatever her reasons, we're the lucky ones. He's a gift to us."

I could see from the glow on her face that she meant every word. It sounds sappy, but I couldn't help wishing that one day I'd find someone to love me like that. Whether it was from a foster parent, or a boyfriend, or maybe just getting closer to my friends. The yearning inside me was so great my throat ached. Just when I was certain I would burst into tears, Emily set her knitting aside and gave me a rueful smile.

"Enough maudlin talk for now. I'll make up a list of things that need to be done and instructions. And of course, if you have any questions, I'm always here." She gave a short laugh. "Guess I'm not going anywhere for awhile." Seeing my worried expression she added, "Don't take it so hard. As I said before, it was just an accident. Now I'll have time to catch up on my knitting. I needed a break." After the inadvertent pun, I couldn't help but laugh too.

That night as I lay in bed I thought about my father and how different my life would have been if he hadn't gone away. I knew I wasn't alone in wondering that; the other Lunatics all came from broken and dysfunctional families as well. Even Carla, who had both parents and tons of money, had her own issues with her father.

Though my dad was a faceless figure to me, when my mother had spoken of him it was with love and pride at his sacrifices. One day Tyesha became annoyed with me for referring to my father as 'my father the hero,' because the way I said it made it sound as if it were an official title. Soon she had Carla and Deanne, both apparently bored with my reverence for my father, colluding by making gagging sounds and sticking their fingers down their throats whenever I mentioned him.

Once I'd gotten over feeling offended, we all agreed it was pretty funny. Carla's nickname for her dad was 'God's Gift to Women' because he'd remarried so many times. Tyesha had never known her dad so gave him the title of 'Father Mystery.' But Deanne squirmed and appeared uncomfortable, refusing to participate. After that, whenever we started getting silly or bitching about our fathers, she'd disappear to the school library and stick her nose in a book until she felt the conversation had taken another turn.

As I lay there, I began to feel better about myself and my life than I had earlier in the day, especially just after the accident. I made a mental list of all the things I could do around the ranch to make things easier for the Thompsons until Emily was well and I could finally go back to Stark. I vowed to spend more time teaching Jonathan games and reading to him. But when I went to sleep, it was Jared's scowling face that came into my dreams more than once.

There's a line that goes something like 'Nobody notices what I do until I don't do it,' and that was true of Emily. I had no idea how much work she managed to cram into her day. Every day. I soon learned. It started with feeding and turning out the horses each morning, cleaning the stalls, and then bringing them back into their stalls for their evening meal. There was the feeding of the dog and the cat, making sure all the water bowls and troughs were full, watering and weeding the little garden, it went on and on. And that was just outside the house.

There was a lot more to do inside the house. I actually enjoyed being outside with the animals, but indoors it was laundry, dodging Jonathan who asked a million questions though rarely waiting for an answer, then meals, dishes, making beds, dodging Jonathan again, and assisting Emily if she needed my help in getting around. I rarely had a chance to ride Honey. I couldn't risk getting hurt because if Frank wasn't home and something happened to Emily or Jonathan, there would be no one to look after them. I began to feel like a servant again, something I hadn't done since before I'd arrived at Stark.

In the evenings, too tired and antisocial to spend time with Frank and Emily, and exhausted from dealing with Jonathan, I'd sequester myself in my room to record the days' events in my journal. I wrote long letters to each of the Lunatics, telling them about the accident and Jared's standoffishness, chronicling my days. I tried not to sound lonely and needy, though I knew I was. But so far no one had written back to me. The possibility existed that the teachers withheld my letters, or maybe the post office didn't know I now lived at the Double-T and had sent my mail back.

I started getting anxiety attacks every time the postman came, wondering if there was a letter for me. I would race to the mailbox before anyone else had a chance, only to be disappointed each time. I made excuses for the Lunatics, attributing their lack of communication to a multitude of reasons: slow mail, being too busy, they might be on vacation with family members. Things that happened during holidays and summer break. But I was starting to get worried that they'd forgotten me already.

Jared came over occasionally to help, but always managed to avoid me. The Thompsons had hired him to start on Diablo's ground training. Afterward, he would perform the rest of the chores that were too strenuous for me or required skills that I apparently lacked. Then he'd go back home without even saying hello. So much for Emily's idea that he'd enjoy company his own age.

Secretly, I watched him work with Diablo from the obscurity of the barn, taking note of the way he handled the stallion. Then when he was gone I would mimic what I'd learned: leading Diablo, getting him to back up, do haunch and forehand turns, and rewarding him with carrots. If Emily wondered why her carrot supply was depleting faster than usual, she didn't mention it. Nor did anyone appear to notice that it was me that Diablo now whinnied for.

Once I overheard Jared enthralling Emily with tales of the internet and how she could download recipes and knitting patterns. That got me thinking about asking if I could borrow his computer to e-mail the Lunatics. With no television or internet, and the only newspaper being a local rag whose editorial content consisted of real estate ads and photos of mutant vegetables, I had no idea of what was going on in the rest of the world outside the ranch.

I waited for him one day when I knew he wouldn't be able to evade me and cornered him while he was working with Diablo. He had him in the steel round pen lunging him at a canter, and whenever the horse pulled, I could see the hard muscles in his arms flex under his white T-shirt. Diablo's head was tucked under, his nose almost touching his chest. But when his spirit yearned to break free he would explode with a leap into the air, twisting like a bronco at a rodeo. I watched until Jared had him under control and was cooling him down before I approached.

"Hi." I leaned against the corral, trying to look poised and nonchalant. He gave a grunt of acknowledgment but didn't take his eyes off Diablo as he walked him around the corral to cool him out. Diablo reached out to nuzzle me, perhaps carrot hunting. Jared pulled him back, seemingly unaware of how friendly the horse and I had become.

"I wondered if I could come to your house some time to use the internet," I ventured.

He avoided looking at me and didn't seem to give it much thought before replying. "I don't think my grandparents would let you."

I felt my heart sink down to my stomach. My bottom lip quavered and I waited a few minutes so I would be sure my voice wouldn't break. The last thing I wanted was for Jared to see me weaken. It didn't appear as if he were about to continue the conversation in any way unless I forced him to. I took a long breath and figured what the hell, I had nothing to lose.

"Is it your grandparents who wouldn't let you, or is it that you don't want me there?"

He stopped, then gave a short jerk on Diablo's lead rope and brought him to a halt. He turned to face me.

"Okay, if you must know, I don't want you around."

I felt tears burn my eyes but I forced them back and kept my voice steady. "What did I ever do to you?"

"You didn't do anything. I just don't want to hang out with someone who's..." He stopped when he saw my perplexed expression.

"Who's what?"

"Never mind. I have work to do. Doesn't Emily have something in the house for you to take care of?"

"No," I retorted. "I'm free for the time being. Just what is it you've heard about me?"

"I haven't heard anything other than that you're from a state school, one that has a pretty bad rep."

"Stark?" I gave a short laugh. "What's wrong with Stark?"

He gave me a look of sheer disbelief. "I know someone who went there and I've just heard things, that's all. It's been in the news a lot lately."

I shook my head. I'd never heard anything bad about Stark, but of course, I had been on the inside. I didn't read newspapers, or listen to the media. At least I hadn't since I left Portland.

A thought came to me about a mystery that Jared might be able to provide an answer to. "Have you ever heard the name Kevin Palola?"

Startled, Jared dropped the lead rope attached to Diablo's halter, snatching it back up just in time before the horse pulled away. He turned to me, frowning.

"How do you know about Kevin?"

"I found his name carved in the bottom of my chest of drawers. I also found a homework assignment that was hidden in my room." I stared at Jared quizzically. "Who is he?"

Jared shrugged, tied Diablo to the hitching post and began grooming him. "You should ask Emily, not me."

I crossed my arms in front of my chest and moved beside Diablo so Jared couldn't avoid looking at me. "I'm asking you."

He took a deep breath and studied me carefully, as if searching to find out how much I already knew. "Kevin was Frank and Emily's first foster kid. Before Jonathan even. They told my grandmother that they can't have any kids of their own and they wanted a son. Well, let's just say he didn't work out."

"What happened?"

He set down his brushes and gave me his full attention. "You really should talk to Emily if you want to know. He was not a good kid. He hurt a lot of people, including me." He narrowed his eyes. "He went to Stark School before he came here. I'm glad the Thompsons had to send him back and I hope no one around here ever has to deal with him again. And that's all I'm going to say."

"So you're forming an opinion of me and my school because of the way another foster kid behaved? That's really narrow minded."

It occurred to me that perhaps Jared's feelings about me might not have anything to do with Kevin Palola. He might have heard about my history with the school, the fire, Mr. Simonson, and who knew what else? But Mrs. Watkins had said she hadn't told the Thompsons, so how or what could he know? If he would tell me what he'd heard, I could explain; on the other hand, if I told him what I'd done, I'd only make myself look worse. There was no way out. I'd just have to let him believe what he wanted. And for some reason, that made me very sad.

Jared was quiet for a long time, then finally set down the brush and unclipped Diablo, who took off at a gallop. Then he turned and leaned back against the fence rail. I was dying to ask more about Kevin, but he'd been reticent about sharing information on that subject and I didn't want him to brush me off again. Except for our brief, stilted exchanges, it had been weeks since I'd talked to someone my own age.

"Stark isn't like that." I said it as a statement but I ended up sounding less confident. The truth was, I really didn't know how Stark appeared to the outside world. To me it was my home, and the only one until recently where I'd been happy.

"There are a lot of great teachers. And the only friends I have are still at Stark. Don't you think you should give me the benefit of the doubt before you condemn me for something I have no control over?" I looked at Jared with the question in my eyes.

He shrugged. "Yeah. There are good schools and bad schools, just like everything else."

Jared scrutinized me for a few moments as if seeing me for the first time. "You're right," he said. "It's unfair for me to judge you when I don't even know you, even after what happened to Emily and the rabbit." He smiled suddenly and it lit up his face, making my pulse rate speed up. He held out his hand. "Truce?"

I shook his hand, feeling a rush of heat travel up my hand to my face. "Truce," I replied, my stupid voice coming out in a sort of croak.

TWELVE

With Emily out of commission and Frank busy in the fields mowing and baling hay at first light, no one had been to town to do any shopping for a long time. Judging by the macaroni and cheese we'd had for dinner three times that week I figured we must be nearly out of groceries. Not to mention, I was out of girl things and was reluctant to ask Emily if I could borrow some.

When I went out to help Frank feed the chickens I searched for a tactful way to bring up the subject of shopping. Frank didn't talk much to anyone, let alone me, and about the only thing we had in common appeared to be Emily and Jonathan. He wasn't scary, just didn't have a lot to say, I guess. Finally a brilliant and subtle idea came to me.

I grabbed the five gallon bucket of chicken pellets and grain he'd set out and struggled to hand it to him. "There's a recipe I'd like to make for dinner as a surprise for Emily, but I need a couple of ingredients we don't have on hand," I said. "Next time you go to town, can I come?" I shot him a big grin that drew an even bigger one from him. Say what you will, suggestions of food will work with men of all ages.

"I need some parts for the tractor," he said, "you're welcome to ride along with me. I'll take you to the grocery store where Emily usually shops. She probably has a list of things she needs."

I quivered all over with excitement. I ached to get away from the dirt and dust of the farm, away from the solitude of country living. Ecstatic at the possibility of an adventure, after I finished helping Frank with the rest of the chores, I danced all the way to the house.

Emily thought my going to town with Frank was an excellent idea. "Here's a list of groceries and a few sundries. You know most of the brands I use. Do you think you can handle the shopping? Frank knows exactly where to go in a hardware store, but shopping for food and women's things scare him, so he's not much help in that department."

After reading the list, I laughed out loud. "No problem. I can tackle this easy." I took the list and money she handed me and tucked them into my pocket. Then as I started to head to my bedroom to change my clothes and fix myself up a little, I saw Jonathan staring at me with hopeful eyes. Uh, oh, I thought, he wants to come with us. I chewed my lip and glanced at Emily. She shrugged and gave me a look that said, 'it's up to you.'

I stifled a sigh and turned to Jonathan with a forced cheerful smile. "Would you like to come with us?"

He threw his arms around me, and giving me a gap-toothed grin, squealed, "Thank you! Thank you, thank you!" I caught Emily's sad eyes over the top of his tousled head. Apparently we all had cabin fever. Without fully comprehending what I'd just done, I felt the selfish thoughts that had been coursing through me before disappear completely. Anyhow, taking a little kid along to town wasn't the worst thing that could happen, was it?

Frank was his usual taciturn self as we made the one-hour drive into town. Jonathan kept the silence from becoming awkward with a constant babbling commentary on virtually everything we passed along the way, which consisted mostly of animals and signs. After listening to him announce the speed limit for the tenth time, I could feel a migraine coming on. Frank must have been suffering from the same stimuli overload as me for he finally began to talk.

He cast a brief glimpse in my direction. "How old are you now, Breeze?"

Startled by the unexpected question, I replied, "Sixteen."

He nodded, looking introspective.

"You're old enough to get your driver's license. We could start giving you driving lessons around the farm, if you'd like."

Would I? I couldn't believe what he'd just offered. "This truck is pretty big, though, I'd be afraid I'd smash it."

He laughed. "I was thinking of starting you on the tractor first." My heart sank. Of course. Farm work. That was what it was about. Just another way to find more chores for me to do. I felt him looking at me, taking in how my previous elation had switched to downcast in milliseconds. I forced a smile so he wouldn't think I was being ungrateful.

"Not to do farm work," he said, reading my mind, "tractors are just kind of fun to start out on and small enough for you to manage the concept of steering and parking." I could feel my mood lighten and I relaxed back against the truck seat. "That and they're pretty hard to tip over." He let out a rare chuckle.

"That would be way cool," I said, meaning every word.

"Twenty-five mileths per hour," Jonathan announced.

Frank slowed the truck. We had entered the city. I had no idea where we were. The town appeared to only have one long main street, with a couple of car dealerships, strip malls with the inevitable Starbucks and McDonald's, and a large hardware outlet. Frank pulled into the parking lot with a Fred Meyer store and began looking for a parking space. Then, almost as if we were choreographed, all of our heads turned toward a bright yellow Hummer, parked in a disabled parking space, just in front of the store.

Nolan Barker was leaning against the fender of the Hummer, talking to a young man, probably not much older than Jared and me. He had on the same uniform that everyone around here wore: jeans, cowboy boots and pastel plaid shirt. Unlike Barker and his ten gallon hat, though, the boy's head was bare, showing off shoulder-length black hair pulled back in a ponytail. He was thin and reedy, towering over Barker who had to raise his head whenever he spoke to the boy. Though at this distance it was hard to see a resemblance, I wondered if he could be Barker's son.

I stole a glance at Frank, whose lips were pursed in a pensive line like a Muppet mouth. He whipped the truck around in such a tight turn that Jonathan and I were thrown against the doors.

"Sorry," he mumbled. "I think we'll go to a different store this time." Then he drove up to the street lights and when they changed, into the Safeway parking lot. He pulled into a parking space, and without looking at me, took a big deep breath as if composing himself. Finally, he said, "Will you be all right going into the store alone? I'll get my supplies and join you. If you're finished before me, wait at the entrance."

A little unnerved by the abrupt change in plan, I nodded wordlessly. I got out of the truck and held out my hands for Jonathan. Together we walked toward the grocery store. Just before we entered the building I glanced back over my shoulder and saw Frank leaning up against the truck. He pulled a pack of cigarettes out of his pocket and lit one. For a moment, the entire picture swam before my eyes like a surreal painting. I'd never seem him smoke before. It made me wonder if Emily knew, and if she would disapprove.

I grabbed a cart and let Jonathan push it while I piled groceries and other items from Emily's list inside. Soon we'd managed to find just about everything and it hadn't taken very long. Frank was nowhere to be seen so he was probably still wandering the aisles of the hardware store, something Emily had warned me about. I looked down and noticed Jonathan squirming. I heaved a sigh.

"Do you have to go to the bathroom?" He nodded in a guilty way that made me squeeze his shoulder. I held back the usual admonishment of 'why didn't you go before you left home?' and whispered, "It's okay. I see where the restrooms are."

With no other choice but to wheel the cart along with us,

I led him to the door of the Men's Room. "Okay, you go in, use the bathroom and don't talk to anyone. I'll wait right here for you." Then he disappeared into the Men's Room while I stood watch at the door.

Jonathan had only been in the bathroom for about a minute when I heard my cell phone ring in my purse. My heart jumped a beat. This was the first call I'd received since I left Stark. Excited, I glanced at the screen but didn't recognize the number. Then I realized it could be Emily or Frank, as they both had my number. As I probably had service in town, they would try it if they needed to reach me. It was most likely Frank, ready to leave and waiting for us.

"Hello?" I said into it, but all I got back was static. I glanced at the phone face again, and started to walk toward a window to get a better signal. "Hello?" I said again.

"Breeze?" Deanne's tremulous voice came through then broke off.

I nearly dropped the phone in shock. "Hello? Deanne?" There was no reply.

Frantic, I kept repeating, "Hello? Can you hear me?" all the while walking alongside the wall of windows, pushing the cart and trying to hear her. But then without warning the line went dead. I'd lost her. At that moment I wanted to smash the phone to the ground and jump on it, except she might try calling back. I took a couple of deep breaths and tried to think what I should do. Then I remembered that I'd left Jonathan in the Men's Room. If he stepped outside to find I wasn't there, he'd be terrified.

I rushed back to the store's restrooms, but he wasn't waiting at the door. Fighting the urge to panic and call Frank for help, I gritted my teeth. Then I opened the Men's Room door and leaned in.

"Jonathan? Aren't you done yet?" I called out. There was no answer. A bubble of bile started up in my stomach, threatening to rise up to my throat. I swallowed hard to quell the panic. If he wasn't in the bathroom, where was he?

I heard a small whine coming from one of the aisles

behind me, but couldn't figure out where. Then I heard it again, a soft whimpering sound like a cornered animal. Abandoning the cart, I raced toward the direction of the sound. Three boys, who looked to be in their early teens, encircled Jonathan. His heavy glasses that were held on with elastic had been ripped off him and lay on the floor. His little body heaved with sobs. When he saw me he wailed my name.

"Breeze?" The biggest boy, grossly overweight with long greasy black hair and sagging jeans than hung halfway down his butt, turned, saw me and laughed. "Oh, you're here to rescue the side show freak!" Seeing the anger on my face, the other two boys fell back and glanced away. But the big boy stood his ground.

"Watch who you're calling a freak, Freak!" I snarled. I put my arm around Jonathan and hugged him close.

"Are you okay?" I whispered. Without taking my eyes off the bullies, I squatted and picked up his glasses. He nodded, his eyes as wide and unblinking as an owl's. "Then let's get out of here."

I turned him around, ignoring the words, "Freaky, geeky," coming from the big kid, and headed back toward our cart. At the very least I needed to pay for the groceries and get both of us out of there before Frank found out what had happened. I wheeled the cart around and headed for the checkout. I placed my right arm around his shoulder.

"I'm so sorry, Jonathan. Are you sure you're all right?"

He nodded, wiping his running nose on his sleeve. I handed him his glasses. He pulled them on, wiggling them into place. "Where were you? I was so scared."

But I couldn't respond because I had other worries on my mind: Deanne, and whatever she'd been calling me about that had been so important.

Just before I finished paying for the groceries I grabbed a small packet of tissues from the shelf beside me and tossed it onto the conveyor belt. I paid the bill, then the cashier handed me back my change. I glanced down at the tear-stained Jonathan, took a tissue from the packet and wiped his face. I gave him another and told him to blow his nose. Then I took his chin in my hands.

"Please don't say anything about this to Emily or Frank, okay?" I waited until he nodded, then heaved a relieved sigh. It was hard enough for them to trust me without having yet another strike against me. And I knew how protective Emily was about Jonathan. Suddenly he threw his arms around my waist and hugged me hard.

"I love you, Breeze," he said. I almost burst into tears myself. Just then I saw Frank walk up from the parking lot toward the store. For once, luck was on my side and I couldn't believe the timing. Five minutes earlier and he'd have been in a panic as we raced around the building, looking for Jonathan.

I kissed the top of his head. "I love you, too," I mumbled without thinking, and together we approached Frank, pushing the grocery cart.

"Did you have fun?" Frank asked, not really waiting for an answer as he took the cart from us and headed toward the truck. Jonathan and I exchanged a glance. He giggled.

"Sort of," he said.

The ride home was less strained than the trip down had been. Exhausted, all I wanted to do was sleep, but Jonathan's internal batteries had mysteriously been recharged, probably due to the open box of Oreos I could see spilled all over the back. He was chanting a sing-songy rote, sounding like the flying monkeys from the Wizard of Oz, "O, Ree, O."

Frank started to laugh and in spite of myself, I joined in.

He smiled at me, looking a lot more relaxed than when I'd left him. "I wanted to tell you how brave we all thought you were when you stood in the middle of all those cows to protect Emily," he said. "That took a lot of courage."

Startled, my head snapped around. "I wasn't brave. I just acted on instinct. It was stupid, really. Everything that happened was stupid."

Frank glanced out the window and cleared his throat. "Well, you did the right thing and you probably saved Emily's life."

Emily had said the same, but receiving praise from Frank made me feel better than I should have, considering that the whole episode was my fault. Still, I wasn't about to ruin the moment. It was enough that he and Emily liked me. It was more than I deserved.

I turned back to Frank. "Is Jonathan starting school this fall?"

The knuckles of Frank's tanned hands on the steering wheel turned white as he gripped it. Had I touched on a sore point? Was Emily worried about the challenges Jonathan might have to overcome in public school? That inevitable taunting and teasing that every kid gets, but 'different' kids so much more than others?

Frank didn't look at me when he said, "I think Emily's planning on home schooling Jonathan. But you'll probably have to take the bus to the nearest high school, which is in town."

The weirdest feeling came over me then. Kind of a combination of panic and nausea. I had never thought about going to school here. My plan was that by September I'd be back in the Stark classrooms with my friends, entering my senior year at school. Now the possibility of that not happening seemed so real that it made my head spin.

THIRTEEN

The next few weeks went by quickly, mostly because I was so busy doing Emily's outside chores. Frank and I made a couple more shopping trips to town and thankfully, Jonathan decided he'd stay and 'look after Emily,' as he put it, much to my relief. From time to time, I saddled Honey and cantered around the fields, but I was afraid to venture too far on my own and it was lonely not having anyone to talk to.

Jared came over twice a week to work with Diablo. But a strange thing had started to happen to me whenever I saw him. I'd get a weird tingling feeling, like when you get an itch under a cast that you can't scratch. And it wouldn't leave until he did, which made me uncomfortable enough that I'd busy myself with heavy chores to take my mind off it.

Occasionally I'd give him a hand with Diablo if I weren't occupied with something else. He seemed surprised at how skillful and calm I was in handling the stallion. But of course he didn't know that I'd been working with Diablo whenever I was certain no one else was around. Though I was still a little shy with Jared, he seemed to enjoy having someone his own age to talk to as much as I did. Once he even rode his gelding over and invited me to go for a ride with him. It was almost a date.

Still, there was no way I wanted to stay living at the Double-T and start school here in the fall. So I turned my mind toward other things. The summer was half over. Jared would be back at home soon as the California school year started in late August, unlike Oregon where we went back in

September. In another five weeks I'd be returning to Stark if I could come up with a foolproof plan to land me there and not in another foster home.

One day as I was heading back from the barn after feeding the horses, I saw the bright yellow Hummer that belonged to the man Emily and I encountered the day she'd broken her ankle. The same one Frank avoided in the parking lot the first day we went shopping. Though I was several hundred yards away I recognized 'handlebar,' the man Emily called Nolan Barker, leaning against the Double-T gate talking to Frank. Frank stood with his hands on his hips in the sort of position that barred the other man's passage. Even from that distance I could see the distress on his face. I stopped in my tracks and slipped back behind the house so they wouldn't see me.

"You're going to have to come around sooner or later," I heard Barker say. "You might ask the Shoemakers about the terrific deal I offered them."

"I don't care who else is selling out." Frank's words came out in a low growl, a tone I'd never heard him use before. "My land is not for sale." He took a menacing step forward, causing the other man to stumble back against his Hummer. "Nor will it ever be."

"How can you keep operating this place with almost no income?" Barker sneered, righting himself, looking really angry. "Especially now that Emily is laid up? That Shoemaker boy is going to be leaving soon and the foster kids you have can't do the work. It's time you realized that you're not even scraping by here and once the state finds out that there's not enough money to look after those kids they'll be taken away."

I couldn't hear any more of the conversation because Barker had gotten into the Hummer and started the engine. I emerged from my hiding spot and peeked around. Judging from the dust rising above the road to the north like a jet plume, I realized Barker must be heading home. Frank was nowhere to be seen. As I didn't want to meet up with him lest he think I had been eavesdropping, I slipped back to the barn until he had a chance to talk to Emily.

When I finally arrived back at the house I stopped outside the little porch addition and noticed something that I hadn't seen before. At the base of the door were scorch marks that went half way up the door and then stopped. There was nothing on the ground to indicate that a fire had been lit at the base, only the door was burned. I touched the charred wood and black soot smeared across my fingers. I wondered why Frank hadn't repaired the door or replaced it. I shrugged. Maybe it had been like that for a long time. Or maybe he'd taken a secret smoke and dropped his cigarette before Emily caught him. Kind of like the Lunatics' escapade with the fire. It made me smile to think that adults were often just as sneaky as kids.

After I washed up, I went to my room and thought about Barker's words. They had left me with a hollow feeling at the bottom of my stomach. It had never occurred to me that either Jonathan or I might be *taken away*. Were the Thompsons really so hard up for money? Mom and I had lived hand to mouth, from day to day, and we always managed. But the Thompsons had a lot of other mouths to feed besides just the four of us humans. There were horses, a dog and cat, and those two hundred cattle. Of course, the cattle were now grazing far away on government range land until the fall. So they, at least for the moment, were not an expenditure. The guilt I felt at costing them money was only partly assuaged by knowing I helped out around the place. Whenever I thought about it, I realized that my being here had caused a lot of their problems. My leaving the ranch couldn't be put off much longer.

Emily had been looking forward to getting her cast removed in a couple of weeks. As she healed, she'd become more mobile around the house, even going so far as to hobbling out to the barn to help with some light ranch work. It took a bit of the pressure off my work load because, though he tried very hard and meant well, Jonathan was only able to handle small tasks. And usually after he'd completed them I had to sneak back unseen so as not to hurt his feelings and do them over to make sure they were done right.

One day when I picked up the mail from the battered steel mailbox just outside the Double-T gates, I discovered that one of the envelopes was for me. I nearly dropped it in my excitement. The return address was the Stark School; I recognized the envelope as being from their own stationery. This was the first time I'd received any mail at all. My heart started pounding in anticipation, and my hands itched to open it. But whatever news it might hold could change things for me, in either good ways or bad. Right now, I couldn't let anyone else know. I tucked it carefully in my pocket so no one would ask questions and took the rest of the mail in to Emily.

As soon as I had a moment to myself I went to my bedroom and closed the door, pushing a chair up against it so I wouldn't be disturbed. In spite of missing my friends, the one thing I didn't miss was the crowding and lack of privacy. In my bedroom with the Thompsons I could sing, dance, read; do whatever I liked without anyone else seeing me.

Because no locks were allowed at Stark, not even on our personal property, Deanne had come up with an idea for a safety deposit box of sorts. She'd found a loose floorboard underneath her bed and generously told the rest of the Lunatics about it, though we kept it secret from everyone else. We each stored treasures in a shoe box labeled with our name and had an honor code that no one would touch the others' boxes without permission. Even accessing the items required a Lunatic keeping surveillance at the door until we were safe from prying eyes. I hoped the mail was from Deanne. It made me feel guilty that I hadn't asked Emily to call her back from the home phone after she'd called me that day in town. But so far I'd never told anyone about the Lunatics, not even Emily.

I curled up on my bed, and kicked my slippers onto the floor where they bounced onto the new deep-pile mauve throw rug. As promised, shortly after my arrival Emily and I had poured over the Sears catalog together and found a bedspread and matching curtains we both liked, a fresh print of wisteria and vines that gave the indoors an outdoorsy feel. They weren't that expensive, but after what I'd overheard Nolan Barker say about the Thompson's finances it made me feel even guiltier that I'd let her spend the money.

I looked over the envelope, savoring the feeling of having mail all my own. I didn't recognize the handwriting on the front, but it was probably addressed by an employee in Stark's office. It would have been against school protocol to release a foster parent's address to anyone, even close friends. I squeezed the envelope and felt a small packet inside. I ripped off the end and shook out the contents. A smaller, sealed envelope fell out on my bed.

This time I recognized the handwriting on the inner envelope as Deanne's. A nervous excitement came over me as I began to open it. Just then I heard Emily call my name. Hurriedly I stuck it under my pillow. I didn't want anyone discovering it before I'd had a chance to find out what she had to say. My hands shook as I removed the chair from the doorway. It took several minutes for me to compose myself, but finally when I felt as if I could face Emily without looking like I was hiding something, I meandered into the kitchen where she stood at the counter making lunch. A look of alarm crossed her face when she saw me.

"Are you all right?" She wiped her hands on a towel and reached up to touch my forehead. "You're as white as snow."

I nodded, swallowing hard, my mouth not working.

"You're not coming down with something, are you?" she persisted.

"No, I'm fine," I said finally. "I'm just hungry, I think."

She smiled at that and handed me a sandwich. "I've got good news. I get my cast taken off next week."

I forced a smile, sincerely happy for her. And for myself, as well. Having her out of the cast would take Flipper-Boy off my tail more often. Jonathan, I corrected myself. He was a good kid and in spite of my determination to leave at the end of summer, he and the Thompsons had been nothing but kind to me. I almost gave her a hug, then thought better of it and instead took a big bite of my sandwich.

"We should have a celebration. Maybe a potluck barbeque and invite the Shoemakers," I said as nonchalantly as I could. And Jared could come, too, I thought. But Emily's face stiffened and she quickly looked away.

"It's not a good time for that," she said in a cool voice.

She proceeded to make a big show of busying herself with kitchen work, loading the dishwasher and wiping the table. She didn't look at me again. It felt as if a door had been slammed in my face, but I didn't know why. Had Jared done something wrong? He hadn't been around for a couple of days but I thought it was just because he'd been busy at his grandparents' place. Briefly I wondered if Frank had fired him but decided that it wasn't possible. Jared was a conscientious worker.

I wanted to ask Emily if she knew what Nolan Barker had said to Frank. And what was the 'terrific deal' Barker had offered the Shoemakers. Maybe that's who Frank was talking about when he said "I don't care who else is selling out." Was that the reason Emily didn't want to have them over for a celebration? But if I asked, then I'd have to confess about eavesdropping, which I knew Emily would frown upon. Not to mention, there were the touchy subjects of how much Jonathan and I were costing her and Frank. No, it was better that I left that conversation to Emily bringing it up herself.

Kept busy with my usual chores, it wasn't until after dinner and I'd gone to bed that I remembered the letter I'd gotten earlier in the day. In the privacy of my bedroom I held the envelope up to the light, noting with disappointment the thinness of the paper inside. By now the Lunatics should have had almost two months of news to share with me.

But then curiosity got the better of me so I slipped my finger under the seal and tore it open. Inside was a single piece of white college-ruled paper with perforated edges, like a sheet torn from a notebook. I unfolded it and recognized

Deanne's large looped handwriting. With my stomach bouncing around nervously, I began to read.

"Hi Breeze," she began, "Just in case you come back and don't see me here, I wanted you to know that the school has found me a foster family. They live in Newport on the coast. Can you imagine me with my white skin being out on the beach?" After that she'd drawn a smiley face with squiggly hair, over a stick figure wearing a swimsuit. I smiled to myself.

"I'll send my address as soon as I have it. Maybe they'll let you visit me."

And that was it. Just a couple of lines, no mention of Carla or Tyesha. At least now I knew why she had been trying to call me. At least I thought I did. I glanced at the date she'd put at the top of the page. Suddenly it seemed as if the room was beginning to spin. She'd written the letter a week before her phone call.

FOURTEEN

I didn't sleep at all that night and knew I looked awful because when Emily saw me the next morning, she threatened to take me to a doctor if I didn't tell her what was going on. I wanted to share the news with her about Deanne, or at least, my concerns about the timing of Deanne's call and her foster home placement. Maybe Deanne's call had only been to give me her address. I knew what many foster homes were like. Being lonely in a crowd. Or perhaps she just wanted to talk. Emily might understand although right now it was apparent she and Frank had enough problems of their own.

So until I could figure out what to say, I lied and told her I was starting my period, and kept everything else to myself. I wrote yet another letter each to Tyesha and Carla, and told them what I'd just heard from Deanne. They were the only people who would understand. Her letter had been an announcement, nothing more personal than that to share. They were the only people who knew Deanne and Stark, but either they had moved on as well, or they'd just forgotten about the Lunatics.

Finally, when my anxiety had gotten so bad I jumped at every sound or movement, I decided I would share my concerns with Emily. She was the closest thing to a mom I had right now, and maybe she could think of something to help. It took me a few minutes to figure out how to start. I could feel her watching me as if I was a baby getting ready to poop my diaper and she was trying to potty train me.

"Spit it out," she said.

I played dumb. "What?"

"Whatever it is that's eating at you."

I hesitated. "It's my friend Deanne. I think she's in trouble and I don't know what to do to help her."

"Is she still at Stark School?"

I frowned. It hadn't occurred to me that she might still be there. More likely she was with her new family, although she hadn't mentioned in the letter when she was leaving.

"She's been placed in foster care somewhere on the Oregon coast. I got a call on my cell from her the day Frank and I went to town, but we got cut off. She sounded scared." I hesitated while Emily waited for me to continue. I pulled Deanne's letter from my pocket and handed it to her. "I got this yesterday. But it was mailed before she called. And that's what's worrying me. What if something changed?" I glanced up at Emily, trying to mask the fear I felt.

Emily considered this for a few minutes. "If you like I can call the school, or you can try calling her from the land line."

Instantly, my spirits lifted. I jumped up and hugged her, then raced to the phone. But Stark's automatic answering machine came on and my call just went into the school's voice mail, saying someone would return my call. I left a message asking that Deanne Malinowski contact me asap. All I could do was hope that it would be passed on to Deanne.

Only partly because I wanted to see Jared, I started spending more and more time with the horses. Not so much with Honey and the other three, but Diablo. Jared had started riding him with a saddle but since he was often occupied at his grandparents' ranch, I'd taken over his job of lunging Diablo and cleaning his stall. Every day I took him some kind of treat, usually carrots and pieces of apples. And I'd started grooming him, which he absolutely loved, rubbing my back with his soft muzzle in reciprocation, just as if I were another horse. I couldn't wait to get out to the barn each morning.

Then one day when I was sitting on the wood rail fence and scratching his withers from above, it occurred to me that if I swung my leg over carefully and climbed onto him, he probably wouldn't even care. Stroking his mane to keep him calm, I whispered to him then eased my leg over the middle of his back. He didn't move, though his ears twitched back and forth nervously as if listening for my voice. I grasped hold of the rail with one hand and his mane with the other, gave myself a little push and landed on his back. And the next thing I knew I was lying flat on my back in the dirt, looking up at his muzzle from underneath.

I heard a loud laugh but lay still for a moment, catching my breath and trying to figure out if anything was broken. But apart from a blinding headache emanating from where my skull had hit the ground, I had feeling throughout the rest of my body. Too much feeling, actually. I hurt all over. Finally I scrambled up to see who was laughing and found myself looking into Jared's blue eyes. I blushed as he began dusting off my clothes.

"Ouch!" I shrieked as his hand brushed my shoulder.

"That was stupid," he said. But he was smiling as if enjoying the fact that Diablo had dumped me.

"Thanks a lot," I replied, more humiliated than angry. I started stomping toward the house, trying not to limp from my sore legs and the bruises I could feel working their way up to the surface.

"You know when you fall off a horse you're supposed to get back on again, don't you?" he called after me.

I stopped so quickly I almost tripped over my feet and mortified myself again. I turned around and walked back to where he stood, putting a halter on Diablo and attaching a lead rope. A little smile twisted his lips. He gave me a wink.

"It's so the horse won't get the idea that he should do it again. Why don't we try it the right way this time?"

It was my opportunity to show Jared the kind of stuff I was made of, but I was a little intimidated about getting back on Diablo. He'd unseated me once already; what was there to stop him from doing it again? And with me getting really hurt this time. That wouldn't do me or the Thompsons any good. But Jared was still smiling at me, one hand holding Diablo's halter tightly, the other outstretched to help me climb on the horse. I took a deep breath. And suddenly I was sitting on the stallion's back, and this time Jared was looking up at me in admiration.

"You look good up there," he said. I felt my eyebrows raise involuntarily. Was Jared actually giving me a compliment?

Though Diablo's ears twitched back and forth, and he snorted and sidestepped a few times, with Jared leading him around the corral he made no further move to buck.

Finally, as if Jared realized I was starting to get too tired and sore from the unfamiliarity of riding bareback, he announced, "Okay, that's enough for today. No point in souring him on the idea." He gave me his hand but I had already slid off and began patting the horse.

"The name Diablo doesn't really suit him."

Jared laughed. "What do you want to name him? Buck?" He laughed again at his own lame joke. "We could even give him a last name if you want. Mehoff. Buck Mehoff."

Though I couldn't help feeling self-conscious, I grinned sheepishly, but for a better reason than just being able to take a good-natured joke. I had Jared's respect. And I realized that we were finally becoming friends. I just wished I could find a way to share this tidbit with the Lunatics.

"Do you think we could take Diablo and Honey out for a ride together?"

Jared laughed again. "No, I don't think that would be a good idea." He gave me a teasing smile. "You *do* know where babies come from, don't you?"

I punched him playfully in the arm to hide my embarrassment. "Of course I do, I'm not a kid," I shot back.

He looked me over again and grinned. "No, you're certainly not."

I blushed so hard at that even the roots of my hair felt

hot. That weird tingling had crawled through my body again. I decided to change the subject, trying to come up with any conversational topic to keep him from leaving. I hoisted myself onto the wooden fence railing and Jared climbed up beside me. "Do you like ranch work? Coming to visit your grandparents each summer?"

His whole face lit up. "I love it. My mom and dad only see Grandma and Grandpa when they drop me off and pick me up each summer, but I could stay here forever. I graduated this year. My college major is in agriculture."

Suddenly I felt dizzy. I kept forgetting that I lived here full-time, at least for now, but Jared was only at his grandparents' ranch during the summer. What would it be like during the winter? Going to school here had crossed my mind several times, and not in a good way. If I stayed with the Thompsons I'd probably have to take a stupid school bus full of misbehaving brats and slow-learners, with an hour-long ride each way. That's if I went to school. Because of his disabilities, Emily would be home-schooling Jonathan. Maybe she'd want to home-school me, too. For some reason that sounded even less appealing. I'd never meet anyone my own age.

Jared must have read my thoughts because he said, "Don't worry. There's still a few more weeks left of summer vacation." Then he swung off the fence and held out his hand to help me down. I smiled into his dark blue eyes, feeling the sudden thrill of having someone to talk to and share things with.

At that moment there was kind of an awkward heavy silence between us. It made me so nervous I had to fight the urge to make an excuse to run for the house. Instead I turned my gaze toward Diablo, just as I felt Jared's hand on mine. I turned to face him. His face was so close to mine our lips were almost touching. With a shock I realized he was about to kiss me. Suddenly I was blushing all over.

My joy wasn't to last. At the same time we both saw Diablo's head jerk toward the house and together we followed his gaze. I heard Jared clear his throat. Out of the corner of my eye I saw him sidle away from me. We watched as Emily came striding toward us, still wearing the cast that was due to come off in a couple of days, her face as dark and angry as a thundercloud. The only time I'd seen her so upset was when we'd encountered Nolan Barker the day of the cattle drive. She stopped about ten feet from us and folded her arms across her chest as if she were afraid of coming closer.

"Jared, you need to go home," she said coldly, but Jared was already backing away, throwing a guilty, sullen look my way before he nodded politely to her. Then he got on his mountain bike and pedaled away to his own home. Emily turned to me.

"What do you think you were you doing on that horse?"

I blinked in surprise, having forgotten that Jared had helped me ride Diablo.

"Do you realize you could have been killed? That Frank and I are responsible for you?" Her face had gone white with little red splotches.

"I expected Jared to be more responsible. If he can't abide by our rules, he won't be allowed to work here again."

"Emily, it was my fault, not Jared's," I pleaded. "Diablo threw me off, but Jared got me back on so he wouldn't do it again. Isn't that what expert trainers tell you to do?"

Though she still looked angry, she took a deep breath and said, "You're right," sounding like she didn't mean a word of it.

Then she whirled around and limped back toward the house. I stood there watching her walk away, puzzled and hurt. I'd been so thrilled to have Jared accept me, and finally having someone close to my own age to talk to. Now she'd dashed that tiny bit of happiness. Once again, here I was in a foster home where there was nothing to do but work, work, work, and no joy in my life at all. I missed my friends so much that there was only one thing left for me to do. It was time for me to leave.

FIFTEEN

The biggest difficulty I had in formulating a plan to leave the Thompson's ranch was how I would go about doing so. It was almost physically impossible to run away and hitchhike as the only traffic that passed by the house was the postman and the occasional hay or supply truck. Most of the vehicles I'd seen belonged either to the Shoemakers or 'handlebar.' That didn't help me much. I wished my mother was around to talk to, but of course if my mother was alive, I wouldn't be here at the Thompson's trying to run away. Just thinking about all the 'what ifs' gave me a migraine.

I knew the Lunatics would help me if they could, but I hadn't been able to get messages through to them. Or at least, they weren't responding to the ones I had sent. Deanne hadn't returned my call, nor had anyone else from Stark. I had no other friends or family. There was really only one ally, a new one, who might be able to help me leave. Jared. Except that now he might not be coming over for a while.

At dinner that night the whole family was very quiet. The only noise was the sound of us chewing the steak Frank had barbequed, probably after butchering one of the cows. One down, 199 to go, I though glumly. Frank was almost always completely silent, but tonight spoke less than usual. Even Jonathan, who generally kept us smiling into our plates with his inane patter, seemed to understand that this wasn't the right time to make jokes. I wondered what Emily had said to them, and tried to pretend that everything was normal between us, though I realized I must have really stepped over the line by riding Diablo.

Once dinner was finished, Frank and Jonathan headed to the living room, as if in silent collusion. Emily and I stayed in the kitchen. She washed the dishes as I dried, and for the first time I felt uncomfortable in her presence. It seemed as if every time I zigged she zagged, and I could sense her growing even more annoyed with me. When Jonathan went to bed for the night, Frank headed outside to check on the animals and we were left alone.

"I'm sorry I rode Diablo without your approval," I offered.

She made no reply as we dried our hands and finished putting away the dishes. Then she shook her head, walked into the living room and sank wearily into her chair. Absentmindedly she picked up her knitting. Though she stared at it she didn't work on the stitches. For a long time she didn't say anything, then finally she set the needles down and looked directly at me.

"It's not about the horse, Breeze. It's more complicated than that. I overreacted at first when I saw you with Jared. We should probably have a chat about things like, uh…" she hesitated, obviously embarrassed, "birth control."

It was my turn to be uncomfortable. I could feel my face flush. Bewildered, I said, "But Jared and I weren't doing anything inappropriate. I swear. He was just helping me ride Diablo."

Emily sighed. "I know that. Like I said, it's complicated. You remember that man we ran into the day I broke my ankle?"

I nodded. "I saw him talking to Frank a couple of days ago."

She took a deep breath. A sort of hopelessness settled over her face that aged her. I saw her hands were shaking. "He wants to buy this property. He's nearly talked the Shoemakers into selling theirs."

My heart sank to the bottom of my stomach. The

Shoemakers were thinking of selling their ranch? That would mean they'd be moving. Then Jared wouldn't be coming to stay during summer vacation any more. The plans he'd confided to me about going to college and coming back to run their ranch would never happen. Had he known? If so, why hadn't he said anything?

"Why?" was all I could get out.

She gave a short, humorless laugh. "They're not getting any younger, Breeze. In fact, they've wanted to retire for quite some time. Even offered to sell the property to Frank and me before Nolan Barker came on the scene. We couldn't afford to buy it, though."

"Why does Nolan Barker want this place? Wouldn't he have enough land if he bought the Shoemakers ranch?"

"He wants to buy our property because we're in the middle. If he has ours and the Shoemakers' place, he'll own the size of the estate he needs."

"What is he going to do, put thousands of cattle on it?" I ventured.

Emily shook her head. "Oh no, he's not putting cattle on it. Or horses. Or planting it in crops. He plans to build a casino, and beside it a big resort with condominiums. Basically ruin the land for any kind of farming in the future."

"How do you know what he plans to do?"

"One day he came over and before I could open the door, I overheard him talking to that slimy real estate broker that travels with him. It only took a couple of minutes of listening in to know what his real motives were."

I jumped to my feet and held out my hands in protest. "But if the Shoemakers don't sell, he wouldn't be able to do it, right? Can't we talk to them, get them to see how he's going to ruin everything?"

"It might already be too late," she said sadly. "I told Dennis and Nettie what I'd learned about Barker, but they said they'd like to hear what he had to say before turning him down. I don't blame them. It's not like they need the money, but it's a hard life. Jared will be starting college this year.

Their own children didn't want to take over the ranch. It's unlikely that once Jared finishes college he will either."

"But, Emily," I persisted, "Jared told me that when he finishes college that's exactly what he wants to do. He wants to come back and work his grandparents' ranch. He loves it here." I almost added that I did too, but at the last minute thought better of it. After all, I had no intention of staying here permanently and was still trying to come up with an idea as to how I would get back to Stark.

But she just sniffled and picked up her knitting. Her mouth was turned down at the corners and I could hardly hear her when she spoke. "If they decide to sell it's their decision, Breeze. Let it go."

I finally sat on the sofa, feeling as if all the light had gone out of the room. It would be bad enough for Frank and Emily to lose the Shoemakers as neighbors, but they really loved this place. They worked and toiled night and day to make even the small income they did. And some guy with a 'get rich quick' scheme was going to ruin their way of life for them.

Even as I sat there commiserating with Emily, I began to form a plan to help. For now I would place my preparations to return to Stark on hold. I wondered if Jared knew what his grandparents intended to do and how he would feel about it once he found out. Forgetting my reservations about showing affection, I gave Emily a quick good night hug before retiring to my bedroom. If she was surprised she gave no indication, scarcely looking at me as I left the room. Tonight I'd write a note to Jared. Then first thing in the morning while I was out doing my chores and no one would miss me, I'd walk over and put it in his mail box.

SIXTEEN

The next morning everything went exactly as I had planned. In the beginning, that is. With Frank working in the fields on his tractor and Emily busy with Jonathan in the house, I got all my chores done in record time. I tucked the note to Jared in my jeans pocket, and walked the half-mile length of dirt road to his grandparent's house. I was quite sure no one saw me leave. The one time I heard a vehicle approach, I ducked down into the deep drainage ditch, which luckily for me was dry during the summer.

But I had no sooner finished putting the letter in the Shoemaker's mailbox when I heard another car coming. The high powered engine sounded kind of familiar, if only because it was one that I had heard recently. I hurriedly scrambled into the drainage ditch again and cowered down, waiting until the car went by. Instead, I heard it slow then come to a stop. Thinking it was probably the mailman, I slowly started to rise then I saw the yellow Hummer and knew immediately who it was. Nolan Barker had arrived at the Shoemaker's house.

I watched him ring the doorbell, then Mrs. Shoemaker opened the door and invited him in. Barker took off his ten-gallon cowboy hat and I saw that his head was so bald it glinted in the sun, contrasting sharply with the long handlebar moustache. I shoved my sleeve in my mouth to keep from laughing because once I started to snort it'd all be over. But I was desperate to hear what was being said between them.

Staying low, I crept as close as I could until I got to the outside of the house. Then I tiptoed around the periphery until I was underneath the living room window. I could just barely make out the voices: Mr. and Mrs. Shoemaker, and Nolan Barker.

"What the heck are you doing?"

I nearly jumped out of my skin. My heart pounding in my throat, I turned to see Jared standing behind me, his hands on his hips, a puzzled expression in his dark blue eyes. I raised my finger to my lips.

"Sshhh," I whispered. I took his hand and led him back to the drainage ditch I'd just left. I made him squat down beside me so I could speak out loud.

"When were you going to tell me?" I blurted angrily.

"Tell you what?" He appeared genuinely confused.

"Don't you know who owns that Hummer?"

Jared started to laugh until I held a finger to my lips, indicating for him to be quiet.

"Yeah, that's Nolan Barker. He lives on the property to the north of yours, er...the Thompson's. Never speaks to me directly, only to my grandparents, as if I don't exist. Kind of a jerk."

"That's putting it mildly!" I couldn't help sounding indignant, though I realized he probably didn't know about the most recent history between Barker and the Thompsons. "What's he doing here?"

Jared looked surprised. He made a face and shrugged. "I don't know. My grandpa sold him some cows."

"What does he want cows for?" I persisted.

Jared laughed so loudly I thought the people in the house would be able to hear him. I frowned hard enough for him to stop. "I imagine he wants cows for the same thing we all do. Milk, meat; raising more so he can sell to other people who want milk and meat."

I gave him a rough shove, really upset with him now. "No, he doesn't want cows. That's not what he does for a living. He's a developer."

Jared began to look annoyed and tried to scramble up from the ditch. I yanked him back down again. "Well, that's his business, isn't it? Which means it's none of ours."

Suddenly he remembered my earlier question. He gave me an introspective look. "When was I going to tell you what? I don't know what you're talking about."

"Your grandparents are thinking of selling their property to Barker. He wants Frank and Emily to sell theirs, too, but they won't." I stopped because Jared's face had gone deathly pale.

"You're kidding me." But he could see in my eyes that I was telling the truth. "I don't believe you. They would have told me."

He turned to me with a thousand unanswered questions hiding behind the hurt on his face. I almost wished I hadn't said anything because I was on the verge of ruining the relationship between us that was only just beginning to bud. "Why wouldn't they have told me?"

I could only shake my head sadly. Maybe they didn't know what Jared had planned for his future. Or maybe they knew and wanted out of the ranching business before he could turn around and disappoint them as their own kids, Jared's parents, had done. Whatever their reasons, I was certain it was true that Jared hadn't known about the sale or he would have told me.

"I put a letter in your mailbox," I said finally. "After Emily chewed me out about riding Diablo I decided to run away and go back to Stark. I was going to ask for your help in getting away. But then she told me about Nolan Barker's plan to buy up all the properties adjoining his and turn the entire place into a casino resort. I thought if you didn't know, someone ought to tell you."

He nodded, looking almost as depressed as if his horse had just died. "There's nothing I can do. It's my grandparents' property; they have every right to do what they want with it."

I gave him a shrewd look. "That's if they know what his

plans really are. Maybe they think he's just setting himself up in ranching, buying cattle from them and such. He didn't tell Frank and Emily; they found out by accident. Not that they would have considered selling anyhow," I added.

Jared pulled up a long strand of grass and began to chew on the end of it. He contemplated for a long time before he finally said, "Do you think it's a done deal? That an offer has already gone through and the sale is irreversible?"

"I don't know," I admitted. "It might be too late. But if we can prove that he deliberately misled your grandparents, and they decide that they don't approve of his plans for the property, we might be able to stop him." At that moment I remembered the boy I'd seen with Barker the day Frank, Jonathan and I had gone to town.

"Barker had a boy with him the other day when Frank and I went to town to get supplies. Is that his son?"

Jared frowned. "Barker? No, he's not even married. He hires people to work with him, but I don't think he has any kids. Why do you ask?"

I shrugged. "No reason. I was just curious."

But suddenly Jared's eyes narrowed. "What did he look like?"

I thought about that for a moment. The boy hadn't been particularly distinctive in any way, other than his height and the black ponytail. I described him as best I could.

Jared swallowed hard. "I think you saw Kevin Palola."

"What would he be doing with Barker?"

"I don't know. But you can bet that it's nothing good. I figured he wouldn't be back here again."

But something was still puzzling me. "How well did you know Kevin?"

"Not real well. We hung out only a couple of few times. My grandparents and the Thompsons thought we'd hit it off as Kevin is only a couple of years older than me." His lips twisted in an ironic grin. "But we didn't. To put it bluntly, Kevin is a bad guy. I'm surprised even Barker would associate with him after he got arrested."

"What did he do?"

"What *didn't* he do?" Jared answered with sarcastic rhetoric. "For one thing, he's a pyro."

"What's a pryo?"

Jared laughed. "*Pyro.* Pyromaniac. Likes to set fire to things just for thrills."

A cold shiver ran up my back, causing my arms to roughen with goose bumps. That charred back door: had that been Kevin's handiwork? I'd blamed it on Frank. Holy shit, I thought, he could have killed the Thompsons if they'd been inside. I noticed Jared watching me and forced a smile that I didn't feel.

"Don't worry, I don't think he'd come around here," he reassured me, "last I heard he'd been sent to juvenile detention. He'd be over eighteen now so if he did anything bad he'd be tried as an adult and go to jail. I'm pretty sure he wouldn't want to go there."

At that Jared jumped to his feet. He held out his hand to help me up, reminding me of the day I'd fallen off Diablo. His eyes held a depth of sadness I'd only seen in foster kids I'd met, especially in a lot of those who first came to live at Stark. It cut right down to my heart that this could happen to someone like Jared who'd been fortunate enough to never have known the kind of life we had. "What do we do now?"

I smiled grimly at him because I had absolutely no idea. "We have to decide what to do about Barker and his plans."

"How do you propose to accomplish that?"

"Beats me," I said, "but as soon as I think of something, I'll let you know."

He gave me a long meaningful look that was interrupted by the sound of Barker's vehicle leaving the Shoemakers' property. Once he was out of sight we pulled ourselves out of the ditch. Jared hesitated for just a second before enveloping me in a hug. Then he kissed me on the cheek, warming me all the way to my toes. I would have fallen back into the ditch if he hadn't given me a gentle push in the direction of the Double-T.

When I got back to the Thompson's house I was surprised to see two unfamiliar vehicles parked in the front yard. One was a state police car, the other a brown Suburban with government plates and the National Forest Service logo on the side. At that moment I had the most terrible feeling of deja vu come over me as I recalled the last time I'd seen a police car and a government vehicle in the same place. That day it was to tell me that my mother had been killed.

SEVENTEEN

I opened the door and stopped, frozen in the doorway. Two uniformed men stared at me as if I'd just barged in on a conversation they didn't want me to hear. Emily and Frank's faces held myriad expressions, but neither of them would look directly at me. As I took stock of the situation, noting that Emily, Frank and Jonathan all appeared to be alive and unhurt, I saw that Jonathan's eyes were wide with terror. I went over and put my arms around him, wondering why he wasn't being held by Emily. Then to my horror I saw why neither Emily nor Frank could physically comfort him. They were both handcuffed.

The two men, one in an Oregon State Police uniform, the other wearing the dark green uniform with a U.S. Forest Service emblem on the arm, frowned at me, then glanced grimly at each other. It pleased me when I saw the policeman's mouth twist. He was obviously uncomfortable. I could tell that my arrival had come as a surprise because for several moments no one spoke.

Finally I summoned the courage to ask, "What's going on?"

Emily eyes held a plea as she glanced across to Frank, and then at the Forest Service official. He cleared his throat.

"Are these your parents?"

I sneaked a look at Emily, who made a barely perceptible nod. "They're my foster parents."

He fixed his eyes on me, without changing expression. "Frank and Emily Thompson are under arrest for overgrazing on Federal lands. They have permits for two hundred head, but we keep surveillance on leased property. We've been watching the herd size and grazing habits for some time now. There are at least five hundred cattle with the Double-T brand up there."

I stared at him in bewilderment. We had moved two hundred cattle. Of course, I hadn't counted them; I only knew what I'd heard. This was grazing season on the range land. Could there have been more cattle up there before we moved ours? Stragglers left over from the fall? But even as the questions crossed my mind I knew it wasn't possible. Frank was a more careful ranch manager than that and Emily would have told me. And then another thought, an unwelcome one, came to me: maybe I'd been coached and that number planted for a reason. I shook the notion from my head.

Emily broke through my thoughts. Her unwavering gaze caught mine and held. "It's all a misunderstanding, Breeze. We'll go with these men and answer their questions and when everything is explained and cleared up we'll be back home." She gave a tense smile. "This I promise you."

The state policeman said, "Sometimes these things take longer than expected. If there are minor children who need to be looked after we'll have to contact Children's Services to have them placed in temporary homes until this is resolved."

I saw the fear in Emily's eyes, knowing full well that if Jonathan and I were taken away she'd never get us back. I felt my breakfast swell in my stomach and threaten to break loose. I swallowed away the nausea.

"I'm sixteen," I said, looking the cop directly in the eyes. "I'm old enough to stay with Jonathan until they get back." I saw the tension leave Emily's face for a moment. The policeman squinted at me as if he didn't believe what I'd just said, then searched Emily's face. She nodded.

"She looks after Jonathan a lot of the time." She turned to me. "Breeze, why don't you call the Shoemakers and ask if it's okay to stay with them until we get back?" Behind the officers' backs she gave me an unsmiling wink, then turned to the policeman and said, "They have a grandson her age." Her bottom lip began to tremble and I was sure she was going to cry, but she blinked hard and managed to hold back the tears. The policeman shrugged.

"Fine. We'd better get moving. You can contact your attorney from the courthouse."

All this time Frank hadn't said a word. His eyes wouldn't meet mine, no matter how I stared at him, and I realized he hadn't looked at me since I'd walked through the door. I could almost feel the shame that hung over him like a dark shadow, being cuffed like that in front of his family. I wanted to be anywhere but in the room at that moment, and wished with all my heart I'd never left Stark.

Emily's shoulders were shaking as they left and I knew she was crying. Though I could see the tears running down her cheeks, she forced a smile for Jonathan and me. But I knew her heart was breaking at leaving us behind. I made up my mind to do the very best job I could in looking after Jonathan, and keep his mind off what was happening. At least until they got home. I picked Jonathan up in my arms, hugging him tightly, and ran after them.

"We'll be fine," I promised Emily. "Don't worry. We'll be right here waiting for you when you get back." She smiled and nodded, trusting me because she had no choice. The last we saw of them both was when the policeman lowered their heads into the back of the squad car and they drove away down the gravel driveway.

After they'd gone I took Jonathan into the bathroom and we washed both our faces with cold water. I kept him with me as I went mindlessly through my chores. I needed to keep a constant watch on him because I couldn't be sure he was mature enough to be left alone for any length of time. Later, I made peanut butter and jelly sandwiches for dinner, read to him and put him to bed early. I needed time to think about what had happened and what to do if Emily and Frank were delayed in returning.

I had no intention of calling Jared's grandparents, knowing that Emily's wink had meant 'this is what we want them to think.' I knew if I called for assistance they'd be here in a heartbeat, as would Jared. It suddenly became very important for me to show the Thompsons what I could do on my own.

Before I went to bed I brought Dingus, the dog, into the house for protection, and to give me a feeling of security. Not that he had any traits, or was in any way capable, of behaving like a guard dog. Normally he was forbidden from coming into the house because he had a habit of rolling in all things stinky. But I figured this one time no one would have cared.

As I lay in bed that night, the house eerily quiet with only Jonathan and me, and Dingus yipping in his doggie dreams beside my bed, I thought about what the Forest Service guy had said. More than five hundred cattle. I remember how mind boggling two hundred had seemed to me, and wondered if I had been told a certain number because that's what the Thompsons wanted everyone to think. Surely Mr. Shoemaker and Jared would have known the difference, although they probably wouldn't have said anything. Then I banished the blasphemous thoughts from my head. The Thompsons were good, honest people. Deep in my heart I knew there was no way they would have deliberately done anything illegal.

I stared at the stars in the night sky outside my bedroom window. Somewhere in the distance I heard the coyotes howling their nightly chorus that I went to sleep by every night. How free from care wild animals were, as long as they steered clear of predators, that is. I rolled over to get comfortable and sighed. I guess that didn't make them so free, after all.

EIGHTEEN

Emily and Frank didn't come home the next day and there was no word from anyone else as to when they might be released. I began to get seriously worried. Jonathan and I had only enough food for a few days. Although Frank had given me a few driving lessons on the tractor and I'd watched how he started the truck, I'd never driven it. And it was a little late now to apply for a learner's permit. How we were going to get food and supplies to run the ranch if the Thompsons didn't get back soon?

The following morning there was a loud knock on the door. Startled, I motioned Jonathan to stay quiet while I peeked out a side window. A nondescript car with a government logo on the side sat out in the driveway, but it wasn't like the vehicle that had been here the day they'd taken Frank and Emily away. With a jolt I realized that it was most likely a Children's Services caseworker at the door. Holding Jonathan tightly we stayed crouched behind Emily's chair until the knocking ceased and we heard the car drive away.

By the next day we still hadn't heard a word. Jonathan had started to get on my nerves. He cried for almost no reason at all and refused to eat everything I prepared except peanut butter and jelly sandwiches. After two days of it I gagged every time I smelled peanut butter. I hadn't wanted to call the Shoemakers. Even though they'd been talking to Nolan Barker, I trusted them enough to ask for their help.

Still, they might unintentionally tell someone about

Frank and Emily. And that would put Barker in a better position for acquiring the ranch.

I fully trusted Jared, though. It appeared that he'd been kept in the dark as much as I had. When I found the Shoemaker's home number posted on the fridge, I made the decision to call him, hoping that it would be he that picked up, and not one of his grandparents. I scored on the first try, but burst into tears the moment I heard his voice.

He patiently waited until I'd managed to make my embarrassing, choking sobs sound like a fit of coughing. "Breeze, what's the matter? What's going on?" I could hear the urgency in his voice.

I glanced around to make sure Jonathan wasn't listening. "I can't talk much about it over the phone in case anyone overhears. I need you to come over here as soon as possible, but you have to promise me you won't tell your grandparents."

"What's going on?" he persisted. "Breeze, are you in some kind of trouble?"

"I'm serious, just come as soon as you can, and bring lots of food. I'll tell you everything when you get here." I could hear the questions hovering in his voice, but finally he agreed to come as soon as he could. Now I just had to wait.

Later that morning after Jared finished his early farm chores at his grandparents' ranch, he arrived on his mountain bike with a bulging back pack. Jonathan and I ran out to help him dismount so he wouldn't drop his pack in the dirt. It weighed a ton. I felt a pang of gratitude as I realized how hard it must have been for him to get it out of the house, let alone carry it on his back the half-mile to our place.

"You should have packed it on your horse," I said, taking in his flushed red face, sweat pouring out from under his cap.

He shook his head. "It would have taken too long and someone might have noticed."

Jonathan and I helped him carry the pack inside, and together we heaved it onto the table. Jared emptied the contents, goodies spilling out everywhere. Our own personal Santa Claus, bringing us gifts. He'd packed all kinds of canned soups and food, crackers, cookies and bread. There were even a dozen eggs and a quart of milk, which would last if I used it sparingly. He'd also thrown in a bag of Gummy Bears. I wondered how he'd managed to get it out of the house unseen, or how the amount would go unnoticed.

He laughed when I asked. "As luck would have it, except for the milk and eggs, Grandma had filled a big box with groceries to take to the homeless shelter. I figured you guys were in as much need as anyone else, so I just skimmed a bit."

Jonathan ran over and gave him a big hug. Shyly, I did the same. He blushed, the high red color of his cheeks flaring up the way it did when he was embarrassed. He turned away saying, "I'll help you put it away."

After we'd stowed the groceries in the cupboard, he said to Jonathan, "I want to talk to Breeze for a few minutes in private. Do you mind playing in your room for a while?" He opened the bag of Gummy Bears and gave Jonathan a handful. He watched as Jonathan scampered off, happily sucking on candy, then turned to me.

"What's happened? Where are Frank and Emily?"

I studied his face, taking in the troubled bewilderment in his eyes. I'd only given him the briefest of details, telling him that Jonathan and I were alone and running low on groceries, but not to tell anyone else, or that I'd even called. I explained to him what had happened after I'd last seen him, when we'd watched 'handlebar' going into his grandparents' house. At least I told him what I knew, which wasn't all that much.

"Those are really serious charges, Breeze. Anytime you cheat the government out of anything, even if they only suspect you of cheating, they can lock you up and throw away the key. If there's enough evidence against Frank and Emily, they might not be coming home."

Seeing my face starting to crumple, he put his arm around me and squeezed gently, resting his chin on my head.

I almost burst into tears until I remembered that I was still a Lunatic, no matter what. I didn't cry in front of anyone else.

"But that's just it," I said, my quavering voice making me mad. "I don't know what evidence they have. I don't know if Frank and Emily have an attorney working on their case, or if they think they don't need one because they're innocent. And how do we know they're innocent?"

"What do you mean?" Jared frowned, removing his arm from my shoulders.

I took a deep breath. "The Feds said that they've been watching the herd for some time and there are more than five hundred cattle up there with the Double-T brand. Emily told me there were two hundred; that they have a permit with the National Forest Service to be allowed to graze two hundred cattle on government owned land. Who's telling the truth? Do you know for sure that we, I mean you guys," I corrected, remembering how I'd messed things up and hadn't completed the cattle drive, "drove only two hundred cattle onto range land?"

Jared stared at his hands for several minutes, thinking. Finally his eyes met mine. "I never really gave it any thought. No one mentioned a number to me before now. But I've worked cattle since I was little and there's no way there were more than 250 in that herd, give or take a few. If Emily said it was so, then I'd believe her."

"Okay, then how do you explain the charges?"

"I don't know. And I have no idea how we'd go about disputing evidence the Federal agents claim to have. But I do know this, it's not something you can do alone."

He sat on a kitchen chair and pulled me onto the one next to him. I kept my eyes downcast because I was afraid to look at him, knowing I'd break down if I met his eyes. But he cupped my chin with one hand and leaned close.

"Breeze, look at me." With a great effort I returned his gaze and saw worry and maybe an even stronger emotion there. He moved closer and it seemed as if he were going to kiss me. The heat of his face against mine seemed to sear my skin. I put my arms around his neck. Then I heard a noise in the doorway. I opened my eyes to see Jonathan standing there, looking astonished. We snapped apart like two rubber bands. Jared patted my knee and stood.

"Don't either of you worry about anything," he said. "We'll figure out what to do together." Jonathan smiled tentatively at both of us, as if he were unsure of what was happening, though trusting us completely. What choice did he have? Or me either, for that matter?

After Jared had gone I made scrambled eggs and toast for Jonathan, who appeared in better spirits since Jared had been with us. We played a few games of cards then I put him to bed and sat looking around the room. If I was to clear Frank and Emily I would have to obtain documentation, if such a thing existed, and take it to the courthouse. That would mean snooping in their personal files. Under the circumstances, I was sure they wouldn't be upset with me for doing that.

The other thing I needed to figure out was how to start the truck. After all, I was sixteen, which made me legally able to drive, although I didn't even have a learner's permit. Still, there would be no reason for anyone to question me being allowed to drive the Thompsons' truck. And if I were able to drive into town, there were a million things I could think of to do. Like calling Tyesha, or better yet, Carla. Her dad, Mr. Sutherland aka 'God's Gift to Women,' was an attorney.

NINETEEN

The next morning, while Jonathan created his version of impressionist paintings at the kitchen table with finger paints and a pad of paper, I was free to snoop inside the tall grey steel filing cabinet Emily kept in their bedroom. I found dozens of manila file folders marked with the usual stuff on health and vehicle insurance, one marked Legal Documents containing information on Jonathan and me, and another that said Farm Documents. I figured this was the one that might have any relevant information on how many cattle they bought and sold. I slipped a pen into the space as a place holder and pulled out the file.

After thumbing through page after page of boring receipts I finally found several bills of sale for Hereford cows, which added up to around 125 cattle. While the receipts dated back over several years, I couldn't make the numbers come to any more than that. I thought about this for a minute and then realized that mostly likely half that number would have given birth to calves each spring. That would make up at least two hundred. Then, each year I knew they sold off the male calves. And of course, occasionally cows died, or got butchered. How on earth could anyone keep track of them all, I wondered, especially the Feds who didn't even live here?

I started thinking about how Jared had told me that Nolan Barker was at his grandparents' house because he was buying cattle from them. Emily had said Barker had no interest in buying and raising cattle; he was a land developer.

So why would he be buying cattle from the Shoemakers? If Barker wanted to force Emily and Frank off their land, what better way than to 'plant' extra cattle on the grazing land, then set the government on their tail and seize all their livestock and property? It all seemed crystal clear now, but one giant question haunted me: how would Jared's grandparents react to hearing my theories about Barker?

I put all the receipts back in the file folder, slipped it into my book bag, and got myself dressed in nice clothes: the coral sleeveless tank top Tyesha had given me and new slim fitting black jeans Emily bought for me two weeks ago. I tried to look as sophisticated as I could, and putting on more makeup than I generally used made me appear older. I took extra time with my hair and instead of my customary ponytail, curled the ends and let it bounce loose around my shoulders.

Once all the farm chores were taken care of and Jonathan was dressed, the two of us climbed into the truck and I began a self-administered driving lesson. As I stuck the key in the ignition and turned it, my heart pounded so hard I thought I was going to be sick. But the truck started immediately. I held my breath for just a minute when I put the gearshift into 'drive' as I had seen Frank do. Too late I realized that I should keep my foot on the brake. It lurched forward when I shifted from park, forcing a wide-eyed squeal from Jonathan.

Fortunately for me, the truck had an automatic transmission, so the involuntary jerking that would have taken place had it been a stick shift was minimal. The main problem was that the vehicle was absolutely huge and I had to have Jonathan checking out the side window all the time to see if my wheels were going in the ditch. Wisely, today he stowed his usual babble and concentrated on his task.

As I really had only two choices of direction, I started out where Frank and I had driven when we went into town. Although it was about an hour's drive, it was going to take me longer. As we crawled along the road, people honked at me, giving me angry glares as they pulled around to pass. At one point a man on a large hay baler passed me. I didn't care. The speedometer said I was going 40 miles an hour and that was scary enough. I could feel the power under my right foot and every time I rested it on the gas pedal for just a second we'd zoom forward like a rocket ship.

Finally, after what seemed like hours, I saw signs that indicated we were approaching the town center. I just followed the nose of the truck, slow and deliberate. I'd ask directions once we arrived. Then I had the worst panic attack of my life. Barker's yellow Hummer passed me going in the other direction. But the driver wasn't Barker—it was the kid named Kevin Palola. He gave me a narrowed stare as we passed, but I ignored him and kept my eyes directed to the road ahead of me.

As we got near the center of the city I approached my first traffic light, it was red, and I knew enough to stop. While I'd been waiting for it to turn green I noticed a grocery store on the right, the one Frank had avoided on our trip to town. It had a parking lot large enough for even me to park in. I turned the steering wheel and pulled into the lot. A series of honking horns reminded me that next time I needed to use a signal light.

After I shut off the ignition I paused to catch my breath. It was then that I saw several large signs lining the road from which I'd just turned. They read, "Elect Nolan Barker for County Sheriff." A pounding started up in my head. If I hadn't realized it before, I realized it now. Nolan Barker running for office meant he had connections. We were at a definite disadvantage.

I took a deep breath and turned to Jonathan. "Jonathan," I said firmly, "I need you to follow me and do everything I say without any questions, okay?"

I didn't think I had anything to worry about because so far he'd been quiet and helpful the entire trip. He nodded, eyes as big and round as hubcaps. "All right, then," I breathed. "Let's do it."

I climbed down from the truck then went around to the

passenger's side to help Jonathan out. Then we set off in the direction of the store.

"Can we get some candy?" Jonathan asked hopefully, but I shook my head.

"I didn't bring enough money. Anyhow, we're not here to have fun; we're here to help Emily and Frank."

We walked into the grocery store together and I looked around, wondering where I was most likely to find someone to assist me. I saw a sign in the far corner that said Customer Service and headed in that direction. Overcoming my squeamishness, I took hold of Jonathan's flipper, walked boldly up to the counter and said, "Can you tell me where the Courthouse is located?"

The tiny blonde girl at the counter, who looked close to my age, blinked a couple of times. "I don't know. I'll have to ask."

She turned to a plump, older man standing behind her. He wore a navy bibbed apron over a white shirt with an embroidered pocket that said 'Dick.'

"City or County?" he asked.

City? County? Jeez, I didn't know. Still, I had to keep bluffing. "Well, maybe I'd better just find the police department and they can direct me."

Dick took an interest at that point. "What is it you need? Are you lost?"

I shook my head. "No," I lied, looking at Jonathan, "I'm babysitting this kid and his mother is late picking him up. I think I might need to file a police report." A look of alarm flashed across Jonathan's face, but I squeezed his flipper. Out of the corner of my eye I could see his face relax.

At that the man got really excited. "I'll take you there, little lady." He turned to the girl at the counter and said, "Do you think you can hold the fort?" She nodded, looking bored as she snapped her bubble gum.

And off we went, chubby Dick leading the way, pointing out landmarks, and me dragging Jonathan along by the flipper. Passers by stared curiously at us, and I guess we probably made a weird procession as we walked in single file. Finally we got to a small wood-framed building with fake brick siding that came only half way up the wall. Taggers had spray painted initials in blue and purple 3D lettering on the wood. Someone else had halfheartedly tried to cover it up with streaming white paint, but I could still see a couple of bad words. Jonathan stared at the wall as we passed.

I felt him tug my hand and then he said, "Breeze, what's fu…"

"Shsssh!" I hissed.

Dick stopped when we came to a couple of black and white police cars parked outside a large sandstone brick building with a sign that read 'City Hall.'

"Here's where you need to go," Dick said, pointing toward the entrance, "they'll take care of you." He gave a halfhearted wave and bustled back toward the grocery store.

"Thank you," I called out. He gave another wave, still walking away from me, then disappeared around the corner.

"What are you going to do?" Jonathan lisped, looking worried.

I squatted in front of him and stared directly into his eyes. "I'm going to find Emily and Frank. I discovered some papers that will show that they are innocent of what those guys accused them of, but I need you to be quiet and follow my lead." He stared doubtfully at me. "Do you understand?" I went on. I waited until he finally nodded hesitantly. "Okay, then, let's go."

Together we walked into City Hall, which consisted of five city departments helpfully labeled by overhead signs, like Accounting, Payroll and Court, above the doors. Rows of wooden bench seating lined the corridors, punctuated with end tables covered with City Department newsletters and visitor information. Finally I located the office marked 'Police' and headed straight through the doors with Jonathan in tow. I sat him down on a chair and gave him a dog-eared *National Geographic* magazine.

"Wait here," I whispered, "and don't talk to anyone."

I turned to the Information counter and rang the bell. An elderly white-haired woman with a dark purple pantsuit stretched optimistically across her body walked up. She had an expression of annoyance that, if you could tell by her wrinkles, seemed as if it was permanent.

"I'm looking for two people who were taken into custody three days ago," I stated confidently. The woman seemed taken aback by my boldness.

"Name?"

"Emily and Frank Thompson." She gave me a withering look.

"I meant, YOUR name."

"I'm Breeze Thompson and that's my little brother Jonathan." I pointed to where he sat beside the door.

Out of the corner of my eye I saw a huge grin spread across Jonathan's face. The woman stared hard at Jonathan for a few minutes then uneasily looked away when she saw his hands. Or where his hands should be. She moved to the computer to her left and began punching the keyboard.

"They're not being held here."

"Can you tell me where they are?" I started to get nervous. Neither Jared nor I had seen or heard from Emily and Frank since they'd been taken away. There was no guarantee that they were even still in town. But if not, where would the agents have taken them?

As if reading my mind, the woman spoke. "I could check the state database for you." She began typing again, reading the monitor for several minutes before glancing inquisitively at me.

"They've been moved to the Federal facility in Salem." She gave Jonathan and me another once-over look. Finally she said, "A court date has been set regarding the criminal charges. If you want any more information you'll have to go to Salem."

My head spun. I had no idea how far Salem was from the ranch, but I knew for sure I wasn't capable of driving on a freeway, no matter how well I'd done this morning. Not unless I practiced a lot, possibly with Jared giving me driving lessons. I'd never seen him drive, but being older than me he might even have a license. Still, right now I had to make it look good.

"Can you write the address down for me, please?" I asked. Giving a little huff that further compounded my earlier assessment of her, she complied, handing the yellow Post-It note to me on the end of her finger as if it were a booger.

"Thanks for your help," I said, trying not to sound sarcastic. She had helped, though I knew with a certainty she could have done more had she wanted.

Jonathan looked up at me through those googley glasses of his. "What are we going to do now, Breeze?"

I gave a little shrug because I didn't have a clue what we were going to do, especially since I'd forgotten to call Carla and ask about her dad. I sighed. I hadn't had much of a plan when we left, I didn't have any more now. Lawyers cost money. Even Carla's dad. And even if we were to go to the Federal facility in Salem, and knew how to get there, there wasn't enough time to get there and back home to look after the animals. It would have to be tomorrow. That is, if Emily and Frank still weren't back by then.

I heard a muffled beep coming from inside my purse. As I unzipped it I discovered my cell phone was giving me a warning that it had a low battery. Out of habit I checked the voice mail function, but there were no messages. Then I saw that a text message had come in. I pushed the little envelope icon and saw that it was from Deanne. The text had been sent the same day that I'd received her call. It read, "He's out." Then the screen went black as the battery died. My heart started to pound, but there was no way I could reply until I recharged it at the house. Which was pointless because then I wouldn't have a signal. I sighed, feeling discouraged by just about everything.

"We're going home," I said. "At least for now." I took his flipper again and we headed back to the parking lot where I'd left the truck. For a moment I had a rush of panic as I couldn't remember where I'd put the keys, but eventually found them in the back pocket of my jeans. As I unlocked the truck I breathed a sign of relief. In an hour we'd be home and safe.

Home. It was a strange word to me, one that used to come to mind when I thought about Stark, but now, inadvertently, I was beginning to think of the Double-T Ranch as home. I stole a glance at Jonathan, who had his nose pressed to the window, probably still watching the ditch for me, and bit my lip. Unless things changed drastically, and they'd certainly been heading in that direction lately, in a couple of weeks from now I'd been leaving him and the Double-T Ranch. In spite of all previous resolve not to get attached, I couldn't help worrying about how he'd feel once he found out.

TWENTY

One good thing about living way out in the sticks, I thought, was that there was very little traffic to contend with. Every few miles I had to slow down for an occasional tractor or other farm vehicle, grit my teeth, hold my breath and pray as I finally forced myself to pass it. But other than that, it was pretty uneventful. A few more miles and we'd be back at the ranch.

Jonathan's head had dropped down to his chest. I sneaked a quick look to make sure he was all right. He had fallen asleep from the hypnotic monotony of watching the side of the road whiz by. I smiled to myself and suddenly a flash caught my eye. Then the sound of a siren. I glanced up to the rear view mirror and felt my heart rate surge. A police cruiser was following us. And from the lights and siren I knew that I was supposed to pull over.

I took my foot off the gas and let the truck slow down on its own. There was no shoulder at the edge of the road, only those horribly deep drainage ditches like the one I'd walked in to Jared's house. I didn't dare pull any further off the road. Eventually the truck slowed enough and I put on the brakes, then turned off the engine. The policeman stayed in his car for a few minutes where I could see him writing. Then he finally got out and approached the truck. My heart still pounding, I rolled down the window.

The policeman was an older, heavy-set guy with a bright pink face and a stomach that hung over his belt. What was it with the men out here and their bellies, I wondered. With the exception of Frank and Jared, everyone else looked like they were smuggling watermelons. I was sure that if he didn't have a cruiser he'd never catch a criminal if he had to chase him on foot. He gave me a disapproving look, then glanced at Jonathan, apparently noticing his deformities, and his expression changed slightly.

"License and registration, please." I sat there feeling stupid because I didn't know what or where the registration was, and as far as the driver's license went, I'd have to bluff.

He saw my hesitation and said sarcastically, "It's usually in the glove compartment. Is this your vehicle?"

I shook my head as I reached across Jonathan and popped the glove box open, clutching all the papers that lay inside in my fist. I spread them across my lap, having no idea what I was looking for. But he apparently saw what he needed and snatched a small square of paper from me. He scanned it briefly, then frowned at me.

"Your driver's license, miss."

"I-I left it at home. In my purse," I gulped. From my peripheral vision I noticed Jonathan's eyes slide toward my purse that sat on the passenger side floor of the truck. He pretended to stretch his legs, surreptitiously knocking his sweatshirt over it. A warm wave of affection for him flooded over me, but I pretended I hadn't seen what he'd done. Nor did the policeman, apparently. We were in collusion.

"What's your name?"

"Breeze Jordan. And he's....," I started to say, but the policeman interrupted me.

"He's old enough to speak for himself." He leaned forward to look across me at Jonathan. "What's your name, son?" he asked, his voice softening just a little.

"Jonafon Thompfon," Jonathan replied. *Good for you, kid!* I thought. The policeman turned back to me, the annoyance returning.

"Do you have ANY identification on you?"

I shook my head.

"How old are you?" He turned away from me and stared openly at Jonathan. Jonathan began to look scared, which in turn put me on the defensive.

"Sixteen."

"Really? You look more like fourteen to me." I saw fear spread across Jonathan's face like a rash and tears starting to form behind those thick glasses.

"This vehicle has been reported stolen. I'll tag it and it'll be towed and held until the legal owners can collect it."

My stomach turned over. Stolen? Who would have reported the truck as stolen? No one other than the Feds and Jared knew that Emily and Frank weren't still at home. My thoughts drifted to Jared, wondering if he'd told his grandparents. I forced the feeling of despair and betrayal out of my mind and stared back at the officer.

"It's not stolen," I retorted. "It belongs to Frank and Emily Thompson. Jonathan and I live with them. And if you have it towed away, how will we get home?" I tried to cut the whine of fear out of my voice, but if the police officer didn't let us go soon I was going to start sobbing the way Jonathan was now doing.

"You'll have to come with me," the policeman said. "I'm charging you with unauthorized use of a motor vehicle."

"What's that?" I whispered, terrified now. I dared not look at Jonathan.

"Car theft," the policeman said abruptly. "When we've finished booking you in juvenile court I'll contact the Children's Services Division. We'll find a place to put you both tonight."

"We can stay together, right?" I grasped Jonathan's flipper to reassure him.

"That's not up to me," he replied, but I knew from past experience that it was highly unlikely they'd keep Jonathan and me together. We weren't related and we were foster kids. Without the Thompsons we were back to freewheeling through the foster care system. And now I had a new title to add to my already colorful resume: Car Thief.

By the time I'd finished telling my story to all the legal authorities and they'd figured out what had gone on with me, Jonathan and the truck, including our relationship to the Thompsons, the charges of car theft were dropped. They let me wait in a sort of living room, which I finally figured out was a wing of the juvenile detention center. I lay down on a tattered brown tweed sofa that smelled funny and watched a rerun of Seinfeld. My first TV experience in weeks. I didn't know where they'd taken Jonathan. It had nearly torn my heart out when they led him away because he was crying out for me as if I were his mother. I'd really screwed up this time. I should have stayed home and called the Shoemakers for help. I didn't know who I could trust, so I decided to count on myself.

Finally a skinny young woman with greasy blonde hair tied back in a ponytail came into the room. She wore a red and white shirt and gray pants with the hem of one pant leg hanging down. She gave me a lukewarm but disinterested smile and introduced herself as Amy, a caseworker with Children's Services.

"Get your things and come with me," she said, "we've found a place for you to stay tonight." She turned abruptly and inclined her head, motioning me to follow.

There was something that had been worrying me ever since I'd been pulled over by the policeman. I'd watched enough detective TV programs in my life to know my rights, even if I was still considered a juvenile.

"Is it possible for me to make a phone call?"

An expression of incredulity crossed her face, like as if I'd just told her she looked like Christina Aguilera. Which she did in a kind of undernourished way. "It's not something we usually allow kids to do," she replied, "who is it to?"

"I need to call the Thompsons' neighbors and ask them to look after the animals. They're locked in and don't have enough food or water to last them until I'm able to get back."

If, I ever get back, I thought, but didn't dare speak aloud.

She glanced around and when she realized there was no one watching, handed me her cell phone.

"Make it quick. I'm really not supposed to do this."

Hoping I remembered the number correctly, I called the Shoemaker's house. To my huge relief Jared answered. Without going into detail or mentioning my arrest, I asked him if he could look after the animals until Frank and Emily, or I, got back to the Double-T. He didn't question anything, just agreed to take care of the animals and whatever else might come up, as long as I needed him. There were a few moments of awkward silence. Just as I was just about to say goodbye and hand the phone back to the counselor, Jared whispered, "Are you in some kind of trouble?"

I took a deep breath. "No. No trouble," I lied, glancing surreptitiously at the counselor who pretended not to overhear, though I knew it was her job to do exactly that. "Just look after the animals for me and I'll call you as soon as I can."

I flipped the phone closed and handed it back to the caseworker. "Thank you."

She smiled coolly. "No problem," she replied. "Now let's get you settled in for the night." I had no choice but to follow her and once more leave the decision of my fate in the hands of some impersonal government agency. Just as the destiny of Frank, Emily and Jonathan depended on the whim of other agencies.

TWENTY-ONE

I didn't think I'd be able to sleep. Not only was I worried about Jonathan, I had an overwhelming fear that the room with the fold-out cot that they'd given me was laden with bed bugs, lice or worse. My imagination worked overtime until I had to force myself to throw out the notion that my skin was crawling. Eventually I started to get sleepy. And somewhere during the night I managed to nod off because for the first time since I'd arrived at Stark, I dreamt of my mother.

I found myself standing outside an enormous, old stone Gothic church. Streams of black shrouded, androgynous figures poured through the heavy oak double doors, heads bowed in deference or sorrow. I glanced around the churchyard, surprised at how poorly kept it was. Dandelions and other weeds grew defiantly above the brown and green patches of lawn. Weather worn headstones leaned like concrete and marble dominoes, about to topple. The wrought-iron fence that spanned the perimeter was rusty, some of the rails bent inward from age or misuse, with pieces of fading trash clustered along the inside bottom edge.

Without warning, I felt a gentle push in the middle of my back. A cold chill of terror crept up my spine. I started to shake with fear at the thought of what might be behind me, willing myself against the impulse to move forward. But the prodding came again. I turned to see a figure urging me on, and though shrouded like the rest, I could tell it was a woman.

"You need to see inside," she said. Then a strange mixture of shock and excitement came over me because it was my mother's voice. She gave me another push, this one not quite so gentle. I stumbled forward, following the mourners into the church.

Though all heads turned to stare at me as I entered the building, I recognized no one for they were all draped in the same dark shrouds. At the front of the church, on the stage just behind the pulpit, was a gleaming, black coffin. Surrounding it were enormous bouquets of lilies, roses, and gladiolas, their vivid combination of white, crimson, and purple striking a sharp contrast. Thick cones of incense burned in copper tins beside the pulpit, filling the church with a sweet, nauseating smoke.

All the while the gentle pushing from my mother kept at my back. Push, stumble, push, stumble. Then just as suddenly as it had started, it ceased. Without making a sound, all the mourners in the pews to the right and left stood, beckoning that I should approach the front. I hesitated, afraid of what would happen if I moved closer to the coffin. I whirled around to face my mother.

"I can't," I whispered, petrified now.

"You need to see." She gave me another shove. I half-fell, my heart beating so hard I could hardly catch my breath. At that moment I became aware that as I approached the coffin, the mourners began to burn off like dissipating fog, vanishing from the back to the front. I took a step backward and the row behind me reappeared.

More scared than I'd ever been in my life, I took a few hesitant steps toward the coffin, reassured now that the shrouded figures behind me would continue to recede. I stopped when I reached it. The top half of the lid was open, and though I could now see the pleated cream colored satin that lined the final bed of the deceased, I couldn't see who lay there.

I turned to my mother again.

"Who is it?"

"Look inside."

"Is it you?"

But I dared not look into the casket. Whoever was in there, I had no desire to see them. Then I felt a tremendous shove in the middle of my back. I stumbled over my feet and fell headlong against the coffin, my hands grasping at the sides for support. As I pulled myself up, I was forced to steal a glimpse of the inside. It was empty. And when I turned to look, my mother, and all the other people in the church, had disappeared. All except one. When I faced the casket once more I saw Deanne hovering above it like a misty wraith. She gave me a gentle smile and blew me a kiss. And then, like the rest, she vanished.

"Wait!" I screamed, "Deanne, wait for me!" But I was too late. She was gone. And as I stood alone in the church, the walls crumbled down around me as if they were made of sand.

I reared up in bed, awakening to find myself lying on a cot piled with twisted sheets soaked in cold perspiration, my whole body shaking. I switched on the lights to convince myself nothing else existed in the room to haunt me, willing myself to take slow, calm breaths. When my heart rate returned to normal, I turned on the television and lost myself in a mindless talk show. There was no way I going to try to sleep again.

Around 7 a.m., a pleasant, grandmotherly sort of woman with triple chins and orange-ish hair formed in a kind of beehive hairdo came in and brought me a plate with a couple of muffins and a glass of apple juice. I thanked her and tore into it like I hadn't eaten in days. She watched me devour the food, her hands resting on her hips as she waited for me to finish.

"Where did they take Jonathan?" I asked between mouthfuls. I took a swallow of apple juice to keep from choking.

"He's been placed in a temporary foster home until we can decide where to take him for a more permanent placement."

"Why can't he stay with me? I've had enough experience to be able look after him."

She gave me a sympathetic smile. "Breeze, you're under age. You need to be placed in foster care yourself. You certainly couldn't look after a special needs child like Jonathan."

I wanted to shout at her that of course I could. I already had, but I didn't say a word. I'd play their game, wait it out and see what they had in store for me. As soon as I had a moment, I'd make a break for it. Carla had told me about all the times she'd run away and where a kid could go so they'd never find you. And that was even if you had a lawyer for a dad. I never thought I'd need that information, but it might come in useful now.

After breakfast the woman provided me with soap, a towel, toothbrush and toothpaste, then showed me where I could clean up. She'd also brought me a change of clothes, oversized jeans and a long-sleeved purple T-shirt that looked hideous on me. I scrubbed my face and did the best I could with my hair, but still felt that I looked like a homeless person. The past few weeks of doing all the farm and house chores had made a mess of my hands. Not that I'd have been able to model for Palmolive dishwashing commercials. But at least I'd made grooming a regular part of my daily repertoire.

I smiled to myself, remembering how Carla, shocked at how little we knew about beauty regimens, had shown us how to take care of our nails and hair. Despite her personal choice to downplay her looks, she'd grown up with the luxury of professional French manicures, pedicures and the very best of stylists. Her reading material consisted of smuggled *Cosmopolitans* and *Vogues* she'd stolen from her stepmother and stashed under her bed. She soon educated us by giving us facials and her own version of French-tipped nails. Even the very plain Deanne enjoyed the pampering.

After I'd watched several morning game shows, Amy, the skinny caseworker who had brought me here the night before, asked me to come with her. She looked better this morning. It appeared she'd shampooed and curled her hair and had put on some makeup, which made her mildly pretty. I started to open my mouth and tell her she looked like Christina Aguilera then decided against it. Her night must have been better than the one I'd had as she was actually friendly. She smiled as she approached, though she tried to suppress it when she noticed my outfit, probably so I wouldn't feel she was laughing at me.

"You've had breakfast, I see." As it didn't require an answer I just looked at her, waiting to learn my fate. She half-turned and inclined her head. "You need to come with me."

I scrambled to my feet, rapidly forming a plan while keeping alert to any chink in her armor so I could run for it.

"Can I go back to the Thompsons' today?" I stopped in front of her and planted my feet firmly. "Where's Jonathan? I need to see Jonathan. He'll be scared without someone he knows." She kept her face expressionless at my questions. I felt any hope starting to drain away. "Please," I begged, not even ashamed for doing it.

"I'm sorry, Breeze," she said quietly, taking my arm and looking sadly at me. "I had hoped we could find another alternative. We're taking you back to Stark School."

TWENTY-TWO

I used to wonder what people meant when they said, 'be careful what you wish for, you might just get it.' But suddenly I knew. Going back to the Stark School was what I had been wishing and hoping for ever I'd been told a new foster family was taking me in, the day Frank and Emily had walked into Mrs. Watkins' office to meet me. Now I had exactly what I wanted, but I wasn't sure if I still wanted it.

That's not to say I didn't want to return to the Stark School *eventually*. And it wasn't just because I'd be losing the bet by going back three weeks early. I longed to hear one of Tyesha's sarcastic wisecracks again, or have Carla help me with my hair after I'd finished doing hers, just like two chimpanzees in the zoo. And the very best thing, to be a part of our harebrained schemes. Besides, I was desperate to find out what had been happening with Deanne and her foster home placement. I just didn't want to go now, not with Emily, Frank and Jonathan in trouble and separated from each other.

They'd given me back the folder of papers I'd taken from Emily's filing cabinet, as if they were part of my personal possessions. I'd almost forgotten about them, but even I had no idea how important they might be to us all. One thing I knew for sure, I couldn't let those receipts get lost or fall into the wrong hands. Somehow I had to find a way to use them to help the Thompsons. If not for my sake, then for Jonathan's.

Then there was the other matter of who had reported the Thompson's truck as stolen. It couldn't have been Emily or Frank or they would have shown up to see me, even if they weren't allowed to take me back with them. And I didn't think it could be the Shoemakers who might have noticed the truck missing, because Jared hadn't mentioned anything when I called to ask him to look after the animals. But of course, his grandparents hadn't been forthcoming about giving him information in the past. Maybe this was just one more thing they were keeping from him.

Amy, my current caseworker, was the person who would be driving me back to Stark School. She had a little compact red car with a big dent in the back bumper. The car suited her, though it wasn't very tidy inside, with Taco Bell wrappers littering the floor. She didn't appear to notice or even apologize for the mess. I could see a couple of files laying on the back seat with names on them, probably other kids in the foster care system. Some wild urge made me want to snatch those files and throw them out the window, but I didn't need to be in more trouble.

During the trip she hardly spoke at all, which made for a quiet ride. Her questions and monosyllabic answers emerged strained, as if only to pass the time, until finally there was just silence. That was fine with me. I needed time to think and plan about how I was going to make things right again. At least back at Stark I had three friends with whom I could brainstorm, and who had resources and contacts of their own. And so, as the miles fell away and we got closer and closer to Portland, the more excited I became, until I could hardly sit still in my seat.

We only stopped a couple of times for bathroom breaks, a quick lunch, and to fill her car with gasoline. It wasn't till around dinner time that we reached Portland. Amy wheeled the little car into the Stark School parking lot and turned to grab my file. I would have run straight to my old dorm room, try and find where everyone was hanging out, but Amy took my arm and held me back.

"We have to get some paperwork straightened away. Come with me to the principal's office first so we can find what room they're assigning you to."

My heart lurched at what she'd just said. I'd assumed I'd be back rooming in the same dorm as I had before, but maybe I'd been naïve. The school had probably moved girls around to other rooms as my leaving had created a vacancy. We Lunatics had seen many girls come and go, but the school always took the stance, or maybe just hoped, that any girl sent to a new home would be permanently placed or adopted. It rarely worked out that way, but occasionally it happened. At any rate, some girls never returned. But some did. Kind of like the way some cats will find their way home and some are strays for their entire lives.

Although I hadn't met Amy before last night, she must have been at Stark School at some time in the past because she walked right up to the principal's office as if she knew the way. But for a moment I thought she was wrong. A different name had been engraved on the brass plate on the door. It no longer read 'Eleanor Watkins, Principal.' It said, 'Rex Salter, Principal.' *Rex Salter?* I thought. I'd never heard of him. There must be some mistake.

"Wait," I whispered to Amy, grabbing her arm. "Where is Mrs. Watkins?"

Amy peered at me, frowning. "Mrs. Watkins took an early retirement last month." Her face softened. "But I guess you probably wouldn't have known that."

Damn straight, I thought angrily. Mrs. Watkins and I had some issues in the beginning, but once I'd been at Stark a while we had gotten along very well. I wondered how the Lunatics were handling having a new principal, or if it had made a difference in their lives. I couldn't wait to see them. If that meant cooperating with this Rex guy, then I guess that's how it would have to be.

Amy turned from me and gave a short knock on the door. We heard a gruff, "Come on in," and I stepped back as she held the door open for me. A thin man about forty and nearly bald except for a bad comb-over and a little goatee sat at the desk that used to belong to Mrs. Watkins. He had rimless glasses that he looked over, instead of through, as we walked into the room. When he stood he was almost exactly the same height as me. He held out his hand.

"Hello, Breeze, welcome back." He gave me a warm, encouraging smile. Though he no doubt meant it to be genuine, the goatee gave him a Satanic look that made his smile fiendish instead of friendly. I suppressed a shudder. "Sit down, both of you."

I glanced at Amy but she was thumbing through her papers and not paying attention to me. I did as I was told, while Amy leaned over and handed my large file to Satan. He gave me another smile of reassurance before he thumbed through the papers. Amy finally sat, her eyes flickering sideways to watch me as she waited. To kill time I slouched in my chair, sneaking a look under his desk to see how he had fit shoes over his cloven hooves. He closed the file and opened another one on his desk.

"You're going to be staying in Room 231," he said. "It's just down the hall from the room you used to be in. There have been some changes here since I took over from Mrs. Watkins, but I think you'll recognize a few of the girls."

I almost laughed out loud. Of course I would recognize them! It had only been a couple of months. I couldn't wait to see my friends, completely forgetting that Amy and I hadn't had any dinner yet.

"I think that's about it," he told Amy. "I can take her up to her room if you want to bring in her things." Amy glanced quickly at me and chewed her lip.

"She didn't arrive with much," she demurred. "We'll have to send for her clothes and personal effects later. The circumstances..."

"Yes, I understand," Mr. Salter muttered hurriedly, giving me a once-over I didn't appreciate. "There's plenty of clothes her size here."

I stifled a sigh, then said goodbye to Amy and followed

him down the hall to my new room. Back to the old hand-me-down situation again. If they sent the clothes Emily had bought me down here it would be wonderful, but I didn't expect that to happen anytime soon. At least I was only a couple of doors away from the Lunatics' room. Once things settled down I'd be able to put in a request to share the same dorm. I hadn't forgotten any of the rules.

When we reached Room 231 he stopped and knocked, even though the door was ajar, then we went in. No one was inside, but the drab, boring room was as neat and tidy as we'd always been ordered to keep them. There was the usual row of made beds and one that had a nightgown, bathrobe, a set of towels and some basic toiletries on it. That much hadn't changed. He walked over to the bed and patted it.

"This will be yours, Breeze." He made his way over to the row of metal drawers against the back wall and unlocked one. "And this will be your personal cabinet for your things." My eyebrows raised involuntarily in surprise. Now that was new. Locks. I wondered when they'd decided to do that. Privacy at last! I reached out my hand for the key. But he made no move to hand it over.

"I'm afraid we don't allow the students to have a key," he said sternly. "A room monitor has the keys. She'll lock and unlock the drawer for you when you need to access your things. It's safer that way."

Safer for who? I thought. This wasn't better, this was worse, much worse. The staff had complete control over our stuff and could snoop through it whenever they wanted. I remembered that the Lunatics had always kept their own stash of personal things private by hiding them under that loose floorboard. As soon as I met up with Tyesha or Carla I'd hide the folder with Emily's receipts in there. I shrugged.

"Where is everyone?"

He watched me carefully, as if he expected me to bolt out the door at any minute. If that was what he was thinking, he wasn't far from the truth.

"They're all outside or in the common room right now.

No one is allowed in the dorm rooms during the day. Dinner will be served in about a half hour, if you haven't eaten yet. But you'll have to go out as soon as you've had a chance to clean up."

Another new rule. As long as we'd kept the rooms clean and free of clutter, Mrs. Watkins allowed us to stay inside if we wanted. Especially Deanne who, with her bright red hair and light skin tones, could hardly stand to walk from the bus to the school in direct sunlight without getting sunburned.

Like a vampire, we used to tease. I nodded, resigned to my fate, but only for the moment because I was back now. As far as I was concerned the rules were about to change. Back to what they'd been.

"I'm not hungry," I said. "I just want to see my friends."

Mr. Salter's face remained an unreadable mask though he made no reply. This gave me an uncomfortable feeling deep down, although I didn't know why. He walked me to the closest bathroom and waited outside until a female attendant showed up. I was in the toilet stall when I heard her come in. I could see her feet where I imagined she pretended to be fixing her hair.

After washing my face and hands, more or less under supervision, I was escorted outside to the grounds of the school. Stark School had the same accouterments as any high school: scrubby lawns, especially since it was now mid-August, a kind of commons area with concrete abutments on which to sit, and some little two-person wood benches that had been added as an afterthought, possibly for some kind of privacy.

I wandered around, ignoring the curious stares of the other kids, a lot of whom I recognized, but mostly younger ones. There were a few I hadn't seen before, or perhaps hadn't noticed because I didn't care. But I purposely carried myself in a confident, don't-mess-with-me manner that anyone who has been in a state school can immediately comprehend and respect. So far I had caught no glimpse of any of my Lunatics.

Finally, I was tired from the act of appearing tough, exhausted from the trip back and basically depressed in general. I sat upon one of the wooden benches, sort of hidden from view of everyone else and just watched the comings and goings of the other kids. I noticed a girl about my age sitting on a bench like mine on the far end of the courtyard from me. I didn't recognize her: she had short-short blonde hair, spiked with black streaks, with a ton of black eye makeup I could see even at this distance. It made her look like a raccoon. She wore a green khaki camo tank top and matching baggy combat pants. She caught my gaze and gave me a glare and the 'finger.' Then suddenly her hand dropped down, she stood and began walking toward me.

Uh, oh, I thought, here comes trouble. Now I have to establish myself all over again and then try and keep peace with the new principal. I closed my eyes, dreading the confrontation but knowing that if I didn't hold my ground and protect my territory that I would be walked on all over again. And I wasn't about to do that. I rose, balling my fists into a clench, but keeping them hidden. I knew how to use them if I needed to.

The girl got within about ten feet of me and suddenly covered her face and began to cry. My mouth dropped open in amazement because it was only when I heard her sobs that I realized who it was.

"Carla?" The heavy black eye makeup streamed down her face, making her look like a Halloween ghoul. She threw her arms around me and I just stood there like some kind of a dummy, until finally I realized that there was only her, and me, and no one else at this weirdly altered version of Stark School, who mattered. At that moment, with her sobbing her heart out, I started to cry, too. But for either of us, if they were tears of joy, or sadness, I didn't know. It was okay, though, because I remembered: *Thou shalt not cry in front of anyone other than a Lunatic.*

When she'd stopped blubbering long enough to talk, we sat on my bench and just looked at each other. She was a mess. She sniffled loudly.

"That was disgusting," I said. I took out a crumpled tissue and handed it to her. Then I took my sleeve and wiped away the blackened streaks on her face and couldn't help but laugh.

"Thanks," she said dryly.

"You don't look like you."

She started to sob again.

"I'm sorry. I didn't mean that. If it's a new look you're trying for, well great, but it just kind of caught me off guard."

She stopped crying again and stared at me, drinking in my face as if she hadn't seen me in years instead of only two months. She glanced at the worn clothes that Children's Services had provided that made me look frumpy and dorky at the same time. Finally, she gave me a grin.

"You look different, too," she retorted. "Like a farm laborer."

I deserved that. I shrugged. "I yam what I yam."

She laughed then inexplicably began to cry again.

"What is it?" I asked finally. "Are you having your period, or what? Where's Tyesha?"

She swallowed hard, as if she had a lump in her throat. Her eyes took on a look I had only seen one time in her before: after her father remarried and her latest stepmother had brought her to Stark the last time she ran away.

"You really don't know?"

"I don't know anything." I was beginning to get annoyed and tried to stifle the anger I felt at being so kept out of the loop. "I didn't have any cell phone service after I left, but I sent each of you letters and no one answered me at all. The only person who called or wrote was Deanne, and even that was so cryptic I don't know what it was about." The hurt I'd been holding inside finally came out. "What happened to you guys?"

All the blood had drained from her face and she looked worse than anyone I had ever seen. And suddenly I realized that this was how I must have appeared when the police came to tell me my mother had been killed. I got a cold feeling inside me then and just waited for her to tell me what really had been going on these last two months.

"You know there's a new principal now, right?" she began.

I nodded.

"Well, Mrs. Watkins left. Took an 'early retirement' they told us. It was kind of forced."

"But why? That still doesn't explain where Tyesha is. Have you heard from Deanne since she was placed in foster care."

She blinked hard. "Tyesha's aunt came from Seattle and took her away. She hadn't been able to take her in before because she didn't have a job. Tyesha's been up there for a week now."

"And Deanne?"

Carla got a haggard, faraway look in her eyes that made me edgy. She looked sixty instead of sixteen and that scared the bejesus out of me. She started to bite her nails but I grabbed her hand and gave it a shake.

"What happened to Deanne? When was the last time you heard from her?"

She shook her head. "I only know what they told us. They found a foster family to take Deanne in, but then her father was released from jail. He intervened at the last minute. He finally got permission to take her out of here, even though she fought and screamed and threatened. Mrs. Watkins tried. She really did, but the state overran her and she had no choice but to let her go."

"And?" I persisted.

"About a week after Deanne was sent home Mrs. Watkins called us all into a meeting. She said Deanne had overdosed on antidepressants or painkillers or something. We really weren't given many details." Carla started to cry, her body shaking convulsively. "We could have tried harder. We should have tried something. She always said that if her dad took her out of here she'd kill herself. Why didn't we take her seriously?"

I wrapped my arms around her, feeling the tears streaming down my face, my body wracked with guilt. I thought back to Deanne's frantic call to me, and that I hadn't been able to return it, or even tried that hard. If I told Carla about it now she'd hate me as much as I hated myself. I forced myself to believe that there was nothing I could do. I needed to convince Carla of that as well, if only so both of us could accept her death.

"I know she said that and we believed her. But how could we have stopped them? We have no power. We only had power when we were here together as the Lunatics." She nodded, rendered mute with misery. "Have you heard anything from Tyesha since she's been gone?"

She shook her head. "We're in a kind of lock down now. No correspondence has been allowed in or out since Deanne died. They lock everything away, keep the keys and only let us in to get our things under strict supervision. Tyesha never wanted to go live with her aunt before, and the only reason she finally agreed to go was because of Deanne and the way things have become here since you left."

I stared at my hands, feeling even more guilt stricken. I stole a glance at Carla who was staring off into the distance at nothing, looking horribly miserable. Maybe if I'd made a fuss and hadn't left Deanne would still be alive. But even as I let the thoughts cross my mind I knew it was stupid of me to think that. If Mrs. Watkins couldn't have stopped them from sending Deanne back, what made me think that the Lunatics could have done anything?

I slid my arm around Carla and stayed that way for a few minutes. I ignored the stares and suggestive leers from some of the other girls as they passed, and just gave them the 'look' I used to give any of the kids who thought they could mess with us. Just then I heard a loud voice.

"Girls!" My head snapped up and there was one of the staff, glowering down at us. I recognized her from when I'd lived here before but had never had occasion to talk to her.

"Carla! You know the rules. No public displays of affection." She continued to glare at us until I dropped my arm. She glanced at her watch.

"Time for dinner now. Please head back into the school."

I stood and so did Carla, but we didn't move right away, just watched her go about making the other students' lives miserable. I turned to Carla.

"Is that what it's been like here since I left?"

"Yep," she sighed. "Hardly worth living, is it?" I looked around to see if anyone was watching and gave her another quick 'public display of affection,' reveling in the illegality of doing it and not getting caught.

"We'll just have to regroup, you and me," I reassured her. "Two of us Lunatics are still here, right? We can recruit a couple more, surely."

She shook her head and sighed. "Breeze, I had no idea you would be coming back. "God's Gift to Women" is divorcing my step mom and has asked me to come live with him and make a new start. I told him I would try. At least until he gets married again," she added with a wry grin.

I couldn't believe what she'd just said. There was no way I could survive here without at least one of my friends. Start all over again at this new surreal Stark School that had changed from a place that was the closest thing to home, to, well, to a prison? I could hardly breathe. It felt as if my chest was caving in when I tried to speak. I had trouble forming the words I hardly dared to ask.

"When are you leaving?"

There was a resigned sadness in her eyes. She glanced away and almost whispered, "Day after tomorrow."

I nodded, mute with anguish, though understanding that she had as little control over her future as I had over mine. Together we walked in to the school's dining room and lined up to get our food from the servers before sitting down at the long cafeteria tables. We ate silently, both of us lost in our own thoughts of what was to come and how our lives would change once more. Carla, only half-finished with her meal, pushed her plate away and looked at me.

"Maybe I could ask my dad if you could come live with us."

For a moment my heart surged with hope. Then I realized that even though her dad had always been generous, if maybe only to assuage his own guilt about being a lousy father, there was no way a newly divorced man with a troubled daughter of his own would take on someone else's troubled daughter. I tried to smile.

"Thanks for the offer, but no thanks. I'll figure something out." And I knew I would, because I was still one of the Lunatics and would be forever. But then I had an idea. I could ask him for legal assistance with freeing the Thompsons.

After dinner I grabbed my book bag and headed to the computer lab. The receipts were still in the zipped pocket where I'd stashed them when I'd set out for town days before. I sat at the computer and began a letter to Carla's dad. I explained about the Thompsons' arrest, my suspicions about Nolan Barker and the cattle, and told him of Barker's run for County Sheriff. I made copies of the receipts as I wasn't about the let the originals out of my hands. Then I found a large envelope and stuffed everything inside. When he came to pick Carla up from the school in a couple of days, I'd give him all the evidence.

TWENTY-THREE

During the next two days, Carla and I spent as much time as possible reminiscing about some of the adventures we'd gotten into with Tyesha and Deanne. Talking about Deanne made us sad, but we kept ourselves entertained imagining what Tyesha might be up to. Or if she was miserable without us, too. It was the first time just the two of us had hung out together. I realized then how lonely Carla must have been with all three of us gone.

When Carla's dad came to get her the following day we both kept a brave face. We would not cry in front of him or the staff of Stark School who watched the departure with the faces of prison guards. I made a pretext of thanking Carla's dad for letting her buy us the cell phones, which was now an impossible luxury of the past with the new Stark regime. In that moment of drawing him aside, the staff paid little attention to me. I handed him the envelope and gave him a pleading look that he seemed to understand. This was my one chance. Future communication would be virtually impossible. There were to be no private, unsupervised calls to anyone. Not even other kids' parents. Perhaps it was because of Deanne's death.

Once Carla left, the light seemed to have gone out of my life. I had no one to talk to, actually no one I wanted to talk to. Two of the older girls, Angelina and Heather, who had shared my old dorm with Carla, sympathetically made overtures of friendship. But I wasn't ready yet. Until we'd formed the Stark Raving Lunatics I had been a loner, unable to bond with anyone. I couldn't help thinking maybe that was a better way to be, because nothing had changed for me. Every time I became close to someone I lost them. It would be a long while before I let anyone in again.

But even with my new resolve I couldn't help worrying about Jonathan. And Frank and Emily. There had to be some way to find out what had happened to them, or a way for me to intervene and testify on their behalf if I could. I reasoned that it wasn't getting involved or forming emotional attachments, it was only being a decent human being to want to help. After all, I was quite certain that I had held the key to the truth behind Frank and Emily getting arrested. The cards were in Carla's dad's hands now. I prayed that he would follow through with the information in my letter.

My mind drifted through useless thoughts about things I could have done differently that might have influenced what had happened to the Thompsons or Deanne. I wondered if the Lunatics had left any of their stuff behind under the floorboards in our old room. We were the only ones who knew about the hiding place. The boxes held mementoes that meant nothing to anyone else but were treasures to us. Had the Lunatics managed to remove their stuff before they left, as I had? Or was theirs still lying there untouched?

After breakfast, when the rest of the school's inmates were ushered out, I hid under my bed. Hiding in the bathroom was pointless because that was the first place they checked. They also did a headcount as soon as everyone was outside, but today there would be confusion. I had just arrived and Carla had just left, which if you understood basic math, came out to be the same number. Seemed logical to me.

Because no one expected a student to still be inside, I was able to move freely without being seen. In spite of this, I took precautions. Eventually I would reestablish myself with the new regime but right now I just wanted to see what was left under Deanne's bed. If I were caught in the act everything would be confiscated and I'd never see the stuff again.

Deanne's bed had been the one nearest the door. I had no trouble crawling underneath and locating the board. It was as dark as Hades under there and more dust that you would give even a state school credit for, but I'd brought a little pen light, and by feeling around I could detect the loose plank. Slipping my fingers underneath the board I pried it up and in the process forced a large sliver under one fingernail. Biting back a scream of pain, I set the board to one side. I'd deal with the sliver later. Then I shone the virtually ineffective light down and groped around in the hole. It was oddly empty.

I had known there would be, at the very most, three boxes. I had taken mine with me when I'd left with the Thompsons. Squinting hard in the dim light I saw that there was only one shoe box pushed to the far back of the space. A size 8 Nike running shoe box that had once contained one of the many clothing donations to the school, and by the size I knew it belonged to Deanne. Tyesha and Carla were 9's and 6's respectively, and they must have taken theirs when they left.

Realizing probably not much time remained until they detected my absence I opened the box to examine the contents and shone the pen light into it. There were a couple of envelopes, a small coil notebook, a folded T-shirt, and the bracelet Tyesha had created for her. There was no way I could conceal an entire shoe box once I went outside, so I slipped the bracelet on my wrist, and stuffed the envelopes in my pocket, leaving out the T-shirt. Then I stuck the box back under the floor and pulled the floor board back into place.

Once I was out from under the bed I slipped off the shirt I was wearing and pulled on Deanne's T-shirt that she'd hand-embroidered with her "SRL" logo, and replaced my shirt over top. At that moment I heard voices and footsteps approaching. Deanne's notebook still lay on the floor by my feet. My heart jumped. I didn't dare be discovered here. I slipped off my shoe, stuck the notebook inside and shoved my foot back in, wincing in pain as the end of the wire coil pierced the sole of my foot. I rolled back under the bed just as the footsteps stopped outside the door.

"Have you looked in all the dorms?" I heard someone say.

"I checked them when everyone went out about a half-hour ago."

"Well, do it again. She has to be here somewhere," the first voice came back in angry exasperation. I dared not breathe lest I be discovered, but the housekeeping staff, never particularly diligent at Stark, had left a lot of dust bunnies under Deanne's bed since she'd been gone. I felt a sneeze coming on.

Suddenly I was reminded of the last time I'd sneezed at an inappropriate time and the disastrous results that had followed. Just as the door opened I pinched my nose and forced myself to take slow quiet breaths. I saw a pair of sneakered feet walk to the middle of the room, hesitate for a few minutes, then turn around and walk back out. Then there came the sound of the door being locked. I let out a ragged sigh of relief.

But still the voices and sounds of people checking the rooms continued out in the hallway. Finally, not finding what they were looking for, me presumably, the noises disappeared as they made their way to another floor. This was my chance. I crawled out from under Deanne's bed and tiptoed to the door. Fortunately for me the door locked from the outside so I was able to escape, but once I'd closed the door I wouldn't be able to return.

I peered around then sneaked down the hallway. Limping toward the bathroom because of the metal coil pressing under my foot, I headed to one of the stalls. Once inside I pulled the piece of wood out from under my fingernail, gritting my teeth to keep from squealing in pain. Then I stuck my finger down my throat and made a lot of loud fake vomiting noises and flushed. When I went to wash my hands I held my breath until my faced began to perspire and turn red. By the time one of the staff burst into the bathroom I looked like I'd just been sick.

"What are you doing in here? Why aren't you outside?" demanded the angry older woman, whose name was Anne. A mouth breather, her breath stank of cigarettes. She was the only woman I'd ever seen with a crew cut, and a gray one at that. She glared at me, hands on her wide hips.

"I wasn't feeling good. I came into the bathroom and was sick." Lying about being sick didn't worry me at all because I knew I looked the part. There really wasn't much the staff could do if you were sick. We Lunatics had become experts at mastering that craft. The last thing the staff at Stark wanted was to clean vomit from the furniture and floor, a fact that worked to our advantage very well. I knew I had her with that.

"Well," she blustered, "you look fine now. Unless you need to go to the sick room, get outside with the others."

I nodded and scurried down the hall. She'd probably write me up for it and I might have to go to the Nurse's Room, but I could blame it on the food. They never had much of a rebuttal to that excuse. Besides, I was aching to see what was written in Deanne's notebook.

TWENTY-FOUR

Out in the common area girls clustered together like preening flocks of pigeons. A few sat on the wooden benches in the shade, but most lay in the center of the lawn on their backs, their T-shirts and shorts rolled up as high as they could to get a tan. Apparently acquiring skin cancer was not on the school's banned list. As I walked out into the sun I received a variety of looks from the other girls. Some appeared obviously angry because my vanishing act had been a disruption; others appeared to give me a grudging respect because they realized a new maverick had arrived. Whatever their feelings, they enjoyed entertainment as much as the next kid, especially when the punishment went to someone else.

I could see boys from the other building, the boys' Stark School, peeking through the wire fence, trying to catch a glimpse of skin. A couple of male staff members were sharing a forbidden cigarette near the far corner of the building, and also appeared to be leering at the sunbathing girls. I sighed, feeling sadness and embarrassment wash over me. This little scene would never have been allowed if Mrs. Watkins was still the principal. The rules had become an odd mix of rigidness and debauchery.

At least with everyone apparently watching the girls, who if they were aware of it didn't seem to mind, I was able to freely examine the treasures I'd taken from Deanne's shoe box. I glanced down at the bracelet I'd put on my wrist and swallowed back a lump in my throat. We'd agreed to never voluntarily take them off.

I fingered the bright copper coils on Deanne's bracelet. My own bracelet was back at the Double-T. I had to stop wearing it to keep it from catching on something while doing farm chores and had actually forgotten about it until I saw this one. I wondered if Carla and Tyesha still wore theirs, or if they had outgrown the whole concept of what it had meant to us at the time. I glanced up to see what everyone else in the courtyard was doing but the staff had finished their cigarettes and the girls had turned over to tan their backs. I pulled the envelopes from my pocket.

There were several letters from me to Deanne that I had sent a month ago. Then there was a letter addressed to me from Deanne, but it had never been posted. Apart from the one letter I'd gotten from Deanne, my letters had gone unanswered. Not because the Lunatics hadn't written back, but only because they hadn't been able to send them once Mrs. Watkins had gone. I opened Deanne's letter. It was dated two days after the text message she'd sent me.

To my surprise it began, "Dear Breeze," and that's all it said. She must have begun the letter and didn't know what to write after she'd started. I'd done the same thing many times. You start a letter and don't want to fill it up just bitching about stuff, so you think and think about what good things there are to tell someone, and when there isn't anything at all, you can't write anymore. At least that's how it is with me, and I'm sure it was no different with Deanne.

Despite being disappointed at not being able to read a last letter from her, the pain in my foot reminded me I still had the little coil notebook. I slipped my foot from my sneaker and unwound the coil from my bloodied sock. I stared at the front of the notebook. She'd drawn a skull and crossbones on the red cover and big black letters spelled the words, KEEP OUT! PRIVATE! I laughed out loud, because *anyone* finding it would immediately open it if they read that.

The opening pages were diary entries from when she'd first arrived at Stark, minor notations about teachers and students. Then she began to write about the Lunatics, only at that point we were just fellow inmates. Her initial observations were that Carla was a rich brat and Tyesha considered herself to be superior to the rest of us. Her comment that 'Breeze is the only one I think I could be friends with,' struck a harsh blow. Then, as we began to get closer as a group, there were fewer comments about the girls and more about her hopes that maybe Stark was a place where she could finally feel safe. I skimmed through the rest of the notebook, slightly surprised at the lack of comments about her father.

Finally, close to the end I read, "Breeze was sent to live with a foster family today. I don't know if I can make it here without her. Tyesha is great, and Carla and I have a lot of fun, but they don't understand me the way Breeze does. It's selfish of me to think like this, but I hope she hates it there and runs away and they send her back here."

I felt a burning sensation behind my eyes and my stomach started to ache. If I had known she'd hurt that much I'd have done something that would have stopped the Thompsons from taking me in. Or maybe, and I couldn't hardly bear to think about it now, maybe if I'd known and had shared it with Emily, they'd have taken both of us. I took a deep breath. There was nothing I could do now. At sixteen I still wasn't an adult. What did she expect from me?

Tears stung my eyes as I read on. "They are going to send me back to him. I don't know what to do if he beats me again. I wish Breeze was here. She'd know how to help." Her words hit me like a slap in the face. Why hadn't I comprehended the depth of her fear of her father? She'd had so much faith in me. But I remember her undying loyalty to us once we'd formed our bond. She'd taken it seriously, maybe more than the rest of us. And we'd failed her.

The last page was the worst. And yet, she sounded hopeful somehow. "Okay. So I have to go HOME. Yeah right. HOME. It was never a home with him there. Even Mrs. Watkins wasn't able to stop him. But there has to be something I can do, some way I can get back here because I know that Breeze will be coming home. She said she would after the summer at that ranch. If she can last that long, so can I." And suddenly I realized she hadn't intended to kill herself. At least not at the time she'd left. Deanne had planned on returning to Stark.

Deanne's admission about my coming back devastated me. I hadn't been there to help her when she really needed someone. All the second guessing, all the 'what ifs' wouldn't do any good. Was it the school administration's fault, or even Children's Services, for letting her go back to a place she feared? Could they have helped in any way? But even as the thoughts tormented me I knew that it was too late for recriminations: we'd all failed Deanne.

Though the days when all four of the Stark Raving Lunatics would sit around and talk about the future were long gone, I couldn't help remembering the hopes and dreams we'd shared. Maybe there was still hope for the three of us who remained. And maybe we'd all learn something from losing Deanne, something that could help prevent other kids from feeling so abandoned that the only choice was to take their life. I had new angst radar now, for all the good it did me.

Life at Stark was not what it had been. There were more things we weren't allowed to do than what we were. As far as Stark students were concerned, 'Glee' no longer existed. The only channels we were allowed to watch were the Discovery Channel and Animal Planet. Without television or being allowed to use the internet only for homework, in some ways it was almost like being back at the Double-T. Although that's where the resemblance ended.

And of course, that brought back memories and started me worrying on what was happening with the Thompsons and Jonathan. I had information that could help them, but it was in Carla's dad's hands now. I had to rely on him to follow through, but had no way to contact him to help or push the investigation. There was no one within Stark to help me.

With all the Lunatics gone from Stark, I couldn't think of one reason to stay here. It was time for the unthinkable: I had to run away from Stark School.

TWENTY-FIVE

My decision to run away from Stark was not without problems. How would I get out? The place was locked down tighter than Vacaville State Prison where they kept Charles Manson, the notorious serial killer. Where would I go? Even if I had somewhere to go, how would I get there? I had no money to buy a bus ticket or even food. At sixteen, I was old enough to get a temporary fast-food job, but even if I could bluff about my experience I'd have to sleep in the streets. And technically I wasn't an adult, so the officials at Stark would alert the authorities about my disappearance.

And then when I was just about to give up, I came up with an idea. If I could just get back to the Double-T, I would have whatever food there still was for a while, a roof over my head and until Jared had to go back to San Diego, an ally. If the Thompsons had not yet been cleared of the charges against them I could get more evidence to help their case. And I had the land line to be able to call Carla's dad, Mr. Sutherland, to ask about their case.

I figured it would take me at least a day to get everything I needed, and solicited some help from a couple of girls my age, Angelina and Heather, Carla's former roommates, and who I knew hated Stark. They began taking extra food for me at mealtimes, things that I could carry with me like fruit, bagels and bottled water. Though staff regularly checked our book bags for drugs, alcohol and cigarettes, we were still allowed to use them for carrying books and supplies. The day before I was to leave I packed mine with all the food I could carry and a polar fleece blanket that I managed to intertwine in the straps.

Although Carla hadn't shared anything with her roommates, Angelina had heard about the Lunatics from a few of the other long-time girls, and was sympathetic to my quest. I sensed she wanted to be friends, but there was no time for that. I was on my way out. She gave me a couple of dollars she'd managed to save, which was all she had, and I promised that one day I'd return the favor. She just gave me a bittersweet smile and wished me luck, which both of us knew I'd need a lot if I were going to get away.

The plan I came up with was to leave just after the dinner when the entire school would be milling about, heading to the common room to watch TV or to bed. There wouldn't be a head count until lights out at 9:00 p.m., so I figured I could get about three hours of road time between me and the search party. The girls who were assisting me, and I asked only those two so as to keep information to a minimum, were to start a food fight on my cue, at which time I would slip out.

During dinner my nerves were frayed to a snapping point from the stress of wondering if I would be successful. Though I knew my pilfered rations might not last long and I should eat as much as possible, it was all I could do to force the food down. Angelina and Heather watched me constantly for the sign that I was ready to leave. Though I wanted to delay as long as I could, two things kept me to my schedule: I didn't want to cheat the others out of finishing their meal, and I needed all the time I could before my absence was discovered.

I trained my eyes on the servers and the staff, watching for when I thought they were relaxed and their guard down. But like anything you're waiting in anticipation for, the moment was slow to arrive. It seemed that every time I was ready to give the word, one of the staff was near me or my two accomplices. And then the moment came, several staff left the room to supervise the common room, leaving only two in the dining area. I looked around to make sure no one was watching us then mouthed the word, "Okay" to Heather.

She stood and as she did, picked up the plate she had refilled just before they cut off the food lines, overturned the table, and yelled out, "This food sucks ass!" It took only seconds before the entire room had followed suit, and with my ears echoing from the shouts of "Food fight!" I was able to duck, covering my head, much like all the rest, and sneak out the back door unseen.

Once outside, I sprinted to the bushes where I'd hidden my book bag just before dinner, and slipped it on. Then I raced to the eight foot high chain fence that surrounded the school and, ignoring the wire that cut into my fingers, scrambled up like a monkey and vaulted over to the other side. I landed hard on my hands and knees, but despite the pain that shot through my leg, I knew nothing was broken. I stood and ran as fast as my feet would travel.

Although I passed a few city bus stops, I kept running until I found an eastbound bus where it was just boarding passengers, and climbed inside. I had no idea where it was going, I just wanted to put as many miles between Stark and me as possible. Determined to hold onto the two dollars as long as I could, I ditched the bus a few stops before the end of the line and rode for free. I wasn't intending to be dishonest; I told myself I had no choice, it could mean the difference between surviving or not.

I hopped buses like that for most of the evening, riding for free. It surprised me that no one questioned that a young girl would be riding the bus that late without an adult, but maybe I was being naïve. So far I hadn't been caught freeloading, but on the last bus I realized it was nearing the outskirts of the city, which would mean the end of the route.

As I made my way off the bus I saw signs for the freeway going east and I knew enough to head in that direction. Once at an exit, I would hitchhike a ride. I knew this was a terribly risky thing to do; you never knew who was in the vehicle that picked you up and what their intentions were. But I'd done it once or twice before with my mom when our car broke down, and I could do it again if I had to. I just needed to be choosey about who I rode with.

I purposely didn't stick out my thumb until those I figured were reputable citizens passed by, though it's not like you can identify a serial killer or rapist by their car. Everyone ignored me. Some kids inside the cars even made faces and stuck up their middle fingers at me as they sped away. That was hard to take. But I gritted my teeth and kept trying. I had less than two hours before they started looking for me at Stark. It wasn't until a potato chip truck came along that I got my break.

The bright yellow cube van pulled over in front of me and the side door opened. I walked up and peered inside, staying a safe distance back. The driver was a man about Carla's dad's age, which would be forty, dressed in a plaid jacket and jeans, and wearing a baseball cap. There was a bunch of crumpled potato chip bags on the seat and floor. I wondered if his employers knew, but maybe that was how they paid him. He looked nice, but you could never tell.

"It's against company rules to pick up hitchhikers," he said, "but if something happened to you I'd never forgive myself. I've got a daughter about your age myself. If you want a ride, get in. I'm heading to central Oregon tonight."

I couldn't believe my good fortune. He sounded safe. Well, as safe as anyone can sound, but even though he'd mentioned a daughter, I was wary, making a mental note to remain sharp at all times. "I'll ride with you as far as I can." I climbed up into the cab of the truck and saw that I'd be sharing the ride with an unbelievably rank-smelling, hairy orange dog. That made me feel better. At least there would be a dog between us. I trusted people who owned dogs. "Is he friendly?"

"Sure, if you're nice to him." I petted the dog gingerly, feeling the oil in his hair. The masochist in me was tempted to smell my fingers afterward, but I decided against it and instead just rubbed them on my jeans.

"What's his name?"

"Stinky." He gave a loud laugh which brought on a hacking cough. I laughed too.

"I'm Stan. Stan and Stinky." I laughed again.

"Janice."

"Where are you headed, Janice?" He glanced at my clothes and backpack, and gave me that adult 'you're kidding me, right?' look, which made me nervous. "You look a little young to be out on the road alone."

"I just graduated from high school and I'm exploring the country," I replied. "And I'm going to visit my aunt in the Wallowas."

"Which is it? Exploring the country or visiting your aunt? Seems like a lot of traveling to me." He sort of smiled to himself and I knew he didn't believe me, but that was his problem. I wasn't about to tell him where I'd come from.

Despite my determination not to, I must have fallen asleep because the next thing I knew the truck was coming to a stop. I looked out the window to see we were in a 24-hour truck stop with a restaurant in the parking lot. A jolt of panic shot through me, but I'd remained safe so far. *Just stay aware, Breeze,* I kept telling myself. A lot of other trucks and semis were parked there, too. I figured if I had to I could get a lot of attention fast.

"I need some pie and coffee to stay awake," he said. "Are you hungry?"

Not eating much at dinner and all that running had made me ravenous. I hadn't had time to eat any of the food in my backpack, but I didn't want to bring it out now. And all I had was the two dollars Angelina had given me. I could wait until he was in the restaurant and eat one of my bagels. I shook my head.

"That's okay, you go ahead. I'll look after the dog."

"Come on," he ordered. "I can't leave you with Stinky, you'll asphyxiate. Anyhow, I'm buying. Order anything you want."

I sighed. Maybe it was better if I went inside with him. At least if anything went wrong, someone would have noticed me. We entered into the restaurant together and I walked off to use the restroom and wash my hands free of the funky dog scent. I began to relax, realizing that if Stan was an axe murderer, he probably wouldn't take me into a restaurant where he could be identified if my dismembered body was ever found.

I finished washing my hands then ran my fingers through my hair to make it appear less frazzled. As I gazed at myself in the mirror I was shocked at how much older I looked. For the first time I was actually beginning to see a resemblance to my mother, despite my long nose. When I came out I saw Stan had ordered coffee and fresh apple pie for both of us. It made me feel like I really was an adult.

More relaxed with my stomach full, when we started off again I slept while Stan drove through the night. Just before sunrise he pulled into another all-night restaurant and we had breakfast together. I was grateful that he talked just about nonstop about his daughter, his road travels, his divorce, and pretty much anything else that popped into his head, leaving not much room for me to share anything about myself. It was incredible that he could finish a meal with his mouth moving all the time. He stood and threw some money down on the table to pay the bill, then turned to me.

"We're in Burns now, Janice. This is the end of the line for me. I've got a delivery and then another route to pick up and it's in the opposite direction. You gonna be okay from here on?"

My heart sank. Now he'd gained my confidence, I'd hoped to be traveling with him just about all the way. I masked my disappointment and smiled.

"I'll be fine. Thank you so much for everything." I meant every word. I reached out and shook his hand.

He patted my shoulder and gave me a rueful smile. "Take care of yourself, okay?"

He started walking toward the truck. When he reached it he unlocked the door, grabbed a map from inside and handed it to me. Then he leaned in again and brought out several bags of cheese puffs and potato chips. "These might come in handy. But be careful. A young girl can't be too careful out on the road alone. Right now there's a sixteen-year-old missing from Portland that they've had an Amber Alert on all night." He gave me a wink and hopped in his truck.

As he made a right turn at the lights, he stuck his arm out the window and gave me a wave and a short honk on the horn. I suddenly realized that he'd known all along who I was. A rush of relief and gratitude enveloped me. He could have turned me in at any time and hadn't. Or someone could have recognized us at our stops. Maybe he'd been leaving the decision to let me ride with him up to Karma. But now I was on my own again once more. And the next time I might not be as lucky.

After he'd gone I sat on the curb outside the restaurant and opened the map. As I unfolded the pages, the breeze ruffled them slightly, fanning crisp, cool mountain air on my face. I glanced up to see what the day's weather might hold. The morning sky was the kind of pale green that could go either way: turn to bright blue if the wind was right or black if a storm system came in. The dew on the dusty wild rose bush leaves alongside the road had already dried. From experience, I knew that my best traveling time should be done soon, before the morning sun burned on the pavement and projected onto me.

Judging by the scale of the map, it looked like I was only about seventy-five miles from the town closest to the Double-T. That was about an hour and a half or so by car, but it was forever on foot. Still, at the moment my feet were the only transportation I had. So armed with my book bag and my map, I set off walking on the gravel shoulder of the two-lane highway heading east. If I managed to catch a ride I'd be back at the Double-T by noon.

After about an hour, there had only been one car pass

me and several large semis. One idiot honked his air horns just as he drove alongside me, probably just to see how high I could jump. That made me mad enough to quicken my stride. If the ditch hadn't been so deep and snarled with tangled blackberry bushes and garbage, I'd have walked there instead of on the more dangerous shoulder. I hadn't even bothered sticking my thumb out for a ride. It was a relief to walk and stretch my legs after being cramped up in Stan's truck.

I walked until I got tired, then sat on the shoulder of the road and had some of Stan's chips, one of my bagels and a bottle of water. I consulted the map again, but the last road sign had only reconfirmed that I was on the correct highway. I just wasn't sure if I was going in the right direction or not. I was about to start off again when a rusty green pickup passed me, stopped and backed up to where I sat. A young red-haired woman with a drooling, matching red-haired baby sat in the front. It belched. Curdled milk cascaded down its dirty Elmo bib. Pleased at the relief, it gave me a one-toothed grin.

"You want a ride?" the woman called out.

"Sure," I yelled back, dragging my backpack up to the truck. I clambered in, leaning against the door to avoid the baby's sticky hands grabbing at my jacket. The inside of the truck looked like an IED had gone off inside a 7-11. Fast food wrappers, rolled up disposable diapers and empty cans of baby formula rolled around the floor. I closed my eyes and concentrated on thoughts of Jared and the ranch.

"My name's Gwen," she said. "This is Clove. Who are you?"

"I'm Jordan Johansen." She nodded in a disinterested way. Maybe I should have said Scarlet to see if she was paying attention, but this close to my target I figured I'd better not upset the boat, so to speak.

"Where you headed?"

"The Double-T Ranch. Do you know it?" She frowned. "Not sure. Is it near Nolan Barker's place?" I felt the bottom of my stomach drop to my knees.

"It's the property next door, between his place and the

Shoemakers."

She shrugged. "I know it. I'm going right past there. I work in a real estate office in town. I'll drop you off on the way."

I nodded my thanks, but stared miserably out the truck window. I'd forgotten about Nolan Barker and the role I felt he had played with the Thompsons and the Double-T. I wanted to ask how this woman knew him, if she was a friend of his, or an enemy. But this close to my goal I didn't dare let her know my identity. Fortunately for me, she wasn't the talker that Stan had been and kept busy just driving and making sure the baby didn't aspirate on something. Watching her with the baby made me appreciate Jonathan even more.

A half-hour into the drive I smelled something terrible and glanced at Clove to see her face had become pinched and reddened. I'd been around enough babies while living with foster parents to know what was going on. I glanced at her mother who didn't seem to notice anything unusual. Then I heard a 'brrrep, brrrep' sound and held my breath as the stench got stronger.

Clove's mom winced, aware now of Clove's predicament. "Sorry," she said, pulling over to the side of the road. "If I don't change her diaper we'll suffocate and won't make it to town." At that point I didn't know what smelled worse, Stan's dog Stinky or this diaper-laden baby. I decided right then I was never going to have kids of my own.

Fortunately, Clove's mom threw her dirty diaper in the truck bed, along with a half-dozen others and some of the trash, and once her diaper had been changed, we set off again. Soon I saw the wooden gateposts and the familiar Double-T logo come into view. A million emotions passed over me, but most of all the intense feeling of coming home. Really coming home. But the mobile home still looked dark and empty, although I could see Dingus lying on the steps. He stood and began barking at us as we approached.

Gwen stared doubtfully at the property as we pulled to a stop. "I've heard this place isn't running any more. You sure you want me to leave you here?"

"I'm sure." I could hardly suppress my huge grin. "I am absolutely certain." I grabbed my backpack, said thank you and leapt from the truck.

Gwen observed me carefully for a moment as if she were noticing me for the first time. Clove let out a squeal, and she turned to her momentarily. Then she inclined her head, shifted into drive and the truck was out of sight before I even had a chance to thank her. I bolted toward the house. When I reached the steps I threw my arms around Dingus, hugging him hard enough to make him yelp.

"I'm home, old boy," I said, laughing and crying at the same time. "I'm home to take care of you." Then I set off to retrieve the extra key that Emily kept hidden above the door to the add-on porch. After I'd checked out the property and looked after the animals, I'd get started on making things right again. And then it would be time to call Jared and find out if he'd heard anything about Frank and Emily.

TWENTY-SIX

Before directly heading into the house, I checked around the outside perimeter to be certain nothing had been changed or moved since Jonathan and I had last been there. Then I went out back to see to the animals. It appeared that Jared had been meticulous in taking care of the horses, but they still whinnied to me like I was an old friend they hadn't seen in a while. I took a little extra time petting them, especially Diablo. He'd missed me as much as I had him, rubbing his head on my chest and nuzzling my neck. I scratched him behind his ears, kissed his muzzle then headed back to the house to get all the evidence together.

But as I passed the barn I sensed that something had changed. I returned to the big sliding barn doors and just like outside the back door of the house where I'd noticed the charred area a couple of months ago, there was evidence of a new fire. I stared at the embers for a couple of minutes, puzzling this over. Despite being late summer, so far this area had not suffered from the usual drought-induced forest and grass fires. I bent down to inspect it more closely and saw an open book of matches that had been tossed aside. I picked them up and stuck them in my pocket. Then I saw the Double-T branding iron that Frank used to brand the new calves with each spring. Wondering why it would be out here and not in his tidy shed, I tossed it toward the barn to take care of later.

When I reached the house I attempted to unlock the

door, but it opened easily at my touch without benefit of a key. I swung it open and called out, "Anyone here?" thinking Jared might have come up while I was with the horses. But there was no answer. Jared must have forgotten to lock up last time he was here, I told myself.

Once I'd made my way into the kitchen I saw that Jared had stacked the mail from the past week on the dining table. I flicked through it absently, discarding the catalogs and junk mail and piling up the bills. This was just routine procedure because apart from that one letter from Deanne, I never received any mail.

I tried calling Jared's number but when his grandmother answered I hung up, praying they didn't have Caller ID. I killed some time making sure Dingus had food and water and threw a stick for him to fetch, but both of us soon became bored with that. Then I dusted around the house and swept the floors just to keep me sane until I tried again about a half-hour later. Jared himself answered this time. For a moment I couldn't think of anything to say, my heart was pounding so hard.

"Did you just call here?"

"Yes, I'm sorry. I need to talk to you alone. I don't want anyone to know where I am."

"Well, where are you?"

"I'm at the Double-T."

"What? How? When did you get there? Don't you know that your school has police in every county looking for you? They were here last night asking my grandparents if they'd seen you."

"I figured as much. That's one of the reasons I need to talk to you, Jared. And there's so much more. When you come to look after the animals we can talk then."

"Are you all right? Do you need anything?" He sounded genuinely concerned. I smiled to myself. Under different circumstances I'd be elated that he cared. Right now it was hard to feel anything other than stress and the pressure to get the Thompsons back home.

"I'm okay," I reassured him. "Just get over here as soon as you can."

With Jared due to arrive in about an hour, which was his usual schedule when he came to work with the animals, I realized I was running out of time. I ran to my room and got showered and cleaned up, putting on tan cargo shorts and a black tank top, brushed my hair and let it hang long and shining instead of in a ponytail, and put on a little makeup.

When I opened my dresser drawer I saw my own bracelet lying there. Carefully I removed Deanne's from my wrist, twisted the two together then put them back on. They actually looked pretty good, like real jewelry. I put some fake diamond studs in my ears and gazed at myself in the mirror. Not too bad, I thought.

When I was as satisfied as I could be about my appearance, I sat at the kitchen table, and decided I would use the time to organize the paperwork and receipts from Emily's files. I removed the receipts from my book bag, then headed into Emily's bedroom and over to the file cabinet to see if I'd missed anything. I pulled the first drawer out and my mouth dropped open in surprise. Most of the files were missing. I tried another drawer, then another. But all the documents that Emily kept tidily stored away had been removed. Could the Feds have confiscated them to prove their case?

I slid the last file drawer closed, then stopped. I could have sworn I heard a creaking sound coming from the closet on the other side of their bed. As I turned to look I felt my pulse slow, then begin to quicken erratically. Frank and Emily's queen sized bed was unmade, the covers tousled onto the floor. When I'd left it had been perfectly made up, the pillows all in place.

"Is someone here?" I called out. Which was a stupid thing to say because if anyone was in the room it was unlikely they'd respond. My mind raced through the possibilities. News of a vacant or abandoned house traveled fast in the underworld.

My eyes roved the room in search of an object I could

use as a weapon. But there was nothing obvious to me. Frank kept a rifle stowed safely away somewhere in case of the unfortunate circumstance of having to put an animal down. I just didn't know where he hid it. I prayed it wasn't in the closet. In this tiny room there was only one place left to look. Under the bed.

I crept toward the bed, keeping my eyes on the closet all the while as I sank to my knees. Still scanning the room, I reached under the bed and groped. At first I couldn't feel anything, so I knee-walked forward and stuck my hand further underneath. Something grabbed my wrist hard and jerked hard. I fell forward, smacking my head on the bed frame rail. Then everything went black.

The pain in my forehead woke me. For several minutes the headache was so vicious that I had trouble focusing. I raised myself unsteadily to my knees, feeling as if I were about to throw up. Slowly I backed out of the room and pulled the door closed. Then I raced to the bathroom, locking the door behind me.

I sat on the toilet for what seemed like an eternity, trying to work out what had just happened. A warm trickle worked its way down my cheek. I raised my hand to my face and it came away bloody. Grabbing a wad of toilet paper I dabbed at my forehead and tried to focus. Someone besides Jared had been in this house while I was gone. Someone who had taken files and possibly even slept here. A squatter maybe? But why would a squatter come here, in the middle of nowhere? Then I remembered that Kevin Palola had once lived here. And how would he know the house would be empty?

I heard Jared's voice just then, talking to the dog. There came the sound of the key in the front door lock, then his footsteps. And finally silence.

"Breeze?" he called out. I closed my eyes tightly, took a deep breath, and willed myself to be calm.

"I'm in the bathroom," I said, my voice barely above a squeak. "I'll be right out."

There came the sound of a chair scraping across the

floor as it was pulled out, then as Jared waited, I emerged from my hiding place with faltering steps.

He gave a low whistle when he saw me, making me blush. Then in an instant he saw in my face that something was wrong. He leapt up and grabbed my arm, pulling me onto a chair. I almost collapsed then, spots starting to form in my vision. He put his hand under my chin and tipped it up until I was staring into his eyes.

"What's wrong?" he demanded. "You look like you're about to pass out. And what happened to your head? You're bleeding!"

I swallowed hard. "I'm okay," I said, though I was still seeing black spots. "Are you the only person who's been in this house? You haven't given anyone else a key?"

"Of course not! Not even my grandparents have been over." He squinted at me. "Why?"

"I think there's someone in this house besides us," I whispered. "I think they're here right now."

Inadvertently he glanced around as if they would emerge at that moment. "What makes you think that?"

As I told him about the file cabinet, the mussed up bed, and that someone had grabbed me, his frown grew darker. He stood and took my hand, then led me out of the house and to his grandfather's truck. He reached behind the seat and removed a shotgun. Then he opened the glove compartment and brought out several shells.

"Get in the truck and lock the doors. I'm going to check the house and make sure no one is there."

"I'm going with you." He started to protest but I was determined. Whatever or whoever was in that house we would face together. With me creeping behind him, we headed toward the house and threw open the door. We sent Dingus in first.

We started with Emily and Frank's bedroom, searching the tiny closet until it was apparent all it held was clothes and shoes. The sliding window was open, but I couldn't remember if it had been that way when I entered earlier.

Then we checked under the bed, but other than the occasional dust bunny, it too was clear. One by one we searched all the rooms but found nothing. Finally we ended up back in the kitchen where Jared sat while I took a couple of Cokes out of the fridge.

"Wanna tell me what this is all about?" he said after taking a swig of the Coke.

"I thought I heard a noise in the closet, so I looked under the bed. I felt something grab my arm. I fell forward and hit my head on the bed frame."

"Well, we didn't find anyone. And other than the unmade bed and the missing files, there's no evidence that anyone was or still is here."

I thought about that for a moment. Then I remembered the burned door and the fire that had been set near the barn. I reached into my pocket and pulled out the book of matches, handing them to Jared.

"I've found a couple of burned patches around the property that are not where you'd normally find fire. These matches were beside one at the barn."

He turned the matches over in his hand, staring at them. Half of the matches were missing, leaving only the stubs of the used ones behind. "With both of us handling them the police probably couldn't get any prints, even if they would agree to do it."

He glanced up at me. "I think most likely some homeless person realized that the house was empty and decided to stay here until people returned."

I wasn't convinced but I didn't have any better answers. I'd had a pretty good scare and my head still throbbed like crazy. I tried to smile, though I felt more like bursting into tears. Jared placed his hand over mine and squeezed it reassuringly.

No longer focused on the possibility of an intruder, I went back to the bathroom and washed my face, pinching my cheeks to erase the pallor. I returned to the kitchen to see Jared giving me a welcoming smile.

"That's better," he said. "Come over here." I moved toward him and he reached up, pulling me onto his lap.

I laughed, realizing he was wearing shorts, and I was sitting on his bare legs. He leaned toward me and kissed me gently on the lips. I pulled back to look at him.

"I've been waiting a long time to do that," he said.

I didn't know what to say. Anything I said now would sound stupid, so I just stayed quiet. But I stayed sitting on his lap, his arm encircling my waist protectively. I was delirious with joy.

"You've changed. You look older," he said. I raised my eyebrows.

"Is that good or bad?" I didn't want to sound flirtatious, not that I knew how to flirt effectively, I seriously wanted to know.

"It's a good thing." He couldn't avoid the embarrassed grin that crept up. He turned his head slightly to hide it, and blushed.

"Maybe it's because so much has happened in the last couple of months."

He shot me a look as if he wasn't quite sure what I meant.

I was at a loss for words with us sitting there together. Finally I managed to squeak out, "Thanks for taking care of the animals while I was gone."

"Don't forget, Emily and Frank hired me to take care of them before, when Emily had her accident. As far as I know, I'm still employed." I felt his fingers stroke the back of my bare arm. I shivered, but not from cold. It unsettled me for just a second, forcing me to lose my train of thought.

"So you haven't heard anything from them? Or about them?"

He rolled his neck as if taking out kinks and stretched out his long legs under the table, nearly unseating me. I took that as my cue to move to a chair. "Not much. Barker told my grandparents they're being held without bail in Federal prison on environmental charges, which are pretty serious."

"Nolan Barker? How would he know anything?"

Jared shook his head, frowning. "He's in contact with the County about building and development permits and keeps up on things around this area. Takes a personal interest in local politics, I guess. He's actually being a pretty good neighbor. Last week he noticed Frank's truck was missing and reported it stolen."

"It wasn't stolen!" I almost shouted. "I took it to town to see if I could find out where they'd taken Frank and Emily. That bastard had me arrested!" The anger and frustration that I'd kept welled up inside me threatened to boil over. Then I remembered seeing Kevin Palola as he drove past me into town. My hands formed into fists. I jumped to my feet and started pacing angrily.

"What?" Jared sat up straight in his chair. "What are you talking about?"

"When I called you a few days ago I didn't tell you why I wouldn't be able to look after the animals. Jonathan and I went to town to try and find Frank and Emily. On our way back to the Double-T we got pulled over because the cop recognized the truck as having been reported stolen. I was arrested for car theft and driving without a license. Jonathan was taken into custody by the Children's Services Department and I haven't seen him since. But I just remembered that I saw Kevin Palola driving the Hummer."

Jared's face turned a chalky white and he grabbed the edge of the table as if he were about to rip a chunk out of it.

"Why didn't you tell me this before?"

"I called you from the Juvenile Detention center. After I spent the night there I got sent back to Stark. I ran away yesterday and hitchhiked all the way here. That's why the police are looking for me."

Jared dropped his head into his hands and violently rubbed his forehead in frustration. Finally he said, "You probably should have stayed there. There's nothing you can do to help Frank and Emily. My grandparents are really torn up about it and can't figure out why they were charged. We all know they don't have more cattle grazing up there than they have permits for."

I stared him straight in the eyes. "Do you think they would be willing to testify to that? Would you?" His eyebrows shot up and he gave a short laugh.

"I don't know what good that would do. It would be our word against the Feds'. They're the ones who claim to have evidence that the Thompsons are lying about the numbers."

"They're not lying," I replied defiantly, "and I can prove that they only own two hundred cattle. I have the receipts. I made copies for my friend Carla's dad, Mr. Sutherland, who's an attorney. I wrote him a letter explaining everything that has happened. I think Barker bought cattle from your grandparents to put them with Frank and Emily's property so he could frame them and force them off the BLM land."

"Receipts for the cattle they have would only be proof the Thompsons owned those." A doubtful frown furrowed Jared's brow. "And why would Barker do that? He's not a rancher. He's a developer."

"That's just it. Frank and Emily won't sell. It was the only way the land would come up for sale and now it will be auctioned off, along with all the cattle, horses and farm equipment. And who do you think will be the first or highest bidder?"

Jared stared at me with admiration shining in his eyes.

"Wow," he said slowly, dragging out the word. "You may be right. But how would you go about proving it?"

Triumphantly I patted the file folder containing Emily's receipts, and hugged it to me. After all I'd been through, and the miles I'd traveled, it wasn't unrealistic to say I'd protect it with my life.

"Your grandparents will have additional records of all the cattle sold and who they've sold them to, whether it was the Thompsons or Barker.

"You'd have to take into account any that have been sold after that, or died, and any newborn calves," I added, "but even if someone has stolen Frank's records, he has a good memory for what cows have calved, and which he's sold or had butchered."

"How would we prove that Frank and Emily didn't get more cattle from a source other than my grandparents? Or maybe paid cash so there were no records?"

I stared at him shrewdly. "What if we had the Feds do DNA testing on the cattle?"

He shook his head. "Too time consuming and not in their interests. And what would it prove? That our cattle are family?"

I frowned and chewed on a fingernail as I tried to analyze the problem the way a detective would. "Maybe we should take a ride up to the range lands and count those cattle for ourselves. We can take pictures. Right now all we have is the word of those Federal agents."

Jared laughed out loud. "You've given this a lot of thought." He smiled at me with new respect. I blushed, pleased with myself. Suddenly he seemed flustered, as if he wished he hadn't said what he had. But inside I was thrilled to pieces. He shrugged it off.

"How about we ride up tomorrow? If you pack the lunch I'll bring a camera and binoculars."

I nodded, mentally assessing what I had left in the house to make a lunch. It would take some creative scrounging, but I'd figure out something to impress him.

"I'd better take those receipts you have to my grandparents and let them take care of Barker. The sooner we get Frank and Emily out of prison, the sooner you can get Jonathan back home."

He reached for the file but I placed my hand over his, stopping him before he could take it. "These are the originals. Right now this is all we have to exonerate them. I have to call Mr. Sutherland and see if he thinks there's enough evidence to defend them. If he won't take the case I'll give these to your grandparents, but you have to promise me that they won't fall into the wrong hands. Or worse, disappear forever. Then we'd never get the Thompsons released."

He looked me straight in the eyes. "I swear to you that this will go to the proper authorities, Breeze." He stood and only then noticed my bracelet jangling against the table top. He touched it, turning it over. He peered at me from underneath his lashes, curious.

"That's pretty. Where'd you get it?"

"It's a bracelet that one of my friends at Stark made for a few of us." My lower lip trembled as I stared down at Deanne's bracelet, now intertwined with mine. "I connected mine with hers. She left it at Stark and I found it before I came back here."

He threw me a questioning look and I glanced across the room, tears stinging my eyes. "Did something happen to her?"

"She died," I said, and felt hot tears gushing freely down my cheeks. I didn't know how to tell him about Deanne, or any of the other Lunatics for that matter, and so I didn't say any more. A sob caught in my throat.

He moved closer and encircled me with his right arm to comfort me. At that moment all I wanted to do was have him hold me. I threw my arms around him and this time he didn't appear embarrassed at all. It might have been my imagination because I heard him whisper something against my ear that I couldn't hear. I felt him kiss the top of my hair, and then my ear and my neck. I snuggled closer, reveling in his warmth.

My tears made damp stains on his T-shirt and suddenly I realized I'd forgotten one of the paramount rules of the Lunatics: Thou shalt not cry in front of anyone other than another Lunatic. Heaving a contented sigh, my sobs subsided. I smiled to myself as I stood there, held tight in Jared's arms.

TWENTY-EIGHT

I'd been so exhausted with the happenings of the previous day that for once I had no difficulty in getting to sleep. I awoke to the ringing of the telephone and had to scramble to get to the kitchen to answer it in time, momentarily forgetting that it might be the police or CSD trying to track me down. But to my relief and joy I heard Jared's voice.

"Are we still on for today?" he asked. "I realized after I left you yesterday that you probably didn't have any food in the house to make lunch so I had my grandmother pack us something."

"You didn't tell her about me being back, did you?" I demanded anxiously.

"Relax. I just told her I was heading out on horseback to check the Double-T and I'd be gone most of the day, so to make lots of food." He chuckled. "She's used to me going on long rides and doesn't worry. Or at least she says she doesn't," he added. "She is a grandmother."

"Did you ask your grandparents about the cattle?"

"Not yet. Let's see what we discover up on the range land before we start asking questions that Barker can just refute. If we get all our information and documents ready to be presented in a professional way, it'll have more impact. In the meantime, get the horses fed and I'll be there in an hour."

I laughed, impressed by the planning he'd put in already.

"Yes, sir," I said. "We'll be ready and waiting."

After hanging up the phone I took a hurried shower, put

on a little mascara, dressed in riding clothes and raced to the barn. I fed all the animals and while they were eating, on a whim groomed Diablo for the ride to come. By the time I had him tacked up, Jared was trotting up the driveway on his big paint gelding, the saddle bags bulging so heavily with supplies they didn't even jiggle as he rode. He skidded to a stop in front of us just as I was getting ready to put my foot in the stirrup.

"Are you crazy?" he said when he saw the saddle on Diablo.

I shrugged and pointed to the 'SRL' logo on my shirt. "I've been a lunatic for a while." At his puzzled expression, I said, "I'll explain later. Anyhow, he's got to get used to the trails some time, and what have I got to lose?"

"Limbs? Brain function?"

I stuck my tongue out at him and swung easily into the saddle while Jared watched me with an 'oh-my-god' look on his face. I grinned from atop the stallion that was now pawing in anticipation and jigging in place.

He sighed. "All ready?"

I nodded, thrilled to be on this adventure with him. We set off at a sedate trot so as not to tire the horses too quickly and though Diablo was shorter, he had no trouble keeping up with the larger horse's stride. I yearned to let him out in a gallop, but today wasn't the day to take chances.

We rode in an easy companionship as we headed toward the mountain range where the cattle would be grazing, both horses moving side by side as if they'd been pastured together all their lives. We were making much better time than if we'd had a herd of roving cattle to move. I worried that the day would pass by too quickly and soon Jared would be on his way home. As if he were reading my thoughts, Jared shot me a big smile and the brilliance of his eyes mesmerized me until all other thoughts melted away into the dusty trail behind us.

Around noon we found a couple of scrubby looking fir trees, ground tied the horses and set out a picnic lunch in the shade. Mrs. Shoemaker had packed a half dozen sandwiches, layered beef and turkey, Swiss and cheddar cheese, lettuce and tomatoes. There were Ziploc bags packed full of chocolate chip and oatmeal cookies, as well as a few apples, and homemade fruit leather. I ate until I thought I was going to burst. We fed the apples to the eager horses then washed everything down with water from the canteens on our saddle.

"We'd better get moving," Jared said. "The sun is starting to set faster these days and we don't want to get stuck out here over nightfall."

We climbed back into the saddles again and made our way deeper into the mountains. Nearly an hour later we came upon a small valley tucked at the base of the hills, an alpine meadow of sorts, dotted with Indian Paintbrush and purple Fireweed. An enormous herd of Hereford cattle grazed peacefully amid the long, lush grass. They lifted their heads watchfully as we approached. Calves darted to snuggle close to their mothers, who tossed their heads in a defensive measure. I rode a little closer and saw the Double-T brand on their haunches. Diablo wasn't used to being in such close proximity to cows and started to jig nervously, so I kept a tight rein on him.

"We shouldn't get too near just yet," Jared warned. "Don't want to spook them." He made a kind of an 'oops' face at that, because we both remembered quite clearly the last time that had happened.

I stared at the herd, trying to discern anything different, something to set one apart from the other. But except for the obvious varying sizes of cow and calf, those with horns and those without, they really looked all the same. Before we'd gone on the cattle drive I'd watched Frank brand some of the calves. They all bore the ranch logo: an upright 'T' and an inverted 'T' beside it. For the first time I realized the significance of the inverted 'T': Emily was from Australia, occasionally called 'down under'. I smiled to myself, wondering if anyone else had ever figured it out.

At that moment, a couple of adult cattle moved forward and occluded my vision of the calves. They were slightly darker in color than some of the other Herefords, but I dismissed it, thinking, cattle are cattle. Cautiously, I backed Diablo away from them, though I was still easily able to see the mark on their flanks. They too, bore the Double-T brand, though something about it looked different.

"Jared, come here for a minute and hand me your binoculars." As he rode up I snaked my arm across the saddle, not taking my eyes off the herd. Jared passed the binoculars over and I focused them to my eyes.

"What is it?"

"Have a look." I handed them back to him. "There's something strange about the brand on that cow."

He stared for a couple of minutes then lowered the binoculars. "Looks like the Double-T brand to me."

"Look again," I ordered impatiently. "Then compare it to the ones on the cows in front."

He shrugged and raised the binoculars again, then suddenly turned to me. "You're right. It's supposed to be the Double-T brand, but it's not quite right. I've watched Frank dozens of times when he branded the cows and would know that brand anywhere. The T's are spaced too far apart and don't meet at the tips the way the Thompsons' do. Like someone was trying to copy it but didn't quite get it the same." He pulled a digital camera from his jacket pocket and began taking pictures, then slipped it back into his pocket.

"Let's ride quietly around the herd and see if we can find a few more. You spot the fake brands and I'll photograph them for documentation. It looks like someone has been slipping in bogus cattle to make it appear that the Double-T have more occupying the grazing land than what their permits allow."

"And we know who that someone might be," I said triumphantly.

Jared nodded then focused in on some more cows as he nudged his horse forward.

I followed on Diablo, scanning the herd. "There!" I said, pointing to a few more with the counterfeit brand. "Maybe that's why Emily and I met Nolan Barker that day. It's because he was tracking us to see where we were putting the herd."

"I'm sure you're right," Jared agreed. "Along with those receipts, we might have enough evidence here to show that whoever owns those other cattle has set Frank and Emily up. The Feds wouldn't have been looking for fake brands, and Frank and Emily would have had no idea what he was up to."

Suddenly I remembered what I'd found when I'd returned to the ranch. I could have kicked myself for not paying more attention at the time.

"I found a branding iron near the barn. It was around the same place I found those matches," I said.

Jared raised his eyebrows. "What did you do with it?"

"I tossed it near the barn. I didn't look at it too closely so it might be Frank's. I thought it was odd to find it there because he always puts his stuff away."

"Someone might have used it to copy. Or maybe it wasn't Frank's. Maybe it's the counterfeit brand."

I blew a wisp of hair away from my eyes.

"Let's get those photos back to show your grandparents. They'll know what to do with the evidence."

Jared tucked the camera carefully into a zippered pocket and once further enough away from the cattle so as not to spook them, we took off at a gallop for the Double-T. And this time we didn't have to worry about saving the horses' strength because they seemed as anxious as we were to stretch out and show what they could do.

TWENTY-NINE

Although Jared offered to spend the night sleeping on the sofa at the Double-T to keep me company, I didn't know how Emily and Frank would react should by some chance they arrive home and find him there. Instead I began organizing the receipts and for safekeeping placed them in my chest of drawers. There was no danger now, Mr. Sutherland had copies and once we showed him the photos, I felt we were building a solid case to exonerate the Thompsons. Suddenly I had a premonition, and though I couldn't say what it was, decided not to put them in the drawer after all. Instead I went to the kitchen and found a coffee tin, emptied it and stuffed the receipts inside.

After I'd taken care of the animals, I headed back to the house and locked all the doors. I left Dingus outside because earlier in the day he'd rolled in horse manure. For dinner I ate the last of the lunch Jared had left with me, then I popped a DVD in the player and lay back to relax and watch a movie.

I must have dozed off because I awoke to find the movie had returned to the credit screen and the room was dark. I'd forgotten to turn on the lights. The LED clock on the DVD player said it was 4 a.m. Unwilling to stand with my legs still stiff from the ride, I extended my arm to flick on the living room lamp. It was just out of reach. I sighed and leaned forward to push myself out of the chair when, in the sickly beam from the yard light, I saw a shadow pass into the kitchen. I froze.

For a second I thought it was Jared, but he would have wakened me or called beforehand. Whoever it was didn't want to be seen or they would have turned on the lights. Feeling as if my heart were in my mouth, I forced myself to breathe normally so as not to make a sound and give myself away. If the intruder knew of my presence I wanted him to think I was still asleep.

Then a noise came from my bedroom. The sound of cabinet drawers being jerked open. Was it the same person who had ransacked Emily's file cabinet? And what were they looking for? If they were looking for the receipts, they wouldn't find them in the drawers. But they'd continue to search and that spelled danger for me. My cell phone was useless and besides, it was in the bedroom. If I used the land line the person would hear me. I had two choices. I could turn on the lights and face the intruder, or I could attempt to sneak out unseen and try to get to the Shoemaker's house for help. I chose the former.

But at the same time that I flicked on the living room lamp I smelled smoke. There was a fire burning and the smoke wasn't coming from outdoors. Someone had set a fire in the house. I needed to get out fast. Intending to quickly shut off the light so as not to be seen, I stopped when I heard a sound from behind. I spun around. There, coming down the hallway from my bedroom, was the boy I'd seen with Barker. Kevin Palola.

For what seemed like an eternity we stood staring at each other. This was the closest I'd ever been to him. He had an unhealthy sallow complexion speckled with pimples, and tiny, deep-set black eyes. Soulless eyes. His greasy pulled-back hair and pointed chin with its stubble of hair gave him the appearance of a rat. Involuntarily, I shuddered. He began to move toward me and I started to back toward the door.

"Where did you put the receipts for the cattle sales?" he said, giving me a smile that chilled me to the bone.

"I don't know what you're talking about. I don't have anything to do with the cows." Staring defiantly at him I continued to back up.

"Well, I know that's not right because Nolan saw you on the cattle drive with Emily," he sneered. "I get the feeling you and Emily talk about all kinds of stuff. You see, I know about the receipts because I lived here when the Thompsons bought their cattle."

As I inched backwards I suddenly found myself up against the living room wall. But Kevin kept approaching, with a kind of crazy, half-excited look in his eyes that scared the shit out of me.

"I know that you took them from the file cabinet because Emily and Frank didn't have a chance to when the Forest Service came to haul them away."

I stopped hard in my tracks. "What do you mean?"

He laughed. I'd never heard anyone laugh like that, kind of a weird high pitched cackle that seemed as if it was coming from somewhere else. Or someone else.

"You might be stupid," he conceded, "after all, you are a Stark kid, but you must have figured it out by now. I'm working for Nolan Barker. I copied the Double-T brand and branded the cattle that Nolan bought." He shrugged. "Nolan's not what you'd call a hands-on guy, but Frank taught me real good." He appeared to brighten at that. "We ran those cattle to the high country just the same way Frank and your pussy boyfriend took the Thompson's cows up. Then we called the Forest Service. They became real interested in the Thompsons."

As he continued to advance toward me, I noticed that the smoke behind him was getting denser. Then a flicker of flame licked through the hallway and up the side of the wallpaper. He followed my gaze and glanced back to me.

"Guess those receipts are gone now," he said. "I figured you probably stashed them in your bedroom." He cocked his head. "Used to be *my* bedroom. See you found my homework assignment, too. How'd you like that bit of writing?"

By now I'd reached the door. Groping for the knob with my hands behind me, I circled my fingers around it then stopped. I needed the receipts that were in the cupboard, but I also had to put out the fire. Whether the Thompsons had insurance or not was immaterial; they couldn't afford to lose any more. I began inching toward the kitchen.

"You know, Kevin," I said, forcing myself to be calm, "if you help me put out this fire, I'll let you out of here and we can forget this happened. Otherwise you're going to go to jail."

He really cackled at that. "Seriously?" he said. "I don't think so. Barker is on his way over here right now and as he's rewarding me nicely for my work, I think I'll have to decline your offer."

The thought that Barker would be arriving any time made me more nervous than just being here with this maniac and the encroaching fire. I was now backed against the recliner that Emily sat in when she knitted. I kept my eyes trained on Kevin's, hoping that a remnant of sanity would come to him, but I didn't hold out much hope. I leaned against Emily's chair and felt something cold and hard standing behind it, pressing against my leg. Jared's shotgun.

I waited. At that moment a loud pop came from the bedroom, the sound of light bulbs bursting, or synthetic fabric catching fire, I couldn't tell. It was enough of a distraction that Kevin whirled around to look. I grabbed the shotgun and raised it to my shoulder. When he turned back I had him in the sights.

He giggled nervously. "You don't know how to use that," he cajoled. "You see, I've been watching you for a while. I know your limitations and no one here has taught you how to fire a gun."

But he was wrong. My mother had bought me a BB gun when I was ten and on weekends together we'd go out to the desert and pick pop cans off fence posts. I knew there was a shell in the shotgun; I'd seen Jared put it there. I gave Kevin the same frozen smile he'd given me. Then I fired. When he fell, I threw the shotgun behind the chair and ran for the garden hose, praying I wasn't too late.

Jared arrived about a half hour later, just as the glow of the rising sun turned the blue mountains into indigo cones. His cheeks were flushed with excitement and he smelled like horse. I looked out the window and realized he must have galloped over on his big paint gelding because the horse stood tied to the Double-T poles, pawing at the dirt. I was surprised he'd arrived before the police but then, we were out in the sticks and there was only one local cop that I knew of, and he worked 9 to 5.

"I gave those photos we took yesterday to my grandfather…" he stopped, taking in my disheveled appearance and the dank smell of wet smoke and burned synthetic.

"What the hell is going on here?" he said. "Are you okay?"

I nodded, sinking to Emily's chair, exhausted. "It was a rough night. Kevin Palola is gagged and tied up in my bedroom."

His eyes narrowed. "What?"

I filled him in on my adventure during the night. The trauma hadn't really sunk in yet and as I related the events I realized I sounded like a robot.

"The police are on their way. But before I called them, I had Kevin write out a confession," I said matter-of-factly. He stared at me as if I'd suddenly gone insane. And maybe I had a little. It's amazing what a person can be capable of under extreme conditions.

"Kevin's a punk," I continued. "He has no love for Barker. He was just in it for the money and to get back at the Thompsons. After I fired your shotgun at his feet he fainted. So I ran and grabbed the garden hose and put out the fire. Then I tied him up."

Jared was still staring at me, a sort of reluctant admiration in his eyes, but there was anxiousness, too. I didn't want to scare him. I sighed.

"Everything's okay," I said. "At least I think it is. I need to call Carla's dad and see if he's willing to take the

Thompsons on as clients."

A loud groaning sound came from the direction of my bedroom. Jared and I shared a glance. "I'll go," he said. He stepped carefully around the hole in the floor made by the shotgun blast, then moved into my bedroom. I heard his voice but not the words. Kevin wouldn't be saying much as he had duct tape over his mouth. Jared emerged a couple of minutes later.

"He peed himself." He moved to the other recliner and sank into it, stretching his legs.

"Whoops. Sucks to be him."

Jared shrugged. "He'll live." He leaned across and took my hand. "What I came over to tell you," he waved his other hand in the direction of the waterlogged carpet with its massive hole, "before you filled me in on all this, is that my grandfather talked to someone in the District Attorney's office about Barker. Grandpa said to apologize to you for not taking Emily's warning about Barker wanting to buy the land from them to develop a resort. He thought Barker was going into ranching because that's what he said when he bought the cattle from him."

"That's what he told a lot of people."

"How did Emily find out that he wanted to develop the property?"

"That I don't know, but Emily is a pretty shrewd judge of character. If she thinks someone is a bad person, I'd be inclined to follow her lead."

"You're right about her judge of character," said Jared, smiling broadly. "After all, she got rid of Kevin and chose you, didn't she?" I felt my face flush all the way down my neck.

Just then the police arrived, two of them this time, probably given the seriousness of the situation. One went to check on my prisoner and hustle him into the squad car while the other took my statement. I handed him Kevin's signed confession though he mentioned that if it was made under duress it might not hold up in court. That didn't matter so much to me. With Kevin's arson rap sheet he was pretty much cooked, so to speak, for a few years. As he passed me in the kitchen, his hands in cuffs instead of the baling twine I'd used, he threw me a poisonous glance.

Once the police had taken Kevin away Jared stayed to help me clean the house. First I needed to call Carla. I could feel my pulse pounding all the way up to my head as the phone rang several times. When she came on the line I almost broke into tears. I quickly filled her in on the events since she'd left Stark and I'd returned to the ranch. Uncharacteristic for her, she was speechless for a couple of minutes. Finally she said, "You really need to talk to my dad." Then Mr. Sutherland came on the line and I explained what had taken place the night before, as well as Jared's information about the District Attorney's office. Then my big question.

"Do we have enough evidence for you to defend them?" His answer almost made me drop the phone in relief. I shook so hard Jared had to take the receiver from my hand. Unabashed, I threw my arms around him.

"What did he say?" he asked, extricating himself to look at me.

"He said that with Kevin's arrest, the receipts and photos we have, and with me and your grandparents testifying, the charges against the Thompsons will probably just be dismissed. Even if Kevin's confession doesn't hold up."

It was Jared's turn to hug me. He kissed the top of my head. "You're amazing," he said. "Probably a bit crazy, though."

"I can't deny that," I replied agreeably. "Now let's get this place cleaned up before anything else happens."

In the excitement of tying Kevin up and calling the police, I hadn't had a chance to take a good look at my room. It was a mess, but the majority of damage appeared to be to the chest of drawers, which had burned beyond repair and scorched the wall behind it. The carpet would have to be removed and the sheet rock would need to be replaced and repainted, but all things considered, it could have been worse.

I didn't know what we could do about the hole in the living room floor, but I figured Frank would have a solution, once he got home. He might have to put in new living room carpet, or if funds allowed, maybe it was time for renovating and redecorating. I thought about that for a few minutes. If I was going to be staying here it would be a great project for Emily and me.

When we'd cleaned up the house to the best of our ability, I opened the fridge and brought us both a soda. We settled down at the kitchen table, dirty and sweating, but pleased with the results. Jared took a swallow from his Coke then set it down, absentmindedly looking at the label.

"So are you finally going to tell me what's been bugging you?"

I froze. I'd been dreading this conversation. "What do you mean?"

"Your friend Deanne. What happened to her?" Suddenly he held up his hands. "Hey, I'm sorry, this is none of my business. You don't have to tell me anything if you don't want to."

But then I realized I did want to tell him. I wouldn't hide anything from Jared now because I didn't want him to ever misjudge me again. And there was no way I would lie to him about a person who had been so important to me.

"Children's Services failed her," I said bluntly. "They were supposed to protect her from her father but they put her right in his hands."

"Oh!" Jared was at a loss for words, looking embarrassed that he'd asked. "I'm sorry."

"Well," I said slowly, "maybe I'm putting the blame in the wrong place. It's the system that's flawed. Deanne wrote to tell me that she was being sent to a foster home in Newport, on the coast. At the time her father was in jail. But then he was released. As soon as he got out he went looking for Deanne and took her home." I paused, trying to find a way to share what Deanne had told me what seemed like a lifetime ago, but was actually only a couple of months.

"Deanne once confided in me that he beat her. He'd done the same with her mother, and she'd run away, leaving Deanne with him."

Jared's forehead wrinkled in barely suppressed anger. "Did you tell anyone about the abuse?"

I sighed. "Deanne made me promise not to but I went to our school counselor anyhow. I told her some of it, although not the worst part." My guilt weighed so heavily on me I found it difficult to look at Jared, so I just stared at the Coke can.

"Didn't they do anything?"

I shook my head sadly. "No, they let him take her away. She told us long ago that if she was ever sent back to her father she'd kill herself. I don't think anyone really believed her."

I sneaked a glance a Jared.

"Did you?"

"Not really. Then I found her diary when I was sent back to Stark. She wrote that she was being sent to live with him again but she actually sounded positive for the future."

I hesitated for a few seconds, trying to find the right words, afraid to share with him that I had been part of that hope.

"I think that the abuse must have gotten so bad, and without anyone to talk to or help, her belief that she would ever get free from him began to fade." Looking him straight in the eyes, I confessed the depressing truth. "But we'll probably never know."

Scalding tears welled up in my eyes, blinding me. Then I felt Jared's arms fold tightly around me. The aching pain I felt for Deanne began to dissipate into the warmth of our bodies as we stood there together for what seemed like an eternity.

Finally Jared pulled away and was just about to speak when we were both startled by the ringing of the telephone. The Thompsons got so few calls that every time it rang we'd all nearly jump out of our skin. I glanced warily at Jared but he just shrugged and said, "Better answer it."

And I was glad I had because the voice on the other end brought a flood of more happy tears. After I'd hung up the phone I turned to see the question on Jared's face.

"That was Emily," I said, giddy with excitement. "She and Frank are being released tomorrow."

After Jared rode back to his grandparent's place, I practically flew around the house. We'd cleaned it as best we could but I still needed to rearrange Emily's bedroom from the ransacking Kevin had given it. Then I went out to the barn, cleaned the stalls and groomed all the horses, including Diablo. By the time it got dark I was exhausted, but so happy I could hardly get to sleep.

First thing the next morning I got showered and dressed, and fixed my hair in a ponytail. Then I made homemade chocolate chip cookies. The ones that got a little burned I ate for breakfast. Still too excited to relax, I went about doing all my daily chores again, hardly able to sit still until they arrived.

Finally, late in the afternoon I recognized the Shoemaker's big silver Cadillac drive up and from my perch at the window I could see four heads. Then Jared's grandparents emerged from the front seat, and from the back came Emily and Frank. I met them halfway across the yard and we almost fell over in a group hug.

Emily hugged me the longest then as everyone else headed toward the house she held me at arm's length. I expected a scolding but instead she asked, "How on earth did you ever think to look for receipts on those cattle?"

"I just started adding up the cows, and the charges they filed against you didn't make sense," I said shyly. "Somehow it seemed that it would be the kind of thing an unscrupulous developer might do, frame someone so they could get what they wanted. His conscience probably didn't even bother him because he knew that you'd be released eventually, but by that time all the cows and horses would be auctioned off and he'd be able to snap up the property."

Emily hugged me again. "You are one very intelligent girl. Not to mention, extremely pretty."

I blushed, and gave her my rehearsed response when I was embarrassed by compliments. "Pretty is what people call you when you can't qualify for beautiful."

She laughed out loud at that. "Well, you're a beautiful girl, too, inside and out."

I grimaced. Giving her a playful punch in the arm, I said, "Are we going to be able to get Jonathan back?"

Emily nodded. "There's red tape involved, of course, but seeing as the charges were dropped, Mr. Sutherland doesn't anticipate any problems with Children's Services. Jonathan was in temporary foster care so it shouldn't be difficult getting him home."

Relief coursed through me. Poor Jonathan. He'd been through a lot, as well. Suddenly I remembered the last time we'd been together. "Did you hear about your truck?"

"What about it?" She steered me in the direction of the house and we started walking.

"When Jonathan and I went to find you Nolan Barker reported it stolen so he could get me out of the picture, too."

Emily opened the front screen door, turned to me and gestured toward their red truck sitting in the driveway. "It looks fine to me. Home safe and sound. It doesn't look like it ever left the yard."

Once the Shoemakers had gone home Emily said, "Do you want to talk about what this has all been about? I mean, the cattle grazing rights and all?"

"You don't have to explain much. It didn't take too long to figure out what Nolan Barker was up to."

She nodded. Frank, as usual, sat quietly drinking a cup of coffee while letting his wife do the talking.

"But you probably don't know what happened this afternoon," she continued.

I shook my head. "Barker was arrested for lying to public officials, fraud, forgery. And get this: misuse of public lands. He had more growing on his property that just cattle, if you get my meaning. I think we've seen the last of him. He won't be developing anything around here any time soon." At that she started laughing so hard I thought she'd cry. I only partly understood what she meant, but it made me laugh, too.

Suddenly her voice took on a serious note. "I know you and Jonathan went through hell when we were taken away. Jonathan might have some residual effects from the trauma of witnessing us being arrested and from being taken into custody when the police stopped you. They tell me he's seen a child psychologist a couple of times. I think he'll be okay. How about you, Breeze? Are you going to be all right?"

I sighed. "Yes, I'll be just fine, but there have been some unusual things that have happened since you left. I got sent back to Stark School. I think they want to take me back."

Emily's face turned a pasty white, and she looked as shocked as if I'd struck her. "And what do *you* want?"

"I don't know," I admitted. "For once, I really don't know what I want." But I was only partially telling the truth. With all the Lunatics gone I wanted to stay at the Double-T, with Frank and Emily and Jonathan. And Jared coming back to his grandparents' ranch every summer to visit me. When the time was right I'd tell her about Deanne.

THIRTY

The following week passed by in a blur. Accompanied by Jared, I got in all the horseback riding I could, me on Diablo, he on his gelding. In a few days he would be leaving for San Diego, to go back home to his parent's house and starting his freshman year in college. I would be staying with the Thompsons and traveling to school by bus every day.

Nolan Barker had been sent to prison, as had Kevin Palola. Emily was still reticent when speaking about him. I sensed that she felt embarrassment and failure whenever his name came up, but IMHO she had no reason to. Kevin was old enough to change his life and become a better person; he'd just made the wrong choices.

The Shoemakers, still set on retirement, agreed to lease their land to Frank and Emily for the cost of the property taxes, if they agreed to maintain it until Jared had finished college and could come back to farm it. We would be moving into their lovely hacienda until the Thompsons' house was renovated. It was a win-win situation for both families. In the spring Sage and Honey would be giving birth to foals, Diablo's first offspring. Emily looked kind of smug when she said, "You can help me deliver them." But of course I knew I'd probably be at school or asleep when it happened.

Jared and I had one last ride together the day before he left for his home in San Diego. We started out at sunrise and spent the entire morning riding toward those mysterious blue-grey hills that had once appeared so elusive to me. Now they beckoned like an old friend. We rode our horses to the top of the mountain and when we reached the crest we were able to gaze down into the valley on the other side. Below us a herd of maybe a hundred wild horses grazed, oblivious to our presence, the prized Steens Mustangs.

I held my breath, awestruck by the wild beauty of them. I turned to Jared and saw that though there was a smile on his lips, they quavered with emotion.

I inclined my head toward the horses. "Incredible, aren't they?"

He nodded slowly. "You know what bothers me the most?" Without waiting for me to reply he continued, "By spring a bunch of them will be gone, and it won't be because of a harsh winter or lack of food. It'll be because the Feds have decided it's time to cull the herds because they're overgrazing their habitat, or encroaching on a new subdivision. And then one day, there just won't be any."

There was nothing to say. Everything he said was true, but at least we'd staved off Nolan Barker and his plan to turn our ranches into a casino or housing development. For now at least. Unfortunately one day there would be more Nolan Barkers. I turned to see Jared smiling sadly at me. He reached out across both horses and intertwined his fingers in mine. Then he reined his horse close to Diablo, leaned over and kissed me long and hard. It wasn't until one of the horses shifted their weight that we pulled away from each other.

But our eyes were still locked in the moment. In a single movement Jared slid off his horse, grasping the reins in one hand. He led his horse over to Diablo and held him while I dismounted. Wordlessly we walked together to the nearest trees, tying the horses safely apart. As if in silent collusion, we melted together as if we were one person, and for what seemed like a lifetime the world around us disappeared.

Then the stallion from the herd below caught our scent. A hundred equine heads shot up. In less time than it takes to draw a breath they whirled away and became a flying carpet of gold, brown, black and white, nearly enveloped in the dry dust of the August desert. We watched until the horses disappeared and only a trace of the dust remained, until it too, vanished into the hot southeastern Oregon wind.

The next day I called Jared's house to say goodbye until he returned at the end of the spring college term. We'd promised to e-mail each other as Frank and Emily decided that it was time we had access to the internet. Even if the best we could do was a dial up connection. Emily told me that she and Frank had even been talking about buying a television. I wasn't holding my breath on that one.

Later that morning I heard a small commotion outside. A gold Mercedes pulled into the driveway and stopped in front of the house. Puzzled, I walked toward the door and just about fell over in surprise.

"Carla!" We ran toward each other, bodies smashing in a hug. She stepped on my toes and I yelped in pain. Suddenly self-conscious, we let go of each other and our arms dropped to our sides. She had cut the black tips off her hair and now had it cropped short. Though it was spiked, the cut had a feminine look to it that she'd previously avoided. Gone was the black, Gothic eye makeup I'd last seen her wearing. With only a touch of pale blue eye shadow and mascara, she looked young, but very beautiful.

"What are you doing here?" Out of the corner of my eye I saw a tall handsome man with a strong resemblance to Carla walk toward us, smiling. Carla turned.

"You remember my dad, right?" She ran up to him and gave him a big hug. "He called the District Attorney about the Thompsons and turned over the information you gave him. Then he hired an investigator to look into that slimy Barker guy."

I looked up at Mr. Sutherland, my face beaming with gratitude. "I don't know how to begin to thank you. Barker and his accomplice are in jail now."

He laughed. "And with the case we have against them,

they'll probably stay there for a while."

Carla turned to me and took my arm, leading me away from her father, who had gone over to talk with the Thompsons.

"Tyesha called me a couple of days ago. She started working part time at Starbucks and she's taking classes in Community College. She said to ask you if she could come and visit when she's on school breaks."

That made me laugh out loud. "Only if you'll come, too. I know how much you guys like the smell of horses. Although Deanne would have loved it here." My eyes widened, hot with tears that threatened to overflow.

Carla whispered close to my ear, "There are lots of other people around. Remember the commandment: Thou shalt not cry *in front of anyone other than a Lunatic.*"

"I won't have to worry about that commandment in future," I said, giving her a hug. "I have nothing to cry about any more."

THE COMMANDMENTS

Thou shalt not associate with anyone other than Lunatics.

Thou shalt not watch Glee without another Lunatic.

Thou shalt not kill anything or anyone belonging to a Lunatic.

Thou shalt not cry in front of anyone other than a Lunatic.

Thou shalt not steal from another Lunatic.

Thou shalt not tell lies to, or to hurt, another Lunatic.

Thou shalt not covet another Lunatic's boyfriend.

ABOUT THE AUTHOR

Leigh Goodison is the author of *The Jigsaw Man, The Horse Trailer Owner's Manual,* and the 'foodoir', *Goodies From the Great White North, Recipes for Dinners, Delicacies and Disasters.* Her articles, essays, short stories, and poetry have appeared in publications such as *Western Horseman, Horse Circuit News, The Northwest Horse Source, Northwest Rider, Rider's Roundup, NW Family Magazine, Lighthouse, ByLine, Bronté Street, The Willamette Writer,* and many more. For more about Leigh visit www.leighgoodison.com